THEIR

DEADLY

TRUTH

BOOKS BY CARLA KOVACH

On a Quiet Street

My Husband's Wife

Meet Me at Marmaris Castle

Whispers Beneath the Pines

Flame

THEIR DEADLY TRUTH

CARLA KOVACH

bookouture

Published by Bookouture in 2025

An imprint of Storyfire Ltd.
Carmelite House
50 Victoria Embankment
London EC4Y 0DZ

www.bookouture.com

The authorised representative in the EEA is Hachette Ireland
8 Castlecourt Centre
Dublin 15 D15 XTP3
Ireland
(email: info@hbgi.ie)

ISBN: 978-1-80550-277-7
eBook ISBN: 978-1-80550-276-0

*To those who have reached a crossroads in life and are finding it
tricky to decide what to do next.*

PROLOGUE
BAZ

Mid-nineties

I hate my family sometimes. My dad likes to throw his rules around and my brother is a pain in the arse. My hands are jittery so I discreetly pop a tablet into my mouth. I know they're not my tablets but I feel so much calmer when I take one. New starts are scary and right now, I'm scared, but leaving home earlier tonight was the right decision. My life has been pants since the bedroom share. I've hated every moment of it, all because my dad wants a hobby room.

My mate Chipper pats me on the back as he downs the last of his lager. 'Keep in touch, okay, mate? Maybe we can do that Ibiza holiday we keep talking about soon, once you've settled into your new pad.' Chipper won't be going anywhere for years but I might still go. Who knows, I might get a job selling boat trips.

It's late. I gaze at the several pint and shot glasses lined up on our table. The bartender calls last orders. Drinking chasers wasn't the best idea because I'm now feeling like shite. Dad always told me not to knock back shots and to stick to the pints.

I don't tell Chipper that I'll be sleeping in my car for now even though it's cold outside. The bedsit I'm moving into isn't available until a week next Wednesday and I can't bear to stay in that house a minute longer. The arguments have been happening every day now. Those last words before I left are haunting me now. I smile, just to show Chipper that everything is okay even though it's not. I don't need an interrogation tonight. For a second, I wonder if I should tell him what went down at home and maybe stay on his couch. But, then again, there isn't room at his with the baby being due. No, I won't ask. He's already staying with his mum and his pregnant girlfriend is there too. They're all crammed in a two-bedroomed flat. His mum wouldn't be happy. I don't want to put anyone out and I do have my rusty Mini. 'I'm happy for you, mate. You'll be a great dad. We'll do Ibiza one day.'

'Thanks. I'm happy, too, I think.'

'You think?' The room is swaying a bit. I wish I hadn't drunk so much, especially the shots. What even were they? Toffee, coffee, banoffee? Every time I swallow, I taste them again and that taste makes me want to puke.

'Well, it's hard, isn't it? I'm going to be a dad at twenty. I mean, what the hell? We didn't plan this.' He pauses and sighs. 'I best go. I told her I wouldn't be too late. Call me when you've settled into the new place so I can visit. I'll bring you something, maybe a pot plant. That's what people give as a house-warming, isn't it? A spider plant in a macramé basket. God, I'm going to have to get good at this stuff if I'm going to be a husband and father soon.'

I laugh, wondering what the hell I'd want with a pot plant in my room the size of a box. He grabs his hoodie and stands. 'I will do but I'll pass on the plant. Buy one for your mum instead. It might cheer her up with having your smelly arse around the place.'

Chipper nudges me and laughs. 'Don't forget, call when you're sorted.'

With those final words, Chipper leaves and now I need to go. The place is emptying out. All these people are going home to their nice warm beds and I get to cram my lanky legs into the back of a Mini because of my stupid dad. I pull my car keys from my pocket and start the ten-minute walk to the quiet little road I parked in, the one that backs onto some woodland. The bear key ring is an annoying chunk of rubbish that I will definitely remove and bin when I get five minutes, maybe when I get to the woods. Dad bought it for me when I first got given a set of house keys but I'm too old to have a teddy bear key ring.

I figured I won't get bothered by the trees and I can hide under my blanket in the car. I flinch as I replay all the shouting at home over the past week. I hope they're missing me and feel bad that I left home. As I half stumble off the kerb, I replay the argument we had earlier. It was pathetic and the wrestling on the floor with my little brother was even more pathetic.

It's dark and cold. I can't see well but there's shouting ahead. I try to focus on the group of men kicking something on the ground but my vision is getting a bit blurry from the tablet. The closer I get, the clearer the mass on the ground becomes. They're kicking Chipper. I stagger over and muscle through the crowd. 'Get off him,' I yell before pulling one man by the arm and flinging him to the ground. One thing I'm proud of is my strength. All those days at the gym are paying off now, even if I'm verging on paralytic and half drugged up.

A thin man with a missing front tooth is about to lay the boot into Chipper again so I draw back my fist and hit him, the impact of which I'm sure knocked out his remaining front tooth. Adrenaline pumps through me, rendering me almost deaf as my heart beats in my ears.

My friend is curled up in the foetal position, his face a bloodied mess and the other three keep going at him. 'Chip, I'm going to get you out of this.' I grab another man, or is he a boy? Either way I snatch his long hair in my fist and yank him downwards so hard, his face hits the tarmac. The others are shouting about Chipper getting so-and-so's sister pregnant.

Strong arms come up behind me and wrench me back. I elbow my attacker hard in the stomach before turning and punching him on the nose. That's when I catch sight of the police hat falling to the ground, moments before the police officer drops next to it. I just punched a police officer in the face and he looks as unconscious as Chipper does. I'm going to be in such big trouble. 'I was helping my friend. I'm sorry,' I say to him as I attempt to check for a pulse. I only wanted to save my friend. I'm on their side.

I'm dragged backwards by two officers and all the time I can see Chipper. He's still on the pavement as his attackers are dragged away and thrown into a riot van. I can only hope they show me some mercy when it comes to charging me because I never set out to hurt anyone.

The van hops over several speed bumps and I can't fight the wooziness that is coming over me. The tablet is also kicking in fast. I feel worse with every second that passes. Each bend is hell and my stomach keeps churning.

I don't feel like me. I know I shouldn't have taken the Valium I stole from Mum. Either everything is a blur or I'm asleep and all this is a dream. The custody sergeant has booked me in and I'm being dragged into a cell. Everything is fuzzy. The two officers push me and I hit the floor. I turn onto my back and look up and one of them spits in my face. Another officer comes into the cell. 'Get up,' he shouts.

I can't get up – I can barely feel my limbs and the room is spinning like I'm riding the waltzers. My eyes close and their shouting fades into the distance.

My world goes black and I'm enjoying the peace of it all but then I can't breathe. Is it a dream? The more I try to inhale, the more I choke. A flash of memory hits me. Chipper covered in blood. All those men punching and kicking him. The unconscious police officer. I try to inhale but it's a fight I'm losing. My whole body feels heavy – so heavy. I'm not going to make it.

All I can think of as I gasp for breath is my brother. I shouldn't have sworn at him like that before throwing him to the ground and pinning him down in a headlock. He's not as strong and I know I hurt him. I want to tell him I'm sorry, that I didn't mean anything I said or did. He's not a loser or a dickhead. As for Dad, he only did his best and I had to go and walk out in a temper and tell them I was never going back. I love my dad so much.

I want to scream for help but I can't move... or breathe...

ONE

TINA

Thursday, 20 November

Tina opened her curtains to another pleasant morning. Like every year, there seemed to be less and less coldness during winter and more mild yucky rain, and this year was no exception. She glanced through the netting covering the lounge window at the silver Mercedes that was still parked on her drive. The large oak tree that stood like a huge umbrella above half of her drive had shed even more leaves and the car had become swamped under a blanket of them, but that wasn't her problem. That car stopped being her problem four days ago, when the owner was meant to collect it. People really took the pee and she hated it. Her prices were cheap, much cheaper than what they charge at the train station, which is why her space was so popular.

She checked the parking app. Not a word from the car's owner – a woman called Maura Pickering. She paid in full for one night which has now turned into five nights, which now caused her a problem because her next customer was turning up in half an hour. That also meant she'd have to park her car on the road to make room for that car. She hated parking on the road. The last time she left her car out, it got scratched. All this because of one entitled woman. Tina placed her phone to her ear and tried to call the number the woman had registered to the app – again – and again all she got was that dead tone sound. It was obviously a fake number.

'Tina, it isn't going to go away just because you're staring at it,' her mother said, shuffling across the carpet with her walking frame.

'I know. It just annoys me that they do this all the time. I should start issuing fines and clamping them.'

'Maybe we should quit renting the drive out to save our sanity,' her mother said with a little laugh.

She fumed at the attitude of this Maura woman. Who the hell did she think she was? 'We need the money, Mum. We've spoken about this before.'

Her mum's smile downturned. 'It's my fault and I'm sorry. I know I fell but you can go back to work soon. I'm getting stronger every day and I won't use silver foil in the microwave again, I promise. See, I'm not losing my mind. I know I put foil in the microwave.'

Maybe she could go back to work soon and leave her mum at home, just as soon as her mum's leg had healed properly. She spotted a figure coming up the path. 'This must be Mrs Entitled and I'm going to have serious words. She owes us forty-eight pounds so if she thinks she can get into her car and slink off never to be seen again, she's got another thing coming.'

Leaving her mum in the living room, she hurried to the door and snatched it open whereupon the woman handed her a pizza menu from her bag. Tina screwed it up before the woman reached the end of the drive.

'Was it her?' her mum asked from the kitchen.

'No.' She checked her watch. It was now twenty minutes until the next arrival. She hurried into her house and slipped her shoes on, ready to move her car onto the road. After grabbing the keys, she stepped out and pressed the button to unlock her car. That's when she noticed a haze of flies buzzing around the boot of Maura Pickering's car.

She peered through the passenger window and nothing seemed out of order. An air freshener in the shape of a strawberry dangled from the rear-view mirror. A pen and a packet of mints occupied the central console and the car looked to be clean inside. A slight gust of wind blew a few oak leaves at her face. She exhaled, trying to get the debris away from her. Something was tickling her nose. She waved a hand at it and the fly flew away to gather with the others.

Tina hoped there wasn't a dead bird around the back of the car. It wouldn't be the first time she found something dead on her drive. There were a lot of bushes and trees and sometimes the foxes caught an animal and left the carcass behind. After taking a deep breath, she started walking towards the back of the car. Last time, she'd found a dismembered rat, another time it was a half-eaten pigeon. On both occasions, Tina had nearly thrown up.

'Tina,' her mum called from the door. 'I'm doing brunch. Do you want some?'

'I'll get back to you on that in a minute, Mum.'

'Is everything alright? Is it the foxes again?'

'I, err, I don't know.' She peered around by the bumper, only looking through one eye in the hope that if death was lying on the ground, she wouldn't see it in its entirety, but there was nothing. She opened both eyes and stood amongst the buzzing flies. What was going on? 'Mum, do you smell that?'

'Smell what?'

'I don't know, eggs, really bad cheese, drains, or the back of a bin lorry? Take your pick on any or all of the aforementioned.'

'I've just whisked up some eggs. Maybe you can smell them.'

There was no way she'd be smelling eggs all the way from the drive when their kitchen was at the back of the house. She took a step closer to the car boot. As she inhaled, it was as if the rancid smell was coating her nostrils. She stepped back and dry heaved.

'Tina, you don't look well. What's happening?'

She couldn't help trembling. Something was off and it wasn't a dead rat. She bent over to see a fly crawling out of the tiny gap in the boot, then another, and another. The overpowering stench hit her nostrils again. She moved back several steps and inhaled the clean air sharply. She knew that smell. She stumbled back, into her own car. 'Mum, call the police now. Tell them to come quickly.'

'What is it?'

'There's something dead in that boot. Tell them to get here now.'

'Hey, are you going to move one of these cars? I can't get my car on here and I've paid.' The man made her jump.

'Sorry, parking's cancelled.'

Her mind drifted as the man started ranting. She didn't hear a single word. All she could think of was her time working on the farm. Doing the admin for an abattoir told her that the smell coming from that boot was the smell of death. She couldn't help but think of poor Maura, the woman she'd been angry at for the past few days. All that time Maura had been rotting in her own car boot.

TWO

DI Gina Harte sat in her office eating an apple. Her cholesterol was good and her doctor had told her to keep it that way and it would stay good, as long as she kept eating like a damn pigeon. The scent of last night's pizza that the staff had been sharing wafted through the building. She'd never noticed it before but now she noticed it all the time and all she could do was dream of the cheese she shouldn't have. Her healthy diet wasn't really the cause of her frustrations, the main cause was the fact that Detective Chief Inspector Chris Briggs still wasn't talking to her. Since the last case, he'd treated her like she was just another member of staff, not the woman he'd been in love with for years – not that anyone knew because they had done the right thing and kept their work romance a secret. They both loved working for Cleevesford Police so wanted it to stay that way.

She kicked her bin. Another miserable day of him ghosting her had gone by. Nearly three weeks had passed since the case that ruined what they had. How long was he going to punish her for? Scrap that thought, maybe she should stop caring and move on. She got why he was so angry – she really did. Gina had been stupid, she knew that now, but it was easy thinking that in hindsight. She gave her own collateral away on a memory stick to a dodgy reporter to save her own skin and she didn't have time to regret it.

'Gina.' Briggs stood in the doorway. His hair was a little floppy, almost reaching his eyeline. She wanted to reach over to stroke it like she'd done in the past before kissing him, but he'd made it clear that he was her DCI and she was his DI. Despite what he thought of her now, she'd always love him. 'How's the paperwork going?'

Great, all he wanted to talk to her about was paperwork. She couldn't help but meet his gaze, searching for the smallest clue that he still cared, but he looked away. 'Sir... Chris.'

He slammed her door shut. 'Gina, not now.'

'I'm sorry I shut you out, okay. Can we please just talk about it?'

He shook his head. 'No, I said I was done and I'm done.' He opened the door and looked the corridor up and down before closing it again. 'You didn't even talk to me about giving that memory stick to that piece of scum. We talked about everything.'

'I know. I didn't get time to think let alone—'

'There's always time. You make time for the people you love.' He looked away and bit the inside of his mouth. 'Except you, Gina. You do what you want and I'm finding it all too much. I live on the edge when I'm with you and I accepted that things were complicated. I never let you down once. I kept all your secrets. Do you tell me everything or just choose bits to suit?'

She stood and walked over to him. 'You know everything.'

He looked beyond her, out of the window and frowned.

'Are you okay?' She glanced in the direction of his gaze.

'Err, yes. I thought I saw someone I knew, that's all.' He bit his nail.

'Is there something you maybe want to talk about?' She tried to ask as caringly as she could. It was obvious he was going through something.

'No.' He swallowed.

'Is there something you're not telling me?' Her stomach began to churn. His demeanour was making her uneasy. It was easy to blame her for holding things back and being the destroyer of what they had. Was he trying to project? Was he the one with the bigger problem?

He checked his watch. 'I have a meeting in five. Let's just act professionally at work and get the files up to date, okay?' He slammed her office door as he left.

She felt her eyes watering up and her fists clenching. She didn't know if she wanted to hit something or sob her heart out.

Her personal phone beeped and she opened the text. It was her daughter, Hannah, sending her a photo of her granddaughter, Gracie, dressed up as a bauble for the Christmas play she was rehearsing at school. She couldn't help but smile at her granddaughter's happy face. After taking a few breaths and fanning her eyes dry, she screwed up her notebook and threw it at the filing cabinet next to her office door. It bounced into the middle of the cramped room.

'Guv.' Detective Sergeant Jacob Driscoll stood in the doorway and frowned as he bent over to grab the balled-up notebook. He discreetly flattened it out and placed it on the edge of her desk. 'Are you okay?' His neat short back and sides framed his face and was a total contrast to her chaotic hair stuffed in a scrunchie.

The last case had hit her hard and her distance from Briggs had hit her even harder, but she had to be okay. She needed to do her job and get on with the pile of paperwork on her desk because the fairies weren't going to do it for her. 'Yes, sorry. I was just deep in thought.'

'There's just been a call. Uniform attended a scene.

Suspected body in the boot of a car. They've confirmed that it's looking likely that it is a body and they didn't want to tamper with it so they've called forensics. There's the smell, the flies... Anyway, Bernard and his team have already been informed and are on their way over to the crime scene now. Uniform have secured the scene. I said we were on our way.'

She stood and grabbed her charcoal-coloured coat and pulled it on over her slightly tight around the middle grey suit and white shirt. 'What do we know?'

He kept talking as they hurried past Nick, the desk sergeant, and another officer who was having trouble getting a drunken shoplifter towards the desk. 'The car has been parked on the owner's drive for five days now. She uses an app where people pay to park there so she doesn't know the owner of the car.'

They both got into Gina's car where Jacob carried on talking. 'The woman who made the booking is called Maura Pickering and she was meant to pick her car up four days ago. I've left that name with Wyre and O'Connor so they can look into her while we're gone.'

Gina knew that Detective Constables Paula Wyre and Harry O'Connor would do a thorough job and let them know any relevant information immediately. She paused to programme her satnav. 'Where are we going?'

'One Chandelton Avenue.'

'That's right by the train station, isn't it?' She typed the address in and pulled away.

'That's the one.'

After battling Cleevesford High Street and the early lunchtime traffic, Gina pulled into Chandelton Avenue and spotted Bernard Small, the crime scene manager, standing around the back of his forensics van with a crime scene assistant. He towered over everyone as he passed the women forensics suits. He tucked his long grey beard into his face covering and proceeded to step under the outer cordon with his tool box, where he met a fully togged-up crime scene assistant carrying a camera.

PC Smith stood guard at the outer cordon near the end of the drive, holding a clipboard. 'Afternoon,' he said as Gina and Jacob stepped out of the car.

They walked over and Gina stood outside the cordon knowing it was difficult to see what was going on further up the drive. She stepped a little to the left and caught sight of Bernard placing a crowbar into a gap and wrenching the boot open. The fact that the two crime scene assistants and Bernard recoiled and looked away told her that there was indeed a body in the boot. She swallowed at the thought of what they were walking into.

'Or should I say not so good afternoon?' PC Smith creased his brows and looked away from the scene behind him. He took a couple of breaths.

Gina caught the putrid scent as it carried on the breeze, and was glad that she'd only eaten an apple. 'Can you fill us in on what's happened so far?'

'Yes. We also have a team of officers on the way.'

'Good, as soon as they arrive we'll start the door-to-doors.'

'PC Ahmed has made a start. He left about fifteen minutes ago to start speaking with the neighbours.'

'Great,' Gina replied. 'Where's the woman who called the incident in and what do you know about the set-up here?'

PC Smith continued speaking and Jacob started making notes. 'Her name is Tina Wild. She lives with her mother Agatha Wild. She's fifty, her mum is eighty. Ms Wild rents her drive out. A customer called Maura Pickering booked the space and was only meant to stay for one night but the car has been there since which makes it five nights in total.'

'So, the body has been there all that time unless it was placed there after the car was parked up.' Gina knew from previous cases and her training that a body that had been left for five days would have gone through the rigor mortis stage and it would also have bloated because of gasses building up from the decomposition process. If the smell was anything to go by, this was the stage that their poor victim was in at the moment. She glanced up at the lounge window to see Tina, her mum, and a man looking out. 'Who's the man?'

'He was meant to be her next customer. He was about to park his car up when she told him what had happened and he waited with them for us to arrive. His car is parked further down the road.'

'Thank you. We'll head into the house to speak with them now. It looks like Bernard is going to be a while.' She watched as the assistant with the camera took what seemed like a constant stream of photos and the other assistant started placing stepping plates down. A gust billowed through Gina's hair and she wondered just how much evidence they'd probably lost due to the blustery winds. She also didn't envy the team with all the oak leaves and bird droppings covering the car and drive, then there was the body in the car. She took a deep breath at the thought of seeing Maura Pickering's body before having to inform her relatives.

Gina and Jacob walked around the cordon and were pointed towards the back gate by another uniformed officer. They headed alongside the house until they reached the garden and stepped through a barn door that led to a spacious kitchen diner where they were greeted by Tina Wild and the man.

'Is it okay if I go now? If I leave, I might just make my meeting in Coventry and I gave a statement to a police officer called PC Ahmed a short while back.'

Gina turned to Jacob. 'Could you quickly check with PC Smith?' Jacob nodded and left with the man. 'Ms Wild, are you okay to speak with me in here?'

'Please, it's Tina, I prefer Tina, and my mum is Agatha.' She stroked her grey-threaded braid that fell over her right shoulder and poured a couple of glasses of water, before placing them on the small kitchen table. 'Take a seat. I've told Mum to wait in the lounge for a bit. She's eighty and, as you can imagine, she's really upset by what's happened.'

Gina nodded. 'Of course.'

Jacob stepped back into the kitchen diner. 'All sorted, guv.' He sat down at the table with them and placed his notebook down and pulled his pen from his top pocket.

Gina continued. 'This must have been a huge shock so thank you for speaking to us. I'll get an officer to speak to you later about what happens next and offer you some ongoing support. Are you okay to speak now?'

The woman picked up her glass with shaky hands and held it to her lips before taking a nervous sip. 'I just want to get this over with and then we're going to stay with my Aunt Sue until you've finished here. I've already given your officers her address and I packed a few things while we were waiting.'

'I understand. I'm glad you have somewhere else to stay.' Gina paused for a moment, hating the fact that they needed information now and poor Tina looked like she could really do with a bit of time to process what was happening. 'It would really help us if you could tell me how the booking system works and about this booking in particular?'

Tina sipped her drink again and almost spilled her water on placing the glass back on the table. 'Err, yes. What day is it? I'm so sorry. This has thrown me.'

'It's okay,' Gina replied sympathetically. 'It's Thursday.'

'Okay.' Tina picked up the iPad on the table and logged in to the app. Her hands began to tremble even more.

'Do you need a moment?' Gina knew that shock hit people in different ways.

Tina closed her eyes for a second, then continued. 'No. Right, here's the booking. Maura Pickering was meant to arrive on Saturday evening and then pick her car up by midday on Sunday. The booking was made at ten-fifteen p.m. on Friday the fourteenth of November.'

'Do you have her address and phone number?'

'I have access to a phone number but not an address. The number isn't in use.'

'Do you know the purpose of the booking?'

'No, but most people I speak to use our space to catch the train into Coventry or Warwick. Our space is cheaper than what the station charge and it's not always safe to leave a car on the street here. The roads are a bit tight and cars get damaged and scratched.'

'Do you have CCTV?'

Tina shook her head. 'No, it's so expensive.'

'How about a camera doorbell?'

'No. Mum loves the one we've had since nineteen eighty-nine.'

'Did you see the car and its driver arrive?' They still had no idea who was in the boot of the car and couldn't assume it was Maura Pickering. Maura could be the perpetrator or her car could have been stolen.

'I was already in bed. Mum wakes up about five every morning in pain so I have to tend to her. She had a big fall and has taken a while to get back on her feet properly. It's been one thing after another so I've been off work for a while caring for her.'

'What time did you go to bed on Saturday the fifteenth of November?'

'Around nine thirty, just after putting Mum to bed. I usually go up at that time.'

'Was the car on the drive then?'

'No, I looked out to see if it had arrived and it wasn't there.'

'Did you hear it arrive later?'

She slowly shook her head. 'No, I fell asleep around ten and

I didn't hear anything before then. I would have heard it pulling up if I'd been awake because the drive is right under my bedroom window.' Gina waited for Jacob to note down the times.

'Would your mum have heard anything?'

'She sleeps in the bedroom overlooking the garden and she'd have taken her hearing aids out. I did ask her while we were waiting for you but she said she was asleep by then anyway.' Gina knew they'd have to ask Agatha Wild but made a note for uniform to do that.

'When did you wake up on the Sunday?'

'As I said, it would have been around five. I would have had to have gone down to get Mum's pain medication around that time. She's normally desperate by then. I don't leave it with her because she can forget she's taken it already and I don't want to risk her overdosing.'

'What time did you first notice the silver Mercedes parked on your drive?'

'I gave Mum her tablets and looked out the window. It was maybe about six that morning. The car was there. It was dark but I could see it parked up. I didn't take too much notice of it being there. I never do take any notice when anyone parks up. People can come and go and I often never see them. They pay through the app so there's no need for me to greet them or be here.'

'How long was the booking for?'

'The car was meant to be off our drive for midday but it was still there. This happens sometimes. People often take a bit more time and think it's okay to pay when they return. I get angry after a couple of days and mark them down on the app. As I said before, I tried to call the number attached to the booking but it doesn't work. I've given this information to your PCs. I guess I should have realised something was wrong and called you then but I've been busy with Mum.'

'What made you check on the car today?'

'I had another booking. I was well mad by then because I knew I'd need to start looking for somewhere safe to park my car on the road. I went outside around ten, maybe ten thirty this morning to move my car... that's when I was... I saw...' She swallowed and looked away. 'I saw the flies first, and then there was the smell and I just knew, then I called you around ten forty, at a guess.'

PC Smith knocked on the open back door. 'Guv, can I have a word?'

'Excuse me a moment.' Gina left Jacob to continue asking the questions and tie up the interview. PC Smith stood on the path waiting for her. 'Is Bernard able to speak with me now?'

'No, guv. He's still working the scene but he said in a few minutes he'll be able to share what they've found with you. PC Ahmed has also found someone who wants to give a statement. They saw the driver of the car. I also heard forensics saying that the victim is not the owner of the car. It's a man.'

THREE

Jacob hurried down the side path to the house to meet Gina at the end of the drive. She peered across at the scene but could barely see anything now the large tent had been erected over the whole car. The gathering in the road had got bigger since she'd pulled up. Neighbours held phones out and a uniformed officer kept asking them to keep back and stop filming but Gina knew the officer was wasting his time. It was like herding cats. She also knew that some inaccurate version of the news would have already hit social media by now before she'd even had a chance to speak to a relative of the victim.

PC Shafiq Ahmed crossed the road and they headed away from the crowd to talk privately. 'Alright, guv. I've been speaking to Mrs Cole at number fifteen who saw the car pulling in and she said she'd like to speak to you.'

'We'll head over now. Thanks, Shaf.'

Gina nudged through the crowd and headed along the pathway until she and Jacob reached the semi in the cul-de-sac.

A woman opened the door. 'Detectives?'

Gina nodded. 'I'm DI Harte and this is DS Driscoll.'

'Come in.' The woman stepped barefoot into her hallway

with a toddler on her hip, her long brown hair falling over her red T-shirt. She nudged open the door to a dining room. 'Have a seat. Can I get you a drink?'

Gina shook her head, hoping to hurry so she could speak to Bernard. She also didn't want to put the woman out, especially as her toddler was beginning to fidget in her arms. She placed the little girl down, her two bunches bobbing as she ran over to a box of plastic farmyard animals and tipped them all on the floor. 'Can I take your name, please?'

'Alia Cole.'

'Thank you.'

Jacob noted that down so Gina continued. 'As you know, we're investigating an incident on your road and one of our officers said that you have some information that might help us.'

'Is Tina okay? I tried to call her but her phone's off. I was getting worried. We're quite close in this neighbourhood and we all try to look out for her mum.'

'She's been speaking with our officers. Hopefully she'll be able to answer your calls soon. Can you tell me more about the driver of the car?'

'We are talking about the silver Merc, aren't we?'

'Yes.'

'I didn't know it was parked on Tina's drive until your PC spoke about it. Her driveway is covered by all those trees and the big oak, but a car matching that description came steaming up our road about midnight last Saturday and I really freaked out.'

'What happened?' Gina gave the woman a moment to compose her thoughts and a cat meowed as it entered the room.

'This is Archibald, our very senior cat. He was out that evening. Our daughter had woken us up. While my husband was soothing her in the nursery, I came downstairs to put the kettle on. Moments later, I heard Archibald wailing, then a fox joined in. I got worried so I opened the front door and

Archibald was nowhere to be seen. A moment later he darted into the middle of the road, wailing, just as that silver car sped into our road like it was competing in the Grand Prix and I don't know how it missed my cat, I really don't.' She let out a long breath.

'Did the driver pull over? You live in a cul-de-sac.' Gina noticed that there had been cars parked all around the loop, almost bumper-to-bumper with only gaps left for drives.

'No, the driver kept revving the car while doing a three-point-turn before speeding back out. I must admit, I was a bit shaken so I grabbed the cat and ran back in. We thought about reporting it but the car had already gone. I didn't catch the number plate and no one was hurt. This kind of thing doesn't normally happen around here.'

The toddler passed Jacob a plastic horse. 'Thank you. I love your horse,' he said.

The little girl smiled and shyly put her knuckle in her mouth.

'I just can't stop thinking, what if that happened in the daytime and what if we were outside getting into the car and he ran her over.' Alia looked at her daughter.

'It doesn't bear thinking about.' Gina paused. 'Did you see the driver?'

'Only briefly. We have a fair few street lamps. I'd say male, white, but he was wearing a dark sweater or hoodie – squarish jaw – I think. Oh, he was wearing a baseball cap which obscured his eyes as he seemed to be looking down.' She shivered. 'The whole incident is now giving me the creeps. I just read on social media that they found a body in the car, is that right?'

Gina felt her fists clenching. Of course, someone had already seen something from afar or had been watching through the trees next to the house, close enough to hear what the team had been saying. 'We're just starting to investigate so I can't discuss the case. There will be a press release soon.'

'Sorry, you're right. I shouldn't be so nosy. I'm just scared, that's all. I worry about a lot, especially after becoming a parent.'

Gina glanced at the little girl who sweetly gave Jacob a plastic sheep. 'That's understandable. It's a horrible thing to happen.' Gina paused for a moment, then continued. 'Is there anything else you can tell us about the incident or that night?'

'I'm not sure if it's relevant.'

'If it isn't that's fine, but please tell us because it might be.'

'The day before, I was walking back from a friend's house and I walked past Tina's drive. I thought I saw smoke or fog. It wasn't too late, maybe about seven on Friday evening... I was sure I heard rustling in the trees alongside Tina's house. I got scared and ran the rest of the way home. My husband went out to see if anyone was there but he said there wasn't. I don't know...' She frowned. 'I just got this feeling someone had been watching me approach and that they'd accidentally moved and drawn attention to themselves. It sounds odd but it's like I felt a person's gaze on me despite not being able to see anyone.' Alia dismissively waved a hand. 'Maybe I'm being silly.'

'Where did you hear this noise coming from?'

'By the trunk of the oak tree. It's huge, perfect size to hide behind. When I heard there had been an incident, I wondered if there had been someone there that night, scoping the place out.' She shivered. 'I feel sick at the thought now.'

Jacob's phone beeped. He led Gina into the hallway before speaking in a whisper while Alia comforted her now crying toddler in the other room. 'That was Wyre. The owner of the car, Maura Pickering. She died a month ago.'

FOUR

Gina kept up with Jacob as they hurried back to Tina Wild's house. 'So, the car owner died a month ago? Did Wyre say anything else in her message?'

'Only that the car had been SORN.' Jacob checked the road before they crossed. 'We'll have an address to follow up on which is good. Who takes a SORN car that belonged to a dead woman?'

Gina shrugged. 'Relatives, or maybe it was stolen. Can you get Maura Pickering's address? I think we need to head over there next, see if anyone else lives there and find out who had access to the car. Can you also ask Wyre to check the system for reports of this car being stolen?'

He nodded and pulled his phone out. 'I'll call the station.'

Bernard beckoned Gina over. A crime scene assistant handed her a pack containing a white forensics suit, mask, shoe covers, a hair cover and gloves. She removed her coat and Jacob offered to take it while still talking on the phone to Wyre, then she started to feed her legs into the coverall. Once she was all togged up, Bernard led her through the outer, then the inner cordon.

'What can you tell me?'

'Stick to stepping on the plates, as usual,' Bernard replied. He stood outside the entrance to the tent.

Gina glanced over her shoulder at the oak tree. Their witness was right. The trunk was definitely big enough for someone to hide behind, especially as it was set in a carpet of unruly shrubs and bushes. 'Bear with me.' She walked back towards the cordons and PC Smith began to move the tape for her. 'I'm not leaving yet but when the other PCs arrive, can you go with a forensics assistant to search around the oak tree for anything that might have got caught up in the bushes or undergrowth? The witness we just spoke to thought she heard someone lurking around there last Friday evening around seven, that's the night before the car was parked up here.'

'I'll arrange that, guv.'

'Thanks.' She hurried back to the tent. 'Sorry about that.'

'It's okay. You can step inside but be warned, it's up there with the worst.'

The smell was already permeating through her mask. She took a deep breath and stepped under the canvas cover with Bernard. 'What can you tell me?' She glanced at the bloated man in the boot and caught sight of the wriggling maggots on the body as Bernard spoke. She looked away and batted the flies around her face away with her hand. Her stomach took a few seconds to stop churning. Someone had done that to him, left him like that. He was someone's son. She clenched her fists and not for the first time that day.

'The victim is a male aged forty-five to fifty-five. Blond hair. Blue eyes. It's hard to estimate weight or height. As you can see, he's still scrunched up in the boot and his body is bloated. The post-mortem will tell us more and we're obviously keen for that to get underway. As for his clothing, you can see he's wearing track bottoms, a blue T-shirt and no footwear.'

Gina couldn't see anything. She didn't want to look. She

wanted to hurry up this conversation, escape the smell and get this man's killer off the streets. 'How did he die?'

'Not in the car,' Bernard replied. 'When he died, his blood pooled on the right side of his body. He's scrunched up in the boot with his left side touching the base of the boot which tells us he was placed there post-mortem. There is also a length of cord in the car and you can see signs of restraint on him, such as marks on the wrists and ankles. There are cuts on his arms that are consistent with defence wounds. I can't actually confirm the cause of death from this scene. Again, we need to conduct the post-mortem to get more information.'

Gina took a shallow breath to try and ease the light-headedness that had crept up on her. 'When will that be likely?'

'He's in an awkward position and moving him is going to be messy but we need to get the body out of here as soon as we can. I'm just waiting for more reinforcements as it's going to be a delicate process.'

Gina didn't envy Bernard's team right now. Her heart started to thrum. She needed to be able to take a full breath soon, before she passed out.

'As for the post-mortem, I'd say tomorrow, late morning.'

'Thank you. In the meantime, if you find anything else out that might be useful to the investigation, can you contact me straight away?'

'Of course.'

'Have you or your team found anything inside the car that might help us?'

Bernard cleared his throat and to Gina's relief, he stepped outside the tent. 'We're still working our way through it. We're in the process of taking swabs and looking for all kinds of trace evidence. Again, anything we do find will need to go to the lab.'

Gina took several deep breaths but the scent of death had already coated her nose and throat. Her heart banged harder. 'I'll get the results fast-tracked.' She knew fast-tracked didn't mean as-fast-as-she-wanted but faster-than-run-of-the-mill was better than nothing.

Several uniformed officers had started scouring the bushes and trees by the house. 'Thanks, Bernard. I won't keep you any longer,' Gina said as she half jogged across the stepping plates, away from him. As soon as she escaped the confines of the cordons, she sidestepped Jacob and headed towards the officers searching the bushes, not to help but to remove her mask and inhale several deep breaths of fresh air. The sight of the maggots sent a shiver through her as she bent over and kept breathing.

'Guv…' Jacob came up behind her.

She jumped. 'Sorry, I didn't want to be featured looking this green on "What's Up Cleevesford".' The community social media page tended to report every bit of gossip first. And she didn't want to see her face plastered all over it.

'It was that bad?'

'One of the worst. How anyone could do that to a person and leave them like that…' She stood up straight before inhaling and exhaling slowly. 'Did you get Maura Pickering's last address?'

'Yep. Sandalwood Road, so not too far.'

'Great, we should go.' Gina peeled her crime scene suit off and popped it in the waste bin, happily leaving the scene to Bernard and his team. She had seen enough. She sniffed the arm of her suit jacket. She wasn't sure if it stank of death or if her nose was too far gone to tell. She removed it and took her coat from Jacob before putting it on, hopefully trapping any odours on her person underneath it.

Gina stopped at the car and stared out at the crowd, wondering if whoever murdered that man was watching on as the scene unfolded. Why? Was it gang related? Drugs? Personal? She gazed at the people loitering at the back. There were a mix of onlookers. Old, young, teenagers, people with dogs, a woman in a wheelchair and another woman with pink hair. No one stood out or looked to be alone or suspicious. She opened her car boot and threw her jacket into it before slamming it closed.

Just as she and Jacob were about to get into her car, PC Ahmed called her. 'Guv.' He ran across the road to them. 'We've found an illegal disposable vape by the tree. We've bagged it up for the lab.'

'A vape is good. The neighbour we just spoke to mentioned seeing smoke or fog coming from those trees last Friday.' Gina imagined someone loitering outside Tina and Agatha's house, vaping while watching them. The perp would have been able to see right into Tina's living room from that vantage point. They may have seen how busy looking after her mother she was to care if a car had been left on her drive for several days. Gina wondered if the perp had already killed their victim by this time or had they been there preparing for the deed? A shiver tickled the back of her neck. It felt up close, personal and calculated, and she was glad that Tina and her mother were staying with a relative for a few days.

A CSI beckoned them all back over towards the cordons. Gina ran across the road with Jacob, her knees slightly shaking at the thought of having to go near the car again. The CSI held the clear evidence bag up so that Gina could see what was in it. 'We found this in the victim's pocket, the one he was lying on in the boot. We could just about reach into it.'

Gina read the name on the photo driving licence. She looked at the small photo of the man with the blond hair and blue eyes. His name was Kain Pickering.

FIVE

JUSTINE

It was almost three in the afternoon. Justine tried to call Craig again but he still wasn't answering.

'Mum, have you seen my footie boots?'

She flinched and put her phone away. Craig might not return her call for ages. Maybe he was in yet another meeting. All day? She second questioned everything now. He'd been travelling back and forth to Newcastle for weeks trying to set this new accounting system up for the multinational company he worked for. She looked at her boy, almost the spitting image of his father with his green eyes and flaming-red hair that she loved so much. He too always wore a cap to tuck his sprawling mop into, which she hated. Both he and Craig had gorgeous hair.

'I put them in the garage. They were getting mud all over my lovely floor and Pixie was trying to lick them. I didn't want her to get sick.' She nodded to their very old bulldog who lay snoring in her basket.

'But I need them and I'm late.' Danny slammed the back door to go to the garage.

She shrugged and she didn't care. For years she'd cleaned

his boots and his kit but he was an adult now, he could do those things for himself and if he couldn't, his dirty boots and trainers would live in the garage. After heading upstairs to her office, she turned her computer off. The bridal shop video edit could wait until later. For now, she had her yoga class to attend and she wasn't going to miss that for the world. She lived for the smoothie bar there and the time spent with her friends that came after.

The house shuddered as Danny slammed the front door. She glanced out of the upstairs window and watched her son running towards the bus stop. Late – always late. Not bearing the mental load of organising his life was doing her the world of good and she knew it would help Danny to become more independent, too. He needed to learn to organise his own life now. She was being cruel to be kind, only he couldn't see that yet.

One last mirror check. She was loving her new crossover jumpsuit in fern green – just perfect. She checked her messages and tried to call Craig again, this time he answered. 'Is everything okay?'

'Are you out of breath?'

'No, but you did get me out from under a desk. I was having a fight with a cable that had dislodged itself from the back of a computer. Is everything okay?'

She sighed, wondering if now was the right time to tell him how much it upset her when he forgot to call her. She felt like just another wife of a man who worked away and forgot she existed. She was a cliché. No, she was turning into her mother. Her father was the type to leave her mum wondering when he'd be home, not only that, he'd been a prize cheater. Her stomach dropped slightly. Deep down she knew that Craig had been cheating on her and when he got home, they were going to have to talk. 'I guess. You didn't call me back last night and you weren't answering today. I thought something had happened.'

'So sorry, love. I've just been working hard to get this project finished so I can come home. I worked late, got back to the hotel and fell asleep. I was out early this morning to battle the traffic. I knew you were working on the wedding shop video and I didn't want to disturb you.'

Disturb her. She'd been trying to call him. No, her gut was telling her not to trust him one bit. This type of job only normally lasted a couple of weeks but Craig had been at it too long for her liking. 'You said you'd be back by now.'

'And everything is running behind. I'll be back soon, I promise.'

'How soon?'

The call ended abruptly. She FaceTimed him instead and he answered immediately looking a bit red and flustered. His freckles were far more prominent than usual, like he'd got hot and bothered, or like whenever he'd been out running. 'Sorry about that. I think the signal dipped. As you can see, I'm okay and I'm working my socks off.' He held a piece of cable up and smiled. 'I've had it up to here with leads.'

'It's just nice to see your face. I miss you.' She tried to peer at the office he was in but all she could see was a blank wall.

'I miss you too.' He blew a kiss at her.

They'd been married twenty-two years which is how she knew something had changed between them. She couldn't put her finger on when things had changed but she could put her finger on the light red scratch on his neck if he'd been in the room with her. 'Have you hurt your neck?'

'Err.' He scrunched his brow and felt the line. 'I did it shaving, the other morning. It's just a nick.'

'How did you really do it?'

His smile turned into a frown. 'Justine, I am not doing this now. I'm at work and people are listening. I did it shaving, okay. I love you. There is no one else. Do we have to go through this every time I work away? It's exhausting. Is that why you had to FaceTime me?'

She let out a long breath. It wasn't good to argue, not with him being so far away. She needed him home. Maybe the sick feeling in the pit of her stomach was just her missing him and everything was okay, but that scratch wasn't caused by shaving and she resented him treating her like she was stupid.

'I've got to go. The boss is coming. Love you.' He ended the call.

She grabbed her yoga mat and gym bag and stormed out the door.

She was going to find out who her husband was sleeping with if it killed her.

SIX

Gina stood at the end of Maura Pickering's drive, half mulling over the murder and half mulling over her argument with Briggs that morning. Was it more about him than her? She hadn't imagined him looking out of the window in the strange way that he did. She shook those thoughts away and took in Maura's house. She owed her full attention to their victim.

Maura's Victorian semi-detached house stood proud from the road and the box hedge that divided it from the path was about eight feet tall, leaving Gina in its shadow. Every curtain was closed and a gate to the left led to an uneven, slabbed path that led to the front door and alongside the house. She knocked at the door and gazed through the frosted-glass panel to see a fuzzy version of the huge porch and an internal door. No one answered. She glanced down to see letters and pamphlets almost spewing out of the open letter box. 'That's a lot of post. It looks like no one has been here for a while.'

Jacob stepped over the moss-covered tiles and nudged the gate with his shoulder, and it opened with a creak. 'That seems odd.' He pointed to the damaged lock that now lay on the ground. Nails stuck out of the wood at head height. 'It looks like someone leaned over and wrenched it off the gate to break in. The wood looks rotten. It wouldn't have taken much effort.'

He led the way and Gina followed him. Ivy carpeted the whole of that side of the house leaving only a small gap for the stair window. A wooden owl peered down at her. She looked away, not wanting to feel unnerved but the closer they got to the back of the house, the more unnerved she felt. As they stepped into the long-overgrown garden she caught sight of a panel of smashed glass in the back door. She stood next to Jacob and peered through. 'Key left in the door.' She pulled a pair of latex gloves over her hands and then popped some boot covers on. 'Can you call it in?'

Jacob pulled his phone out and stood on the patio.

Gina glanced down, checking for footsteps or any other evidence that had been left behind. There was nothing visible to the naked eye. She knew they were standing outside the house where their victim's murder could have taken place. 'What if someone else is in there? They might be inside and hurt.'

'We should definitely check after seeing what happened to Kain Pickering,' Jacob replied. 'He might not be the only victim.'

Gina stepped into the kitchen first. 'Hello. Police. I'm DI Harte,' she called out. A shiver ran through her. It was possible that the killer could be in the house. She held a hand out and placed a finger to her lips so that they could listen in silence. She heard talking coming from upstairs. 'There's someone above us. It sounds odd, maybe they're on the phone.' A loud thud shook the ceiling light. 'Hello. Police,' she shouted again.

Still on his call to the station, Jacob whispered an update before turning back to Gina. 'Backup is less than a minute away. There was a car at the supermarket and they're almost here.'

Gina let out a long breath as she crept between the six-seater wooden dining table on her left and the huge breakfast bar to her right. The Shaker-style kitchen was modern and the Belfast sink full of dirty plates and cups. Another cup sat next to the kettle, dry with a teabag string sticking out of it as if whoever was upstairs had been about to make a cuppa. There was no steam coming from the kettle spout, so maybe they weren't about to come down anytime soon. Her heart began to bang again.

A slight tapping sound coming from the floor tiles between the breakfast bar and back worktop made Gina flinch.

Drip... drip. Then it stopped for a moment before starting again. *Drip.*

She crept around the breakfast bar to see a small puddle of water on the floor. 'There's a leak coming from upstairs.' She pointed to the tainted plaster above where another droplet was about to fall.

'Guv, backup is outside.' He spoke down the phone to Wyre who was still coordinating the officers outside.

'Tell them we entered through the back door and to cover the front and back. We need an ambulance, just in case. There's someone in the house and we don't know if they're hurt.' She tried to listen to what was being said above but the words weren't clear. It sounded like a man, then she heard the tone change and the man began to mutter. 'Keep them on the line. We're going upstairs.' She pointed to the kitchen door and nudged it with her elbow until it opened. She followed the long, tiled hallway, passing the tall-ceilinged lounge. 'Police. We're coming up.'

Again, there was no response. With slightly trembling legs, Gina took the first step and followed that with a few more. 'Keep to the sides. There are drag marks on the stair carpet.' The sight of Kain Pickering's body had unnerved her. She paused midway up to see photos of who she thought had to be Maura in a photo with a man and a woman. She recognised Kain Pickering from his driver's licence photo but she didn't recognise the woman. The step near the top creaked. She stopped walking to pinpoint which room the tinny muttering was coming from. 'I think it's the radio,' she said to Jacob. 'The door's closed.' A scraping sound came from behind it. Gina could just about hear it over the local weather report that started up. She swallowed, wondering if some desperate victim in a poor state had dropped from the bed to the floor as soon as they heard Gina calling up the stairs and now they were scraping at the door. Running towards it, she grabbed the handle and let out a small scream as a cat darted between her legs and ran downstairs. She stood at the entrance to the room, her mouth slightly open as she took everything in.

'There's been a struggle here.' She imagined their victim all tangled in the white sheets as he was attacked. Brown streaks that were almost certainly red a few days ago had crusted onto the bed but there wasn't enough blood to have killed a person. 'Bernard said our victim had defence wounds and looking at what we have here, this scene could easily corroborate that. It looks like the victim had been thrashing. He fought back. Maybe he was asleep when the attack happened. Did the perp put the radio on to disguise the noise? Can you ask Wyre to contact Bernard and send someone to work this scene?'

Gina pulled her top over her nose as she spotted the cat faeces in the corner of the room. 'Poor cat.' She spotted a small water bowl under the bay window and next to it was an upturned cat treat box.

Jacob began speaking while Gina stepped further into the room. That's when she spotted the small pale-blue teddy bear sitting on a smear of blood with its head peering above a crease in the sheets. It had to have been placed there after the thrashing around. Maybe the killer had left them a clue or maybe the teddy was merely coincidence. She didn't believe in coincidences. She glanced around the rest of the room. It was as ordinary as ordinary got. Painted cream walls, a wooden wardrobe, a set of drawers, a big old vanity desk and a king-sized bed. There were no other stuffed toys or signs of anything twee like the bear. It stood out in the neat, clutter-free room. 'The bathroom.' She remembered the leak.

Backing out of the doorway to the main bedroom, Gina pointed to the other bedroom door. Jacob opened it. 'Clear. Looks like a storage and laundry room.'

She then turned to the bathroom and opened the door. Without stepping in, she spoke. 'I think we now know how Kain Pickering died.' She knew they'd have to wait for forensics to confirm her theory with water on the lungs but with the shower curtain dragged into the bath full of water and torn, she was ninety-five per cent certain this is where their victim ended up after fighting with his attacker on the bed. The tap still dripped into the full bath, not fast, but fast enough to keep the water spilling slowly over the edges, causing the leak. 'It's possible that he was killed here before being dragged down the stairs and straight out of the front door, then bundled into Maura Pickering's car boot. It looks like the perp then drove Kain Pickering to Tina and Agatha Wild's house to park the car, taking the body away from the murder scene. Were they hoping to come back and clean up? If so, why didn't they? Did they get disturbed?' She had so many questions running through her mind.

'Guv,' an officer shouted loudly up the stairs.

She hurried back along the landing and carefully down the stairs, leaving the scene for forensics to handle. 'Did you see a cat?' She was kicking herself. The cat had escaped and as far as she knew, it might have evidence under its claws or in its fur and it definitely would have been scared.

'We saw a tabby. Was that the one?'

Gina nodded.

'It belongs to the neighbour and it had been missing since last Friday morning.'

'Damn, we need to borrow the cat. I just hope it isn't too

late. It was trapped in the bedroom and managed to slip through my feet. We need to check it for evidence.'

'We have the cat. I called you because that neighbour wants to speak to you about some funny goings-on, as she put it. She didn't call these incidents in but on seeing us here, she wondered if she should say something. She said that the noises have been haunting her but she's been too scared to confront Kain Pickering and she thinks he kidnapped her cat. Not only that, he threatened her and told her if she didn't butt out of his and Maura's life, when she was alive, he'd make her wish she was dead.'

Gina stepped outside to find a woman standing on the path next to the cat that had slipped past her, only this time it was in a basket meowing to be let out.

'I'm so glad Gordon came home. I've been missing him. I made posters and I even put a few up in the bus stops but no one called. I know Kain took him. That man is horrible. Where is the bastard?' the woman asked in an accent that told Gina she was originally from the West Country.

'May we come inside and speak with you?' Gina asked, not wanting to say much more on the doorstep, especially as a few neighbours were starting to come out of their houses, wondering what was going on.

The woman gasped a few times. She pulled an inhaler from the depths of her thick cardigan pocket and began sucking on it. 'That's better. I shouldn't exert myself really but when I saw Gordon, I almost ran back for the carrier. He wouldn't come to me at first but he soon jumped in for a mouthful of treats. Scared stiff, he was.'

'May we borrow Gordon, so he can have a check over and we can take some swabs? He was trapped in a room next door and we have reason to believe something happened in that room and Gordon might be able to help us with our investigation.'

'Of course.' She furrowed her grey wiry brows and allowed one of the PCs to take Gordon. 'You won't hurt him, will you?'

'No,' Gina replied. 'We'll take care of him.'

The woman turned to the PC taking the basket. 'He's hungry and scared. Look after him or you'll have me to deal with.' She raised her brows.

'I'll personally stay with him. I have a cat, too. He's like family. I'll make sure Gordon is looked after.' The PC smiled and gently took the basket.

'And I want him back soon.' The woman plodded along the path, swaying from side to side with each step as she led them into the house next door to Maura Pickering's. Her oversized nightdress fell to her knees over a pair of jeggings. The woman's house was the complete opposite to Maura's. It was bursting with decorative items including soft toys, artificial flowers in vases and a whole gallery picture wall up the stairs – rather than just a couple of family photos. She struggled into her kitchen and fell into the carver chair at the head of the table. 'Take a seat, both of you. I'd make you a drink, but...' She pulled her inhaler out again and wheezed.

Jacob remained standing. 'Would you like me to make you a drink?'

'That would be lovely. Everything is on the worktop. Tea, milk and two sugars.'

A moment later the kettle began to boil and Jacob poured them all a drink. Gina wondered if the woman had anyone who helped her or maybe she only seemed so out-of-breath because she'd chased her cat. He brought the drinks to the table and sat.

'Can I take your name?' Gina asked. Jacob snatched his pen from his jacket pocket and pulled his notebook from his trouser pocket.

'It's Joyce Burton.'

'How well did you know Kain Pickering?'

'Not well but I knew enough.' She tutted and picked her mug of tea up with shaky hands. With each breath her chest rattled. 'Sorry about this. I had pneumonia several months ago and it's lingered like mad. I can't shake it. I miss Maura, we used to look out for each other and most days we'd have a coffee and a natter. I always said, if one of us bangs hard on the bedroom walls, to call an ambulance.' She took a moment to wheeze and cough. 'Neither of us were getting any younger and she had a bad heart.' Joyce let out a long rattly breath. 'I loved Maura to bits, I did. She was my best friend. We went on holidays together and on days out, until I got pneumonia. Soon after, that weasel of a son of hers came sniffing by. He lost his house; thought he could just move in with her and he isn't a good man. She didn't even want him to move in but she was a good mother. She couldn't say no to him despite him being a whirlwind of chaos. He caused her no end of stress with his problems. Is all this fuss to do with him? I wouldn't be surprised if you lot were after him for something.'

'We're currently investigating an incident so I can't say much as yet.' She couldn't tell Joyce that they had found Kain Pickering's body, not before speaking to his next-of-kin. 'Did Maura have any more family members that you know of?'

'Yes, she had a daughter, Lindy. She's lovely. Maura loved her to bits.'

'Do you have Lindy's contact details?'

'No, but I know she lives in the converted post office house on Thornberry Avenue. You can't miss it. It has an old Royal Mail post box attached to the building. I went there with Maura on a couple of occasions.' Gina nodded to Jacob who began to message those details to Wyre and O'Connor back at the station. The sooner they spoke to the victim's next-of-kin, the better.

She needed to know more about what had gone on between

Maura, Kain and Joyce – maybe she knew of someone who may have wanted Kain dead. 'Can you tell me more about the relationship between Kain and Maura?'

'You can ask Lindy all this when you speak to her. She'll back me up on what I say. Kain treated his mother badly. Her once calm house suddenly became full of his drama. She used to get so upset with him, with his drinking, and he'd always try to get her to help him out with money. She gave him quite a lot, and even paid him twice to fit a security system on her house and he still didn't do the work. He'd been taking her for a ride.'

'Is that what he does for a living – security?'

Joyce nodded. 'I don't know if he's on the tools anymore because he kept telling her that one of his team would do it but he has a security firm. He's basically an alcoholic and because of that, his company has been going down the pan. I'm not even sure if he was bankrupt, you know. I think Maura mentioned something. She said if she asked him to leave, he'd have nowhere to go and what mother wants to see her son out on the streets?'

Gina started to wonder if Kain could have owed some money to a loan shark. Maybe that was a motive worth exploring. 'You told our officer that you heard noises and they'd been haunting you.'

Joyce placed her inhaler between her lips and puffed on it again. 'It was a particular noise. I heard a loud bang like the one Maura and I rehearsed in case we were in trouble. One huge loud bang, repeated again after a few seconds. I heard that last Friday and it freaked me out. It was daytime but I know Kain had been lying in until all hours. It was him and it was like he was taunting me that Maura was no longer there.'

In her mind, Gina pictured a panicking Kain, entangled in sheets while fighting off his attacker. He did the only thing he could think of, the same thing Maura would do to try to get the attention of her neighbour in an emergency, only that time, Joyce thought she was being taunted. 'What time was this?'

'I can't remember now. Early afternoon. I don't clock watch these days. It was after one. I have lunch at twelve thirty every day. I'd gone up after my sandwich to iron some clothes. That reminds me, he had the radio on quite loud or maybe it was an audiobook.'

'Did you see anyone coming or going that day?'

'Only Kain. I could only see him from the bedroom but he was wearing his baseball cap. He always wears a baseball cap.'

'Did you see his face?'

'No, just the top of his hat. He was loading something into Maura's car, then he drove off.'

'And when was this?'

'It was dark. I was going to bed at this time but again, I don't know the time, but it was after ten. I was closing my curtains. That's why I looked out.'

'Are you sure it was Kain Pickering?'

'Are you saying it couldn't be? It had to be him; he was wearing Kain's hat.' She sipped her tea. 'You make a good tea.'

'Thanks,' Jacob replied with a smile.

'I only saw the hat and I assumed it was Kain. It might not have been him but if it wasn't him, who else could it have been and why would they be wearing his hat?' She shrugged.

'Did you see any other cars parked outside that aren't normally parked outside on that day?'

She shook her head. 'No, only those belonging to the neighbours.'

'Did Kain have any visitors?'

'No, I never saw anyone visiting him. Maura said he'd been married but they split up about two years ago. She didn't mention any friends of his, only that he stays in all the time and drinks.'

'You mentioned to our officer that Kain threatened you and said that he'd make you wish you were dead.'

Joyce swallowed. 'He scares me, I won't lie. He has these intense blue eyes, really cold and I'm short. I always feel like he's towering over me. I had the nerve to stand up to him, for Maura. I told him that his behaviour was upsetting her, and stressing her out. I asked him when he was going to stop drinking. She was eighty when he moved in. That's too old to be putting up with his problems. Maura had such a big heart but it was a broken one. It was like he wanted her to have a heart attack so he could have her house. I'd hear him shouting at her when the windows were open. She was my friend and I saw her becoming a shadow of herself the longer he stayed. That's why I said something and it really got to him. He did say he'd make me wish I was dead. I don't know what he had planned for me but I knew to keep my mouth shut from then on when it came to him.' She paused. 'Lindy came one day; I caught her before she knocked and I told her all this.'

'And what did she say?'

'She said she'd deal with him.'

'And how was she planning to do that?'

Joyce pressed her lips together and raised both hands. 'I have no idea.'

'When did you last see Lindy?'

'At Maura's funeral. That was three weeks ago, at the crem. It was a beautiful service. Maura would have been proud of Lindy. I didn't go to the wake. Kain kept staring at me. I felt uneasy, so I left them and came home instead.' Joyce's eyes started to water up.

'I'm really sorry for your loss. It sounds like you were really close to Maura.'

'I was. I think it's only just hitting me that she's gone. She didn't deserve all she'd been through over the last few months. If Kain has done something and that's why you're here, bear all what I've said in mind. I think Maura would still be here if it wasn't for him.' Joyce took a deep breath and continued. 'Maura used to love Gordon, too. I think that's why Gordon was trapped in her house. We used to joke that some people did car shares, but we did a cat share, and I was happy to share Gordon with her because she loved him as much as I did. I wasn't happy when Kain kept letting Gordon in. Gordon vanished last Friday and on Saturday, I knocked on Maura's door. I really didn't want to confront Kain and have to accuse him of taking Gordon to upset me, so in a way I was relieved when he didn't answer. It's been quiet there ever since but I did have some odd dreams. I kept thinking I heard Gordon crying sometimes in the early hours, but then I just thought it was the music that Kain always had on, day and night.'

Gina knew that the cat had probably been meowing for help once it realised it was trapped, but the radio would have masked its cries. 'I'm glad he's okay now. I know this sounds like an odd question but did Maura have a small blue teddy bear?'

'No, Maura was one of these people that hated any clutter. I have some teddies and she used to joke that I was a soppy softie for having them.'

'Did you have a small blue teddy bear?'

'No. Why?'

'I'm so sorry, I can't say much about the investigation, only that it's relevant to the case.'

'I understand.'

'I'm going to get a PC to come over and formally interview you in a short while. Will that be okay?'

'Err, yes. It'd be nice to know what has happened? Can you tell me anything?'

'I will get someone to explain everything to you very soon. I'm sorry we're being vague. I can tell you that a serious crime has taken place and you've been really helpful.'

Jacob closed his notepad.

Just as Gina went to get out of the chair, her phone rang. 'Excuse me one moment.' She answered her phone, leaving Jacob to finish up with Joyce. It was one of the PCs.

'Guv, the CSIs have started working the scene and they've found a couple of things.'

She headed to the door and opened it, stepping out onto Joyce's drive before ending the call and speaking to the PC in person. 'What have they found?'

'A business card in the pocket of a torn blue hoodie. There are small pieces of glass caught in the hoodie. It looks like it could have been used to punch the glass out of the back windowpane.'

'What's written on the business card?'

'"Justine Crawford. For all your commercial videography needs." There is a number on it. I took the number down.' He passed the handwritten number to Gina.

She grabbed her own phone and began typing in the number. 'The number's not connected. What size is the hoodie?'

'Large. It looks like a man's hoodie but it might not be.'

Gina called Wyre at the station. 'Can you please look up the contact details for someone called Justine Crawford who is a commercial videographer? Her business card has been found at Maura Pickering's house. In the meantime, we're going to head to the victim's sister's house. She said she was going to deal with her brother. We need to know exactly what she meant by that statement.'

EIGHT

JUSTINE

Justine lay on her yoga mat in the savasana pose, eyes closed as she let go of her stresses over Craig's potential affair and Danny's filthy football boots. She also worried about her son spending so much time gaming at night. He looked more tired than usual lately. He needed his father. Maybe it was girl or friend trouble. Either way, Danny didn't want to speak to her about it.

The feel of the breeze in her hair and the sounds of the ripples coming from the lake in front of them filled her with joy. Despite it being chilly, the instructor had opened the window a little and after the session, it was more than refreshing. She could easily convince herself that the wall-to-ceiling glass doors in front of them were open, just like they always were during the summer months.

She lived for her once a week, lakeside yoga sessions. All her worries were melting away. She thought of her video deadline – what deadline? She had two weeks to get it done. Loads of time. Craig – he came to the forefront of her mind again and she almost felt slightly choked up despite a successful yoga session. She'd blatantly accused him of cheating several times now and it was clearly having a toll on their marriage. She sensed that she'd annoyed him during their last call, which might have been why he didn't answer all the time.

The instructor signalled the end of the session by saying, 'namaste'.

Justine yawned. Every muscle had been stretched and she enjoyed the feeling of improving and being able to hold the poses for longer every week. A bit of quiet chatter started to build up in the room. She turned to her side and smiled at Lindy who scratched her head and sat up. On her other side, Pia was already on her feet and had rolled her mat up.

'How are you not half asleep?' Justine asked. The chill in the air was giving her goosebumps now. She grabbed her sweater and pulled it over her head.

Pia shrugged and let her brown locks fall loose from a scrunchie. 'I feel full of energy. Ready to take on the day after that session.'

'I'll have what you're having,' Justine replied with a laugh.

'You will, because I have something for both of you. Feeling rough, it's a cure all. Tired, it'll fix that. This will add some bounce to your steps and who doesn't want more bounce in their lives?'

'Ooh, tell us more.' Justine was up for more bounce in her steps but she doubted that Pia's hocus-pocus inventions were really the cure for anything.

Lindy piped up as she stood while readjusting her sports bra. 'Yes, don't keep it a secret, I need all the help I can get.' Lindy yawned and gazed ahead at the lake, her focus seemingly on the run-down building on the other side.

Justine stretched, giving Lindy a moment to enjoy the view. The next bit, the chats and the smoothies were what she really came for. She was aware that Lindy had been struggling to come to terms with the loss of her mother so it was helping her too. It had been a huge risk bringing Lindy into her and Pia's friendship duo because three was always a crowd her mother used to say. She thought of Craig again and swallowed. Who was their number three? Justine let out a long breath. Lindy had been new to the class and offering her friendship had been the right thing to do.

Pia broke Justine's rambling thoughts. 'Well, the product I need to share with you both is our new kombucha flavour and I'd appreciate it if you could drink it before you have your smoothies because I need your palates to be clean.' Pia led them to the changing area and pulled her bag from a locker. 'I have Berry-Cherry-Nice with Hibiscus. It has a green tea base and it should fizz and zing on your tongue. It's refreshing and zingy, and best of all, it should put a spring in your step and keep that gut healthy. Who doesn't want perfect gut bacteria?'

'You sound like a walking advert, Pia,' Justine said. Pia was a walking, talking health guru, always perfect and glowing, holding some qualifications in nutrition that Justine had never heard of.

Lindy laughed properly for the first time since the funeral.

'Someone has to shout about it. If I left it to Simeon, our kombucha would never get sold. I'm already talking to some health food chains. We're going to have to drastically scale up our production if I get a contract. That's a big if.' She passed them both a can. 'I'm not knocking Simeon; it's just his skillset isn't selling and we need to sell more.'

Justine had never told Pia that she really didn't like kombucha and she felt Simeon's pain because he too didn't seem to like kombucha whenever she'd seen him with a can. She hated the tartness and Pia's kombucha was too vinegary. She didn't know if they were all like that because she'd never tried any other brand but she had a duty to be positive for her friends and their businesses. She opened the can and took a sip. The zing caught her nose and she sneezed. 'Mm, lovely. I can taste the cherry.'

'You know, everything is in it for a reason. My mum was sick towards the end and I know kombucha really helped her. It could have been worse. My view is though, we need to drink it now, eat more fermented foods if we're to get protection down the line.'

Justine wondered how Lindy was taking all this after losing her mum so recently. She seemed okay. Maybe she appreciated the return of normality in her life following her mother's death.

'Who doesn't want protection? Bottoms up.' Justine glugged it all down in one and tried to avoid gurning at the taste. 'I'll tell you if I feel better when I've had my shower. I'll meet you at the bar.'

As soon as Justine had changed, washed and dressed, she headed to the bar to meet the others. Lindy and Pia were chatting and laughing, like they'd been friends for years.

Justine watched Lindy glance at her phone. 'Damn, is that the time? I've got to get home. I've got some work to do.' Lindy grabbed her gym bag, then Pia pulled her ringing phone from her pocket.

So much for having time to chat. Justine really wanted to talk to her friends about Craig but that wasn't going to happen today because Pia had just answered her phone to a potential customer and the charm had been turned on. Their little meet up was officially over. Justine's phone pinged. She too said her goodbyes and as she went to leave, she read the message from a withheld number.

Do you really know where your husband is, who he's with and what he's getting up to? You suspect, don't you? Never trust a man with betrayal in his heart. X

NINE

Gina knocked on the door of the old post office. While waiting for someone to answer, she admired the post-box-red ledges. The owners had restored the property beautifully.

'I don't think anyone's in, guv.' Jacob exhaled.

A car turned onto the drive and a woman stepped out.

'What can I do for you both? Has something happened?'

'May we come inside?' Gina held her identification up. 'I'm DI Harte, this is DS Driscoll.'

The woman's pale face began to redden at the neck, her straight blonde hair damp and up in a messy bun. She led them into the snug. 'It's Kain, isn't it? What has he done? Damn, I should've known something was wrong. I haven't heard from him in days.'

As soon as Lindy was seated, Gina swallowed and began. 'We found a body this morning. We have reason to believe it is your brother, Kain Pickering. We're so sorry for your loss.' Gina waited for her reaction but all Lindy did was stare into her lap.

'How... I mean, what happened?'

'That's what we're trying to find out.'

'Was he drunk? Did he hurt himself or fall over? It wouldn't be the first time. I sat with him for several hours in A&E once, waiting for him to have a cut on his head stitched up.' Her eyes began to water.

'No, I'm also sorry to tell you that we believe he died under suspicious circumstances.'

'You mean he was murdered?' Lindy's breaths quickened.

'Is there someone you can call, to be with you?'

She shook her head and wiped a teary trail from her cheek.

'There's something else we need to tell you. We also suspect that he died in your late mother's house. Police and forensics are there at the moment.'

'You mean there are people going through the house? Why did no one call me?'

'Sorry, we didn't know who to contact until we spoke to your late mother's neighbour. Our investigation led us to the property and we suspected that there may have been someone else who needed help on the premises, which is why we had to enter. Also, the back door was already open. The house had been broken into.'

'I should have gone over there and checked when I couldn't get hold of Kain. I should...' She let out a sob.

'Again, please accept our condolences.' Gina paused, giving Lindy a moment to take everything in. 'Can you tell us a bit about Kain? The neighbour said there had been some conflict.'

'That's an understatement.' She sniffed and continued. 'Kain was sucking everything out of Mum and I hated seeing her shrink. He took every ounce of her energy and money. Our arguments came to a head after Mum had paid him for a second time to get a CCTV system fitted to her house. There had been a few burglaries and she was scared. But he didn't do it. He pissed her money up the wall and the things she told me will make your blood chill. She'd started to realise that Kain was never going to fit the system and as soon as he asked her for more money, for better cameras – apparently, she said no.'

'What happened next?'

Jacob turned a page over and was scribbling notes at speed.

'He screamed his mouth off at her, saying that she was a waste of space, that she'd never helped him. She said he pushed her over and then stole money from her purse. I went over to the house and told him he had to leave. I wanted to call the police but Mum begged me not to. In the end, I didn't, only because Mum said she'd disown me if I did and all Kain could do was stand behind her, looking smug.' Lindy leaned back on her settee and stared at the ceiling rose for a moment. When she looked back at them, Gina saw that Lindy's mascara had mixed with her fresh tears. 'I don't know where it all went wrong. In that moment I saw him as nothing but a vicious animal but now that he's dead, all I can think of is my little mop-headed brother with his blond curls and his big gappy smile. The drink changed him. He had no way back and none of us could seemingly help him. I tried so hard and I still had hope that he could deal with his drinking. I never lost hope.'

Gina shivered as thoughts of her own past ran through her mind. Her abusive ex-husband, Terry, drunk and angry as he punched and raped her – the look on his face after she'd pushed him down the stairs to his death. Her knowing that she'd have done it all again to protect her daughter, Hannah, from the monster that he was. She also knew that there would always be that glimmer of the person the victim knew, before they became so cruel and she could see that confusion playing out on Lindy's face. She thought of Briggs again. Only he knew about her past. It pained her to see him rejecting her in such a cold way.

'Your late mother's neighbour, Joyce, said she'd had problems with Kain and that she'd spoken to you about them,' Jacob said.

'Yes, he'd threatened her and Joyce had been worried about Mum. I doubt he'd have really done anything to Joyce. He was all angry talk and no substance.'

'But he pushed your mum.'

Lindy frowned. 'But he'd never have hurt Joyce.'

Gina wondered if Lindy was in denial but the way she saw it, Kain was the victim and Lindy was a potential suspect given the conflict between them. 'Did your mum have a small blue teddy bear?'

She shook her head. 'Mum was an anti-clutter freak, so much so that she got rid of all her knick-knacks. She used to joke and say it was less for us to sort out once she croaked it – her words, not mine. We thought it was funny at the time. Mum had that kind of humour, a little bit morose at times. Is this about Mum or Kain?'

'It's relevant to the case but I'd ask that you don't mention it to anyone else.' Gina took in Lindy's reaction to her mentioning the teddy bear but Lindy didn't react at all. 'Do you know if Kain had any enemies or any fallings out with anyone recently?'

'He had an acrimonious divorce that was finalised a few months ago. He busted a gut to buy a new place and, in my opinion, he overstretched himself with the new mortgage which is why he ended up losing his house. His ex-wife cited his drinking as the reason for the divorce. It was his unreasonable behaviour but he resented her for leaving him and he resented her more for getting together with a man from her past as soon as they'd split up. I don't blame her, though. She deserved more.'

'What's her name and do you have contact details for her?'

'Sheena May. She lives at number fifteen High Street, Cleevesford. I can't see that it would have anything to do with her. She's moved on.' Lindy frowned. 'He was in debt but it was credit card debt. I know he put his business on the line and also burnt his way through a business loan.'

'Could he have borrowed money from anywhere else?'

'Like a loan shark? No.'

'How about friends?'

'Kain didn't hang out with anyone. He preferred to hang out at home and watch TV on his own. He wasn't a pub drinker; he drank at home.'

'Work or business colleagues?'

Lindy shrugged.

'Can I take your surname?'

'Pickering.' She dabbed at the corners of her eyes with a finger.

'What is the name of your brother's company?'

'What's left of it. The staff have gone and the rental lock-up has an eviction notice pasted to the roller shutter. There's nothing there. Mum and I helped to clear the unit out. For what it's worth, it's K Pickering's CCTV and Security Installations.' She cleared her throat. 'I know he took money for jobs then he spent it, letting the customers down. He applied for bankruptcy and they lost their money.'

'Do you know who these customers are?'

'His paperwork and computer is in the spare room wardrobe at Mum's house. I know that because Mum keeps her coats in there and she said that the boxes were creasing them up.'

Gina watched Jacob typing out a message to PC Smith, telling him to mention it to the search team. As soon as they could get that paperwork to the station, they could look into who these wronged customers were. She made a mental note to pass on the information about the industrial unit, just in case anything was left there. 'I'm sorry to have to ask you this but did Kain have any distinctive or unique features such as a tattoo?'

'Yes, he has Sheena's name on the top of his right arm in a heart.' She paused and swallowed. 'I don't want to see his body.'

'That's okay. You don't have to.' Gina was glad. After what she saw earlier, she didn't think it would be possible. The scent of Kain's decomposing body was still coating her nostrils. 'Do you know the name of his dentist?'

'Err, Sparkling Pearls on Caywood Road.' Gina waited for Jacob to message that information back to the station.

'Can you tell me where you were on Friday the fourteenth of November after one in the afternoon?' That was when Joyce heard the commotion coming from Maura Pickering's house.

She shrugged. 'I'm normally at home on Fridays. I was here, probably cleaning up the house.'

'Was anyone with you?'

'No, I was sweeping the drive at one point so someone might have seen me. Am I seriously a suspect?' She started to clench her teeth.

'The questions are routine. All we want to do is find out who killed your brother.'

'Of course. What happens next?'

'We will need to formally interview you at the station. Would you be able to come in later?'

'Yes. There is something you should know about Kain?'

Gina tilted her head, wondering what Lindy was about to tell them. Her phone beeped. It was a message from O'Connor. She glanced at the message while Lindy was taking a couple of deep breaths and Gina almost gasped out loud. Her hands began to shake so she placed them in her lap.

Lindy continued speaking, unaware of the message. 'He used to be in the police. He was a PC in his youth but he didn't stay in the police for long. I don't remember the year.'

Could the policing link be relevant? 'Why did he leave the force?'

Lindy looked away. 'He never said.'

Kain wasn't the person they thought he was. Gina had to find out what changed in his life. What made Kain the PC turn into a man that steals money from his customers and pushes his mother over?

TEN

On arriving back at the station, Gina and Jacob jogged until they reached the incident room. The message from O'Connor kept going through her mind.

Guv. Briggs has just been taken off the case and no one is telling us why. A new acting DCI is being sent from Glouces-ter. You both have to get back, fast!

At the far end, she could see where Briggs had been writing up all their information on the board with O'Connor and Wyre. Stuck in the centre of the largest board was a blown-up photo of Kain Pickering taken from his driving licence. Underneath were a few crime scene photos that had come from Bernard's team. She checked her emails and saw that he'd sent them through about an hour ago. She could clearly see the stretched-out Sheena tattoo on Kain's mottled, bloated arm. It was definitely Kain.

O'Connor sat at the far end rubbing his hand over his shiny head, the cake sat in the centre of the table, that Mrs O had more than likely made, remained untouched. Wyre leaned back, biting her bottom lip and clipping back her straight black fringe. Trainee Detective Constable Jhanvi Kapoor drank water from a bottle before doing up the buttons on her grey suit jacket.

'Why have they taken DCI Briggs off the case? Have you heard anything yet?' Gina asked O'Connor.

'Only that the new DCI will be here any minute. We don't know any more.'

Gina sat near the head of the table, her stomach churning with worry. Yes, they'd argued earlier but that didn't mean she'd stopped caring about him, even if that was just as a friend. Whatever he was going through, she was going to be there for him, just like he had for her in the past. She owed him that much.

Throat clearing echoed through the corridor. Everyone waited silently for whoever was fast approaching to enter. Gina almost gasped out loud when she saw Brodie Fraser. She'd only known him for a year and that year had been her first-year training on the job. She took his features in. He still had his slightly round chin and the same hazel eyes. His once all-brown thick hair was now thinner and greying at the sides, but still he looked like the Brodie she knew back then.

He began speaking in his Glaswegian accent. 'I know you're probably all wondering what's going on so I won't keep you all in suspense for much longer. DCI Briggs is a part of the case now which is why he's not with us at the moment.'

Gina itched to interrupt and ask why Briggs had been sent off the premises but she knew it was best to sit back and wait. She didn't want to be taken off the case, too.

Brodie continued. 'I will be acting DCI and I'll be working out of the office next to Briggs's. Any press releases will be handled by me. I've been going through what we have so far and I know it's early doors when it comes to the case, but can anyone talk me through what we have so far. The clock is ticking and we want this murderer caught.'

Gina popped a hand up and stood. Brodie scrunched his brow and focused on her as if taking her features in. She wondered if he still recognised her. They'd almost had drunken sex as rookies in a pub toilet, not something she was proud of. They'd been on a night out with the team. She remembered falling off the sink unit and then they'd landed in a heap, laughing on the floor of a filthy pub toilet. Terry had been dead for over two years and Brodie had been the first man to get her attention since his death. His wit and sense of fun had seduced her with ease.

'Gina?' He looked down at his notebook. 'DI Harte?'

He remembered her and a part of her wished he hadn't. 'Yes, that's me.'

His smile widened. 'Come to the front and tell me what you have. You've been out all morning at the scene speaking to witnesses.'

She stepped towards the board and filled him in on their morning so far. 'As for the timeline...' She took the pen and began adding to the notes on the board. 'I'll start with the scene where we're almost certain that the victim was murdered. On Friday the fourteenth of November, Maura Pickering's neighbour, Joyce Burton, heard banging coming from the house the victim was living alone in. Later that evening, she saw someone wearing the victim's cap while loading something into Maura Pickering's car boot. I need to add here that Maura is dead – natural causes. We're hoping for a confirmation on the cause of Kain Pickering's death during the post-mortem tomorrow.'

'Tell us about the scene where the car was discovered this morning.'

'It was parked on the drive of one Chandelton Avenue. The car was booked to be there through a parking app but the driver failed to collect the car. Ms Wild, the homeowner, suspected that there was a body in the boot earlier today, so she called us. The parking space was booked for one night but Maura's car was still there five nights later.'

'Suspects or persons of interest?'

'Sister, Lindy Pickering, she's a person of interest. Joyce Burton mentioned that there had been a lot of conflict between the family over Kain taking money from their mother. Kain had recently lost his business so it might be worth checking out his employees or anyone who he owed money too. Hopefully the team at Maura Pickering's house will be back soon with his paperwork and laptop. He had a unit which Lindy claims is cleared of his things but it will need checking out. Kain had an ex-wife called Sheena. He has her name tattooed on his arm.' She pointed at the photo on the board of Kain's tattoo. 'Lindy said that their divorce was finalised a few months ago.' Gina noted Sheena's name down. 'A neighbour saw the silver Merc racing around dangerously on Chandelton Avenue at midnight on Saturday the fifteenth. She also thought she heard someone hanging around by Tina Wild's house the day before at around seven p.m. She saw fog or smoke coming from behind the tree by Ms Wild's house. The team found a disposable vape that has now gone to the lab. That narrows down a time for the car's arrival at between midnight on the fifteenth and six a.m. on the Sunday. If the driver was loading Kain's body into the car around ten p.m. on the fourteenth, then arrived at Ms Wild's just after midnight on the fifteenth, that driver must have parked up somewhere for a day.' Gina quickly updated the timeline on the board.

'We need to check ANPR, see if the vehicle pops up on any of the cameras,' Brodie added.

Automatic Number Plate Recognition had been on her mental to-do list. Gina nodded to Wyre. 'Could you look into that, please?'

Wyre nodded.

Gina continued. 'Going back to Joyce Burton. She has a cat and that cat had been trapped in the bedroom Kain Pickering was using. It had been there for days and the blood found in the room suggests that some sort of attack happened there. We currently have the cat, just in case it's harbouring trace evidence in its fur or under its claws. There was also a small blue teddy bear left at the scene and we don't know if it was Kain's or something the killer left behind. The teddy is out of place. Both Joyce and Lindy said that Maura hated clutter, including teddy bears. As for the scene, it looks like Kain might have been killed in the bathroom as there had been a struggle and Bernard has confirmed defence wounds on his arms. We don't have exact cause of death as yet but given the struggle in the bedroom and the bath full of water, the scene is leading us to believe that he may have drowned. He didn't die in the car; he was placed in the boot post-mortem – Bernard has confirmed that already. We also have another lead coming from Maura Pickering's house. A torn blue hoodie was found there and it looks like it was used to punch some glass out of the door to break in. A business card belonging to Justine Crawford was found in the pocket. She's a corporate videographer. Lindy also told us that Kain was a police officer many years ago but I see you already know that.' She didn't want to add what she was thinking. That was the reason Briggs was off the case. Briggs and Kain had to be connected.

'Yes, we are going to be investigating that angle also,' Brodie said.

'Can you share anything with us yet?' Gina's heart began to bang as she waited for him to answer.

He shook his head. 'No, sorry. We can't jeopardise the case in any way. DI Harte, you're senior investigating officer on the case.' He nodded to Gina to take the lead.

She let out a long, slow breath. She had to speak to Briggs herself somehow. 'Thank you.' She turned slightly to address the room. 'I know you must all be worried about DCI Briggs right now but we have to continue the investigation and get to the bottom of who murdered Kain Pickering. Let's break this down and start following the leads we have. Wyre, you're on ANPR. O'Connor, could you liaise with PCs Ahmed and Smith who are still at Chandelton Avenue?' She turned to trainee DC Kapoor. 'Can you look into Kain Pickering's background, and all of you, when Kain's laptop comes in, can you speak to Garth in the tech department. Also, you will need to start looking through Kain's paperwork. Have a PC check his old unit and look into the debts associated with his business. Jacob, we need to visit Justine Crawford. Can you dig up her address? She has a business so she should be easy to find.'

A hum of yesses told Gina that they were good to go.

'Lindy Pickering is coming in this evening to make a formal statement. O'Connor, Wyre, could you please interview her? We need more details of her whereabouts during key times.'

Brodie turned to leave. 'DI Harte, I'll be in my office, if you need me.'

Gina glanced back. Jacob was pouring himself a glass of water while talking through a few details with Wyre and O'Connor. Gina followed the DCI out. 'Brodie,' she called, just as he was about to turn a corner at the end of the corridor.

'Gina.' He looked away and smiled. 'I can't believe I'm seeing you again after all these years.'

'I know, what a surprise.' Is that all she had to say? She felt a bit silly but she couldn't help remembering all the joking around they did, all the laughing and fun they had all those years ago. 'So, you're a DCI, now? That's amazing.'

'Yes, I've only had this role for about two years and you, you're a DI.'

'And I've been a DI for years. I like getting into the nitty-gritty of it all. I'm maybe too hands on for the role but I can't help myself.' She wondered if she should try asking about

Briggs again but decided not to. He wasn't going to tell her anything.

'We, err... we should catch up properly, have a wee drink while I'm in town... if you're free that is.' His accent sent a pleasurable shiver through her. She'd always loved it when he spoke and she regretted that they'd lost touch when he moved away from Birmingham to work in Gloucester.

She glanced at his hand and he held it up with a grin. 'Divorced twice. Obviously not my fault because I'm perfect.' He let out a laugh and she couldn't help laughing too. He was the Brodie she remembered. If it wasn't for Briggs's predicament, she'd have enjoyed their conversation.

She looked into Brodie's eyes. 'When we get a break from the case, that would be nice.'

'Okay, maybe that's a date, but not a date.'

Gina left him to it and headed back to the incident room. Jacob stood holding a piece of paper. 'Guv, I have Justine Crawford's address. The hoodie is a man's size large and PC Smith is now at Maura Pickering's house and he has an update.'

'What did he find?' She glanced at her watch. It was almost six thirty.

'A tiny bit of torn blue material found under the driver's seat of Maura Pickering's car that matches the colour and texture of the hoodie found at her house. There is a strip of the sleeve missing and what was found in the car appears to be that missing piece. This links the car and the house break-in.'

'In that case, Justine Crawford has a lot of explaining to do. Let's go.'

As Gina hurried across the car park with Jacob, her phone rang. No number came up. 'I'll catch you up,' she called to Jacob as he continued.

'Hello.'

'Gina, I'm going to need your help. I did something terrible, years ago, and it's coming back for me. You have to—'

The call ended. Whatever Briggs had been pulled off the case for, it was bigger than him just knowing the victim. She stared at her phone as Jacob waved to her from the other side of the car park. *You have to – what?* What did he need her to do? Briggs had compromised himself to save her in the past. Could she do the same for him?

ELEVEN
HOMELESS MAN

Certain things happen in life that play on your mind. I remember the things I said to my wife, just before she threw me out. I told her she was a controlling bitch. My sharp outbursts didn't end there. I told my nephew what a talentless twit he was when he showed me his music performances that he'd uploaded to YouTube. Not to mention how I fell onto Aunt Alice's main table at her seventieth birthday party, bringing the whole four-tiered cake crashing to the floor.

I've had a long time to think about all my wrongs and bad behaviours in this godforsaken damp warehouse. Yes, I was wrong. My wife wasn't controlling. My nephew wasn't talentless – he's an amazing young man and I know he'll go far in life, but here, in my heart, I know I took his shine away and that's why I'll never go home. My wife, my nephew and Aunt Alice all deserve better than me. The pain of my past isn't a good enough excuse for all the times I was an absolute arsehole. That is why I'm sitting here watching a rat scurrying across an abandoned warehouse floor.

I hear the sloshing of water downstairs. It must be raining. I didn't think it was raining. I throw the empty white rum bottle to one side. White rum – what the hell have I become? It was all I could pilfer from the corner shop. I don't even enjoy the stuff so it shows how sick I am. My wife used to love a white rum and Coke.

I shiver as I remember why I am this way. Sometimes a person does something so bad that there is no redemption. If they never get punished, they start punishing themselves. That's where I am. I am the deliverer of punishments to me, and I intend to make myself suffer until I die.

After staggering towards my filing drawers, something the previous occupants of the building must have deemed worthless enough to leave behind, I pull out the letters that I've written. If I die, maybe someone will read them. I'd speak to people but they find me scary.

I've often caught my reflection in restaurant windows just as I'm about to bin-dive and I've also seen my manic features become subdued when I've shot up in the town centre loos. The pains and bloating in my stomach, and the yellowing of my skin and eyes tell me my liver is done for, but I will not see a doctor. I don't want my wife, my nephew or Aunt Alice to ever know what became of me.

My eyes water up a lot but I never cry. I remind myself that I don't deserve pity, not even my own. I am exactly where I should be.

As I slide the cabinet open, I see that my letters are still safe. One day, when I don't wake up, my wife, nephew and Aunt Alice will know I'm sorry for everything I put them through.

I squint before glancing along the long building, vacuous areas now only separated by occasional pillars. The wall at the far end has a missing window, one of the only windows where the board has been smashed rendering the building open to the elements and I can't see rain. The window was like that when I got here. There is another broken board downstairs which I smashed in to get access.

I shouldn't have come back to where it all started; I'm just torturing myself. If I look through that window, I will see the building and I can almost pinpoint the room behind the brick façade that looks like it's shouting at me, telling me that it knows what I did. It knows what we did, or what we omitted to do. I talk to one of the others from my past, now and again, but it's getting rarer. He doesn't want to know and once a year seems a struggle for him. We share this burden though and I have something else I need to share with him, and soon.

Three days ago, I thought I saw you, but you're dead. I recognised what I could see of your nose, your eyes and your build as you stared at me. You were far away, a flash of a person in the distance, there one minute gone the next, half shrouded in a cap. Are you a ghost? Have you come back to haunt me or us? If you have, it's working. You won. Were you merely wearing a mask with his photo printed on it or was I seeing things? My memory and perception of surroundings isn't exactly reliable.

Another thing that confuses me is that it's definitely not raining, so why is there a whooshing sound downstairs? Maybe I left the tap on.

I reach the concrete stairs. If I make it down them, I'm going to stay down there. As I take a few steps, I lose my footing and slip down several until I manage to get hold of myself. It's safer to descend the rest of them while shuffling on my bottom. Eventually I'm there so I stagger towards the whooshing with my hands held out to catch a potential fall. It always amazes me how much effort I put in to stay alive when I don't even care about being alive. I don't like pain. If I die, I just want to fall asleep and slip away.

As I nudge the door open to reveal the room at the end, I hear a voice that sends chills through me, but I can't see anyone. The room is pitch-black but my gaze catches a green glow at the one end. 'Who's there?' I step in and the door slams.

Heavy footsteps walk clunkily towards me. I go to turn back – to run through the door but my legs are like jelly and the darkness has made me even less steady on my feet. I'm totally disorientated. With my hands held out, I try to feel for a wall, or even the door I came through, but finding it is impossible.

The green glow comes closer and someone slaps me. I feel like I'm being attacked by bats and they keep coming back. That's when my legs are pulled from beneath me and my upper body crashes to the stone floor. He, she, whoever – they're dragging me. I go to yell but I can't catch my breath, then something hard cracks against my face and nose, rendering me still. The alcohol still courses through me but I feel pain like never before. So much for alcohol numbing everything. I'm being hoisted up and my ankles are stuck together. Blood rushes to my head as I'm dangling on the end of a rope in a dark room?

Something is being wheeled underneath me, then whoosh. I hit the water and the only way is down. My lungs feel like they're bursting. I need to get out. I wriggle and squirm, but it's no good. My strength is all but gone. I'm sorry, is all I can think in my head as my last thoughts go to my wife, my nephew and Aunt Alice. I really did love you all but the ghosts of my past eventually came for me and now I must go.

TWELVE

JUSTINE

'You know what, whoever sent that message is probably just jealous of your lovely life, hun. Don't let them get you down.' Pia passed Justine a steaming cup of chamomile tea. 'Drink that. It'll make you feel better and you'll probably sleep well when you get home. Who needs nasties like sleeping tablets when nature provides?'

Justine wiped her red-raw nose and spotted Pia checking the time on her phone. 'I don't know if someone would do that. I don't think I've upset anyone. It's him. I don't trust him.'

'Look, people do horrible things all the time. I was reading this thing on Facebook earlier – anonymous, obviously.'

'Or made up?' Justine raised her brows.

'Maybe but the point is still there. It could happen. This person, made up or real, was asking if they were in the wrong as they were sending similar messages to a woman they hated, just to upset her and come between the woman and her husband. Have you upset anyone lately? Think hard. It could be something and nothing. You know how stupidly tetchy people get over nothing.'

'No, I don't think so. I argued with the woman living at

number five because she took my bin instead of hers again, and she always throws things in it without bagging first. I think she does it on purpose so that she doesn't have to clean hers and we get ours cleaned every month.' Justine frowned at the absurdity of what Pia was suggesting. 'I don't think she'd send me that message.'

'But she might. People do petty things all the time. There you go, it's probably the result of some silly neighbourly vendetta. She's probably regretting sending the stupid message as we speak. Does she have your number?'

'Yes, I'm in the community hub group.'

'You know what, Craig will be home soon and if you really don't trust him, you'll be able to ask him about the message but don't go in all guns blazing. No need to ruin your marriage over a stupid text.'

Justine bit her bottom lip. 'You know him. Would you trust him? Be honest.'

Pia sat next to Justine, her reflection in every window of the orangery. The faint flickering of the candle's light caught her sparkling blue eyes. 'Look, hun. You and Craig are good friends of ours. How long have we known each other? I make it five years.'

Justine nodded, wishing that Pia would simply get to the point. She wanted to know if her husband was cheating on her and there was Pia stringing the point along. 'Wow. Where has the time gone?'

'Yes, wow. I only have one incident to report here but remember that garden party over on Greenfields.'

An incident. Justine couldn't help clenching her fists that Pia hadn't mentioned whatever happened, earlier. 'Oh, Leanna Jacobson's.'

'Yes.'

'What's she got to do with this?' Justine remembered their stunning model-like host who seemed to captivate everyone at the party. Craig, like all the other men, had noticed her too. The only man who hadn't eyed her up was Simeon, Pia's husband. Justine also recalled telling Craig to close his mouth when Leanna walked by in her tiny lace shorts.

'That woman tried so hard to cosy up to Craig, constantly touching his arm when she laughed. I came out of the toilet and Craig was standing alone outside the front door and Leanna joined him. I saw her drunkenly flinging her arms around him and then she went to kiss him.'

'You never told me any of this.' Justine slammed her cup down, chamomile tea sloshing over the edge onto the glass table.

'It was years ago and I didn't want to upset you.'

'So, it's her. It's been going on all these years under my nose.'

Pia shook her head. 'No, that's where you are wrong. He grabbed her hands, gently removing them, and told her he was happily married. Then, I scarpered back into the party, hoping I hadn't been caught watching them. He followed seconds later. He didn't do it. Nothing happened, so I'm sure you've got the wrong end of the stick. Craig is not cheating on you.'

Justine let out a long slow breath and leaned back on the couch.

Simeon barged in, bags over his arms and a box in his hands. 'Hello, hello. Can you take this off me?' He moaned under the strain of the boxes. 'Hi, Justine.'

Justine forced a smile.

Pia stood and took the box while Simeon placed his bags down against the wall. Sweat had gathered on his forehead from carrying the boxes, pasting his light-brown hair to his forehead. 'Do you have what I think you have in that box?' Pia asked with a smile.

Simeon leaned in for a kiss. 'Version three. Taste it and tell me what you think.'

Justine looked away, envy gnawing away at her and also

hoping she wouldn't have to try another can of kombucha. If only Craig adored her as much as Simeon adored Pia. Justine glanced at the sideboard where a fresh bunch of lilies had been arranged in a vase. He still bought her flowers. Maybe the spark had just gone with her and Craig. Simeon started the kombucha business for Pia. He idolised her and took her away to gorgeous hotels and out for fancy meals. They'd been together forever but he never stopped making an effort. Yuck, she hated how she was jealous of everyone who was remotely happy.

Simeon stood up straight and went to speak to Justine but her puffy eyes were just the cue he needed to leave them to talk. 'Okay, I'm going to unload more cans of this stuff into the garage to package up for the farm shop delivery, then I'm going to have to do some invoicing. Did the gym pay us for the big order?'

'No, I checked,' Pia replied.

'I'll chase them up. Sorry for interrupting.'

'He got the hint,' Pia said, jokingly.

'You're so lucky.' Justine couldn't help letting that thought slip out.

'Well so are you. You have a gorgeous family.'

'Craig never looks at me the way Simeon looks at you.'

'We have our moments like anyone else and let's not also forget that Danny adores you. You're amazing. Besides, we all bicker and get irritated by our partners sometimes. I won't lie, Simeon and I have been bickering because he's stressed with the business.'

'But Simeon would never cheat on you.'

'And Craig isn't cheating on you. He wouldn't.'

Justine picked her tea up to take a sip. Maybe Pia was right. Maybe the message was from her neighbour or some other horrible person who had it in for her. That didn't explain Craig's behaviour though, but that was a conversation for another day. The chamomile was working its magic. She needed her bed. As she stood to leave, Simeon popped back into the room and grabbed an apple from the fruit bowl.

As he held his hand up to take a bite, she saw the leather-plaited bracelet around his wrist. Justine couldn't help the unease that was building up inside her, from her dry mouth to the nausea in her throat. Craig had spent a lot of time helping Simeon set up the accounting system for the kombucha business, maybe too much time. 'I have to go.' She grabbed her bag and fled for the front door.

'Wait.'

She ignored Pia and ran towards her car. 'Sorry, I'll call you tomorrow. Emergency.'

'Anything I can help with?'

'No.'

No, no, no, no, no... She punched a message to Craig into her phone as soon as she'd driven away and pulled over down the road. How could he? All this time she'd been wondering who Craig could have been seeing but it was right under her nose. Back when they met, Craig had just come out of a relationship with a man. It had never worried her that he liked men and women, as long as he chose her to be his forever partner. Pia was going to be so hurt. Craig had to be having an affair with Simeon. Why else would Simeon be wearing the bracelet she'd bought Craig for his birthday? She hit send.

You bastard. How could you?

It had been a long day and she had to fight the urge to pick her nails or pace. Briggs's call had sent off an alarm in her head. What the hell had he been involved in?

She stepped up to Justine's front door and used the heavy knocker. A dog barked from inside. Set in a small estate that had been wedged in between two rural villages just outside Cleevesford, Justine's large house was where Gina thought many families might only be able to dream of living. She knew if it was daytime, she'd see rolling fields as she drove past the street, the same ones that backed onto the house.

'Do you think they're in?' Jacob asked as he stepped closer to the doorstep.

She glanced up again to see if any of the lights had come on. 'It's dark in there.'

Jacob pulled out a slip to post, letting Justine Crawford know to contact them when she got home. As soon as he was about to post it, the dog's barking got louder and light flooded the hallway. A teen boy answered the door.

'Hello, I'm DI Harte and this is DS Driscoll. Is Justine Crawford in?' She held her identification up.

He peered at it. 'How do I know that's real? I've heard of people pretending to be police then robbing things when you let them in.' His red curls were tied up in a bun at his nape.

'Happy to wait while you call Cleevesford Station.' She passed him a card and he closed the door.

'Thanks, but I'll google the number.' Gina was more than happy to wait, it gave her a moment to stare at her personal phone in the hope that Briggs called again. No such luck. A couple of minutes later, he opened the door again. 'Okay, you're the real deal. What do you want with Mum?'

Gina let out a slow breath. 'I'm afraid we can't discuss it with you. We really need to speak to your mum.'

'But she's not here.'

'Do you know when she'll be home?'

He shrugged. 'Could be anytime. She's probably out with one of her yoga friends.'

'Do you have a number for her? The one we have is no longer in use.'

He stood silently and frowned. 'I don't know. She doesn't like me giving her number out. Can you come back tomorrow and talk to her?'

'Do you know which friend she's with?'

'No.'

Gina glanced at an envelope sitting on the console table and it had Kain's name on the front. The boy clocked what she was looking at. 'Is it about him? I know he's always in a lot of trouble. Mum's trying to help him.' He placed his hand over his mouth as if he'd said something he shouldn't have.

The dog barked and scratched from behind a door. Justine's card had been found in a hoodie pocket at the crime scene and the hoodie could easily be a fit for the tall, burly lad in front of her. It could have even been worn as an oversized garment on a smaller frame. She thought of Briggs. She'd occasionally worn his T-shirts and hoodies and they'd almost swamped her.

The business card in the pocket could be seen as nothing more than circumstantial at this point in the investigation. She had to speak to Justine before making any decisions about interviewing the lad in front of her, or anyone else other than Justine. Besides, what would his motive be, when it came to killing Kain? Maybe the answer lay in the envelope. Maura's neighbour, Joyce, had mistaken the killer for Kain because the person loading the car had been wearing Kain's cap. Anyone could have been wearing that cap.

'Why are you here to see my mum?'

'Can I ask how old you are?'

'Why, have I done something wrong?'

'No.' Damn, she wanted to know if he was still a child but she guessed that wasn't going to happen on the doorstep. 'Can you tell your mum to call me as soon as she gets home? We'd really appreciate her help with our enquiries.' The dog barked as it waddled along the hallway.

The lad mellowed at her polite request. 'Err, yes, of course. I can do that.' The snuffling bulldog started nudging its head between the boy's calves. 'Pixie, get back in now. It's not walkies time.' The dog did as it was told. The boy looked at the envelope again. 'Kain wasn't a nice person. I know a lot of people weren't happy with him but Mum is kind, she gave him the benefit of the doubt. You should know this and I don't think Mum would mind me saying. Something went down with his ex-wife, Sheena, and it really upset Mum's friend, Lindy. I don't know what happened but Lindy was crying when she spoke to Mum.'

'Thank you for telling me that.'

'It was about four or five weeks ago, I think. You could ask Sheena. She probably knows more than me or Mum.' His phone beeped. 'Got to go, sorry. My mate's on his way.' With that, he closed the door on them.

'Charming.' Gina sighed as her nose almost touched the door, then she started to walk back towards the car with Jacob. 'I think we need to speak to Justine ASAP and hopefully we'll be able to interview him too. We have a connection. Justine and Lindy are friends. Let's hope Justine calls soon, if not, I think we should come back first thing, then we need to find out what Sheena knows. It sounded like something big went down and Lindy failed to mention that when we spoke to her.'

FOURTEEN

JUSTINE

She ducked in her car as the man and woman who had been speaking to Danny drove away. She saw them holding identification up. Were they police? She checked her messages again and there was one from Lindy to her and Pia sitting in their WhatsApp group.

> *It's Kain, he's dead. He's been murdered. Police came around earlier. Sorry to throw this at you both in a message. I had to tell someone. I feel like I'm going crazy here. First Mum, now Kain. Sorry, sorry – I'm just sad and wanted to tell you both.*

Pia was already typing and a moment later a message pinged up.

> *I'm so sorry, hun. That's awful news. I know you two didn't get along but it must still be such a shock. If there's anything I can do, just shout. You know I'm here for you. Sending huge hugs and lots of love. Xxx*

That's why the police were at her door. Why, though? Why

did they want to speak to her? She didn't even know Kain that well. Lindy had asked her to speak to him, to try to help him because she'd been through similar issues herself, but why would the police want to speak to her? Her heart began to bang fast. She checked her messages. Craig hadn't replied to her accusation. He hadn't even read the message. She threw her phone onto the passenger seat.

Her son, Danny, came out of the house and walked down the road with his head buried in his phone, no doubt on his way to one of his friend's houses.

She swallowed as she tried to process how bizarre her day had got. All she kept seeing in her mind was Simeon and Craig together, making a mockery of her and Pia. She tried to push all that from her mind. There were bigger things to deal with like the police that had come to her house. At least she didn't have to speak to them now while her stomach was doing somersaults. Whatever they wanted; it could wait.

She did a three-point turn and drove down the road and onto her drive, before heading into her house. Everywhere was in darkness. She switched the hall light on and headed to the kitchen. There was a note on the worktop from Danny, telling her to call someone from Cleevesford Police called DI Harte and there was a card next to it. She tried to swallow but struggled. It was like something was stuck in her throat. Her knees began to tremble slightly. The last time she'd been in a police station was when she got arrested for shoplifting while drunk at sixteen. She shivered, not wanting to think back to her past and the amount she used to drink back then. At least she only got a caution.

Pixie barked. Justine opened a tin of dog food and fed her, that's when she noticed that the light was on in the garden room. 'Damn you.' She had told Danny so many times to turn the light off in his makeshift gaming room but still, he never listened. She grabbed the key off the hook, unlocked the back door and hurried to the end of their huge garden. The door opened as she pressed the handle. Not only had Danny left the light on – again, he'd left the door unlocked – again. She pushed it fully open to see his gaming chair positioned opposite his really expensive computer but the only thing on was his laptop.

She nudged the laptop and the screen lit up, displaying two lines of message with a gamer. She read her son's last message to BustYourAss.

Need to talk. Can't live with this shit over my head any longer. You have to meet me now!

All this time she'd been worried about what Craig was up to when her son needed her, and now he was out. How could she even ask him about this message when she'd been snooping? He'd never trust her again. She thought about what it could mean. Can't live with what any longer? She grabbed her phone and tried to call Craig but the call went straight to voicemail.

She ran out of the garden room, locking it behind her, before hurrying back to the house. That's when she heard Pixie barking. 'Pixie... Craig... is that you? Are you home?'

The dog came in from the hallway, snuffling at her feet before continuing to eat.

Had she closed the front door? She couldn't remember. She normally closed the front door. What if Danny had popped back? She hoped he had. They really needed to talk about that message. She walked into the hall and saw a small line of dried mud on the wooden floor. It looked like it had come from the grooves of Danny's trainers, like always. She opened the front door and gazed out. Her car was still there and the road was in silence. She slammed it closed.

The landing creaked like it always did when the house began to get cooler. Then it creaked again. She grabbed her golf umbrella from next to the console table and crept up the stairs. 'Danny, Craig.'

No answer. The bedroom doors were all closed. She flung open the first room, then the second and the rest until she came to her and Craig's bedroom. 'Craig?' She pressed the door handle and kicked it open. Her heart banged hard and she began to breathe rapidly. The umbrella shook in her hand as she stepped in. There was no one in the room. It must have been Danny popping back for something. Her shoulders dropped and she held the umbrella by her side as she hurried back downstairs.

Pixie whined from the kitchen. Justine hurried along the hall and saw what Pixie was whining at.

A hint of pink caught her eye. She walked over to the kitchen table and picked the small pink teddy bear up and hugged it. 'How did you get here?' Pixie began to bark so she threw the teddy for the dog to play with. A shiver ran through her as she watched Pixie take it in her mouth and snuggle in her basket. She gasped for breath. No way would Danny ignore her when she called him, and Craig wouldn't either.

That teddy bear hadn't been there a moment ago. Someone had been in her house. They might still be in her house.

FIFTEEN

Friday, 21 November

Jacob indicated to turn into a road while Gina sat in the car, mulling everything over.

Gina had messaged Brodie through the night, reminiscing about the early days in their careers, partly because she'd struggled to sleep. She had waited in hope that Briggs would try to call again. She knew deep down that he was being interviewed or held and she hated that no one was telling her anything. What had he done all those years ago that was so bad? She pictured him in standard issue clothes waiting in a cell and she wanted to reach in and pull him away from it all. She had no idea what he was going to ask her to do or if she could even do it.

A tiny hint of light began to breach the heaviness of the night sky as morning broke. While Jacob continued driving, she glanced at a photo that Brodie had sent. They both looked happy all those years ago and Gina couldn't believe how youthful she looked back then. After her traumas with Terry, she had been wary of her future but policing had given her a new beginning. In the photo, they'd been out for a department Christmas meal and were all dressed up. Gina had danced the night away, clinging to a bottle of Hooch in one hand while dressed up in her sparkling bootcut jeans and an almost backless black top. Brodie had danced next to her, his reindeer antlers almost getting caught in the tacky tinsel that dangled from the ceiling of the old labour club. She hated that the years had passed in what felt like a flash. Without Terry in her life, things were so much simpler then.

'Any updates, guv?' Jacob pulled into Justine's road.

She put her personal phone away and glanced at her work phone. 'Not yet. I updated the system when I got home last night so we're all working off the same page. Ah, looks like Justine Crawford is home. There's a car on the drive, and she failed to call us when she returned.'

Someone in the Crawford household dropped an upstairs curtain. A neighbour began wheeling her bin onto the road while staring at them as they stepped out of the car and knocked on Justine's front door. She answered, her sandy-coloured hair sticking out at the sides. Gina suspected that she'd been thrashing around in bed all night thinking about their visit. The woman pulled her white dressing gown around her and tied the belt to cover her pyjamas. Gina didn't relish knocking doors at seven in the morning but they had a murder case to solve, and she hoped to catch the post-mortem later. 'Justine Crawford?'

The woman nodded. 'DI Harte?'

Gina nodded. 'We came by last night and your son was in.'

'Yes, I saw a card on the side but it was really late so I thought I'd call this morning. How can I help you?'

'May we come in?'

Justine stared at them both for what felt like a very long minute. 'I suppose. What's this about?'

'Yesterday, we discovered a man's body and we need to speak to you in connection with that.'

Justine grimaced and opened the door wide. Gina noticed that the envelope on the console table had gone. Justine led them into a huge kitchen with an arch that framed an eight-seater dining table. French doors led to a long-landscaped garden with a modern glass-fronted garden room at the end.

'Have a seat.' She pointed at the table. 'I need coffee. Do you want coffee?' Justine yawned and placed a pod into a machine. It started to spew out liquid at the other end.

'Yes, that would be lovely,' Gina replied after smelling it. 'Black, no sugar.'

'White, two sugars, thank you,' Jacob said.

She took the first cup and began making the next drink. 'So, how can I help?'

Over the spluttering, Gina spoke while Jacob started taking notes. 'The body of a man called Kain Pickering was discovered yesterday. We also found that the house he'd been living in had been broken into recently.'

'I heard. Lindy messaged me. It's such sad news. Was he attacked by a burglar?'

'Actually, your business card was found at the scene.'

'Kain is my friend's brother. I didn't even know him. Why would my card be at the scene?'

'That's what we're trying to establish. How well did you or your family know Kain Pickering?'

She passed Gina and Jacob their drinks and sat at the table. 'We didn't. I'm friends with his sister, Lindy. I know that Lindy had lots of issues with Kain. Lindy probably had my card. Maybe she left it there when she visited.'

'Did Lindy ever discuss her brother with you?'

Justine tried to flatten her kinked hair with her hands. 'Now and again. Kain was having a hard time. He'd made their mum's life hell and his ex-wife wasn't happy with him either but it was the drink, not him.'

'Can you tell us more?'

She looked at them both suspiciously before continuing. 'I know they argued about money. Kain had taken a lot from Maura and it had resulted in some big family confrontation just before Maura died. Lindy still puts the stress of it all down to Maura dying. As for his ex, he started some trouble a couple of weeks ago. I don't know the details. Maybe you should speak to Lindy about it.'

'Can you tell me where you were between one and ten p.m. on Friday the fourteenth of November?'

She pulled her phone out. 'I'll just check my diary?' She scrolled as she sipped her coffee. 'I was here, working on a project. I'm a videographer and I edit from home, upstairs in my office.'

'Was anyone here with you?'

'My husband was working away and my son, Danny, comes and goes. I don't keep track of them.'

Gina's mind whirred away while Jacob noted Danny's name down. As far as she could tell, Justine and Danny had opportunity but she couldn't attribute a motive to them. The explanation she'd given to them as to how the card could have been at Maura's house stacked up. 'Where does your husband work?'

'ALV Accounting Solutions. He sets up bespoke accounting systems for companies and that can involve working away for a few days at a time.'

That too gave him opportunity unless they could rule him out through checking his whereabouts with his employers. Gina watched as Jacob glanced at the family photos on the wall and then began accessing the system on his iPad. She carried on speaking to Justine. 'And he's working away now, you say.'

'Newcastle-upon-Tyne. I don't know the name of the company he's working out of.'

Gina cleared her throat. 'When we came last night, we saw an envelope on your console table with Kain's name on the front.'

'Oh, that.' She walked across the kitchen and took the envelope from a drawer before passing it to Gina.

Gina opened it. 'A card.' It had a picture of a man pushing a boulder up a hill on the front with the words, *You can do it*, written underneath.

Justine nodded. 'Lindy asked me to speak to Kain because I've had a problem with drink in the past. It was many years ago, before I met my husband and had my son. I just wanted to help. We spoke a few times and he did want to change. It was just too hard for him. I got him that card and wrote the times, dates and venues for Alcoholics Anonymous meetups. He wasn't in a good place when I gave it to him. He threw it back at me. I tried to help him and now he's...' She inhaled slowly. 'Maybe I could have done more but he wasn't ready for help. I liked Kain. I think there was a good man in there but he couldn't find his way out.'

'So, you did know him well?'

'No. I didn't. I hoped to get to know him better and help, but it didn't work out that way. I've only known Lindy for a few months. She started coming to the same yoga class I go to and we clicked. I really like her and we got on.'

Gina glanced at the back wall, covered in family photos all framed in black on a pale-grey wall. One particular photo caused her to look twice.

'I will need you and your son to come down to the station and make a formal statement this morning. Can you call your husband as we'll need to speak to him too?'

Justine stared and her brows began to crease. The coffee cup in her hand began to shake over her trembling hands. She placed the cup down. 'But my husband is working away. My son's busy and he has nothing to do with all this, and I don't either.'

'It will be easier if you come in voluntarily. We need to have your statements on record. A man has been murdered.'

It was as if Justine had clicked that voluntarily might turn into compulsory. She could see Justine's cogs ticking as she searched for words that weren't coming out of her mouth. 'I best, err... I should try to call Craig.'

Gina sat back and waited. Justine placed her phone to her ear and eventually left a voicemail. 'Craig, it's urgent. Can you please call me back? Danny and I have to go to the police station to make a statement. Lindy's brother, Kain, has been murdered. They need to talk to us, you too. Call me back or just come home, okay.'

'Can we take your husband's work and mobile numbers, please?'

Justine reached into the sideboard drawer and passed a card to Gina. 'He doesn't answer all the time. He's probably still in bed.' She swallowed.

'Do you have the address of where he's staying?'

'No, his company normally book a room above a pub, something like that. I didn't ask for the name of the place.'

'Is your son in?'

After creasing her brow, Justine shook her head. 'He didn't come home last night. He stayed with a friend.'

'Do you know who he went out with?'

She shook her head. 'He has lots of friends and he tends to stay with them when they go to a pub.'

Jacob leaned over and showed Gina what he was looking at on his screen. Craig and Justine's son had a recent conviction for taking a vehicle without consent.

Gina glanced back at the photo on the wall again. 'Is that your husband in the photo?'

Justine nodded.

In the photo, Craig Crawford had a leather-plaited bracelet dangling from his wrist. It dangled at the cuff of his blue hoodie where he stood with their son and Justine on a clifftop, each of them smiling for the camera. It was identical to the blue hoodie found at the scene of Kain's murder, which put Craig Crawford in the picture for Kain's murder.

SIXTEEN

JUSTINE

As soon as the detectives left, Justine almost tripped up over her own feet darting upstairs before half trying to dress and half trying to contact Danny and Craig. She almost toppled over as she stood on one leg while feeding another through her baggy jeans. Craig's voicemail message clicked in, again. 'You know what to do, leave me a message.'

'Craig, call me now. Just phone, will you? The police have left. They want all of us down the station ASAP to give a statement. What the hell have you been doing? For heaven's sake. Why aren't you answering?'

Rage tensed her hands. If she didn't have to try calling Danny again, she'd have thrown the phone across the room. She selected Danny's number. 'Pick up, pick up.'

He answered with a croaky voice. 'Mum. Why the hell are you calling over and over again? You woke me up and it's annoying.'

She suppressed the urge to go off at him. How dare he call her annoying. 'Where are you?'

'I had a drink with my one of my mates so I stayed over.'

'I'm on my way. Where are you?'

'What, no you're not, Mum. I'm an adult. You can't just come here and drag me home. Don't be crazy.'

How dare he call her crazy. If he was in front of her, she'd let him know just how angry she was at that statement. He'd caused her nothing but stress during his teen years, getting into trouble by stealing stupid little things, getting into scraps and, most recently, taking a neighbour's car for a joyride. She swallowed to try and get rid of the rising acid at the back of her throat. 'Did you come back home after me last night and leave a teddy on the worktop for Pixie?'

'I picked her toys up from the floor and put them in her box.'

'Have you ever given her a pink teddy bear?'

'No, maybe Dad did.'

She was still convinced someone had been in the house the previous night, but who and why? She'd searched the whole house twice and no one was there. Someone had left the toy in her house.

'Is all this over a dog toy?'

'No, it's all over the fact that the police have been and the only time the police have been here in the past is because of you. I have something to ask and if you dare go off on some sort of teen tantrum, I'll deliver you to the police myself.'

'What are you on about? I haven't done anything? Is this about the police coming over last night? I left you a note.'

She didn't have time to drag the conversation out any longer. 'You left the light on and the door unlocked in the garden room.'

'Sorry. I got distracted when the police knocked.'

'There was a message on your screen.' There was no way she could ignore what she'd seen. She hadn't gone looking through his personal things. The message had been up there, on a screen for her to see. 'What can't you live with any longer? What have you done, Danny? I know you were angry that I was trying to help Kain, your dad was too, but I need to know what that message was about.'

Danny went silent. 'That was private and none of your business. It's not cool to snoop through my things, Mum.'

'We're about to go down to the police station and you're wrong. It is my business now.'

'Well, it's nothing. It's definitely got nothing to do with Kain being dead but thanks for not believing in me. Thanks a bunch. Did you also tell the police that he kicked you? Didn't think so. No wonder I hated him and by the way, you had no right to make me keep that from Dad. Pick me up outside the sandwich shop on Shore Street. I'll be there in ten minutes.'

She wedged the phone between her ear and head as she pushed her feet into her trainers and scooped her hair up into a messy bun.

He paused before continuing. 'Mum, there is something I need to tell you.'

Her stomach dropped, thoughts going to what her son was about to confess? Had he hurt Kain in anger after he'd kicked her? She almost heaved, then took a deep breath to get rid of those nauseating thoughts that were running amok through her mind. 'What?'

'You're right. I did do something stupid and I need you to go to the garden room and delete that message. The laptop needs to go as well. I trolled someone online, that's all, but the police might use that against me if they take it. I got carried away having an argument with someone. I've deleted that app and only ever used it on that laptop. Everything else has gone but if we're going to the police station, who knows what might happen. They might search the house, take it away and dig up all those things I said, and blame me for something I didn't do. You know what they're like, Mum. I already have a record.'

'Who did you troll?' She hated her son right now but there was no way she was going to throw him at the detectives for

Kain's murder. Did she doubt her son? Yes, he was short-tempered and could be impulsive, and stupid in the moment. Would she do everything in her power to protect him? Yes.

'Just some dude I had an argument with. I went a bit too far but it was all words, nothing else. You have to believe me, Mum.'

She took a deep breath. She did believe him. 'Okay, I'll do it. Now go and get ready,' she said before ending the call.

She needed to take the laptop to her mum's. She would not put her son in the frame regardless of what he'd done. Her mind went back to Craig. He was many things but she was sure he wasn't a killer but... would he do something to cover for their son?

Her thoughts ticked over what Danny had been saying. Maybe Danny did tell Craig that Kain had kicked her. She took a deep breath and tried to calm her banging heart. She shivered as she recalled one of her chats with Kain when he'd been sober. Justine knew it was a mistake to ask her son to help Maura out with a few odd jobs in the garden, especially when Kain had come back really drunk one day. Danny had only tried to defend Maura. It was an accident. He hadn't meant to push Kain into the sideboard, scratching his head. She had to wonder if there was more to that moment or if it had led on to something else. Her forehead started to ache with tension. She couldn't help thinking that Danny had been involved in Kain's murder and that scared her more than anything.

SEVENTEEN

Back at the station, Gina called everyone working on the case into the incident room. Cheese twists spilled out of a torn paper bag onto the centre of the table. She thought of everywhere they needed to be all at once and she swallowed. Justine and Danny would be in for their interviews shortly and she really wanted to speak to Kain's ex, Sheena May. Lindy also still needed to come in and make a formal statement and she was anxious that Justine hadn't been able to make contact with her husband. 'Quick update. Jacob and I have just been to Justine Crawford's house. We've found out that her son, Danny, has a recent conviction for taking a car without consent. Not a biggie in itself but we do know that someone drove Maura's car off her drive and it wasn't Kain given the state of the house and his injuries. While at the Crawfords, Jacob spotted a photo on the wall. In the photo, Mr Crawford was wearing a hoodie that looked exactly the same as the one found at the scene. He looks to be of a very similar build to his son and there's no reason for his hoodie to be at Maura's house.'

Wyre spoke. 'Is Mr Crawford coming in for interview? You only mentioned Justine and Danny.'

'Mrs Crawford couldn't contact him while we were at hers. She said he was working away in Newcastle-upon-Tyne. I have his work and mobile phone number on this business card.' She placed it on the table near Wyre. 'Could you please follow up on that?'

Wyre nodded. 'I also checked the ANPR for Maura's car before it had been parked up on Ms Wild's drive.'

'Did it show up anywhere?'

Wyre nodded and stood. She grabbed a pencil to point at the map so that everyone could see. 'When you leave Maura's house, you turn right onto Cornfield Road for two miles then arrive at the train station which as we know is close to Tina Wild's house, where the body was found. That road does have an ANPR camera and it didn't show Maura's car passing it once. The driver had to have turned left because there aren't any ANPR cameras in that direction. There is only one route the driver could have taken to avoid ANPR and that would have led the driver to take the right turn onto Tina Wild's road. On leaving Maura's house on Friday evening, the journey should have taken no more than fifteen minutes. We know the car was spotted on Ms Wild's road at around midnight on Saturday the fifteenth.'

'Do we have any idea where the driver could have gone in that day?'

'I've just followed up on a call that came in after the appeal. A man called us. He saw someone on Haversham Road, which is in our black spot when it comes to ANPR.'

'What time was this?'

'Around eleven fifteen on Friday. Not long after Maura's neighbour saw the car leave the house. He describes the person as wearing a cap and with their back to him. Our suspected killer was leaning over a farmer's fence and it looked like he was vomiting. He also remembered half of the registration number of the car and we can confirm that it matches Maura's registration.'

'That accounts for just over an hour of where the car had been. O'Connor?'

O'Connor nodded as he chewed what was left of his croissant. A tiny spray of crumbs landed on the table as he exhaled. 'I spoke to PCs Smith and Ahmed, nothing more from the first scene yet but they're conducting more door-to-door interviews today. As for Kain's tech, everything had been restored to factory settings but Garth is doing all he can. As for his paperwork, there were lots of overdue notices, threats of court action for not making loan payments and he had been declared bankrupt. All loans and debts seemed to be with banks so I doubt that a loan shark did this.'

'Great,' Gina replied. 'Kapoor, how about you? Any updates? You were looking into Kain's background.'

'He doesn't have a record. The only thing that flagged up was his bankruptcy. He had a Facebook account but from what I can see, he didn't use it.'

'Has the cat been returned to Maura's neighbour?'

Kapoor nodded. 'Yes, the cat is safe and sound.'

Gina knew they still had to discuss Sheena. 'On speaking to Danny Crawford last night, he mentioned that something had happened recently between Kain and Sheena. Jacob and I need to pay Sheena a visit. O'Connor, would you please attend the post-mortem. I had an email from Bernard's team. It's scheduled for eleven this morning?'

He nodded.

'Wyre and Kapoor, would you please formally interview the Crawfords and make contact with Craig Crawford? If he's not answering, please call his employer and find out where he is. It might be that we need to involve the police in Newcastle. We need to find out if the hoodie in the Crawfords' photo is the same as the one we found at the scene. The best way to do that is to get the family to produce the hoodie Craig Crawford owns. That would rule him out. I feel that finding Justine Crawford's card at Maura Pickering's house and the presence of the exact same hoodie that Craig wears is too much of a coincidence to ignore. If you need to make arrests, then please do so. It'll give us twenty-four hours to investigate them further and we can apply for an extension if we need to.'

Wyre made a few notes. 'We'll do that. We'll also keep you completely updated with any developments.'

'Thank you. Finally, can you please call Lindy Pickering. I'd like to interview her when I return later. There was so much friction in this family, we need to get to the bottom of it. Justine and Lindy are friends. There's something else niggling at me and I can't fathom it out yet. Hopefully the interviews and the post-mortem will answer some of the unknowns in the case.'

Brodie walked in and cleared his throat. 'We have a development.'

Everyone turned to look his way.

'Gina, Jacob, I will need you to head to Kidderminster. A body has been discovered at five this morning by a homeless woman and it's not a pretty sight. A detective from their local office is there and the scene has been cordoned off. There are similarities to our case. The victim has been drowned in a wheelie bin and next to that bin is a small blue teddy bear. It looks like our killer has a calling card.'

Gina's personal phone buzzed in her pocket. 'Excuse me.' She walked out and headed to the toilets, checking to see that she was alone before answering. There was no one else there. 'Hello.'

'Gina, have you heard the latest? They let me go last night and then they stormed in about an hour ago to get me,' Briggs asked in a whisper.

'Why didn't you call me last night?'

'I thought everything would be fine, but it's not. Not now.'

'What have you done?'

'I... I, err.'

'Just say it, Chris. I need to know what I'm dealing with here.'

Wyre burst in and Gina ended the call. 'Everything okay, guv. I didn't mean to make you jump.'

Gina shook her head. 'It's nothing. Just this case.' She left the toilets and stood in the corridor in the hope that Briggs would call back quickly, but he didn't. Once again, she was in the dark. A sick feeling was brewing in her stomach. What line was he asking her to cross?

EIGHTEEN

Jacob pulled up at the large derelict factory unit behind the forensics van. A cool drizzle filled the air and it had caused Gina's hair to frizz. They stepped out of his car and walked towards the PC guarding the outer cordon. She was no longer on her territory which felt odd. 'I'm DI Harte and this is DS Driscoll. We've come to see DI Kempsey.'

The man turned to a group of people who were huddled by a wall and called out. 'DI Kempsey?'

Kempsey emerged from the huddle. The first thing Gina noticed was that his huge grey eyebrows matched his moustache, next it was his crooked tie and creased blue shirt. 'DI Harte?' He raised his brows.

'Yes, from Cleevesford. I hear there are similarities in our cases.' As far as she was aware, Kain Pickering was victim number one. She wondered if their killer had chosen to leave Kain's body in Cleevesford because the area was familiar. If so, was the perp equally familiar with Kidderminster and the factory unit in particular? The abandoned building would be hard to find if the killer didn't know the area.

'DCI Fraser updated me on your case a few hours ago and it

appears we do have similarities. I sent him a photo of the teddy bear and we can confirm that it is identical to the one found at your scene.'

Gina had clocked that there was no label on the bear left at Maura's house. 'Were there any clues as to where the toy may have been bought from, like a label?'

'Yes,' he replied. 'They're really cheap and sold online and in lots of shops. I did a quick search in the hope that it was some person who made them at home. No such luck.'

Jacob stepped a little closer and pulled out his notebook.

'Can you tell me a little about the victim and the scene here?' Gina asked.

'If you both tog up, you can take a look for yourselves. Forensics have already put the stepping plates down and they've been working the scene for a couple of hours. I'll just check with Sheila, the crime scene manager. In the meantime, head over to the cordon, grab yourselves crime scene suits, sign in and I'll meet you there. I'll get Sheila, to walk us all through.'

Gina and Jacob grabbed a suit each and began to tog up. A crime scene assistant lugging a bag over her shoulder and a tripod pressed under her arm nudged past. DI Kempsey led the way. 'Follow me,' he said in a muffled voice from behind his mask.

A metal door leaned against the front wall of the building, leaving a gaping hole for them to go through. On glancing up at it, Gina was faced with a two-storey factory unit. Weeds grew through the gaps in the brickwork and wooden sheets had been nailed over all the windows. She glanced back and saw that the metal perimeter fence had been cut in several places showing how entry could have easily been gained.

'Be careful where you step. There's a lot of needles in the first room.' DI Kempsey stepped into the high-ceilinged dark room, partially lit by a portable light.

To her right, Gina spotted a scattering of syringes and fast-food wrappers. A couple of teaspoons and a portable gas cooker had been placed against the wall.

'The owners cleared a group of squatters out around six months ago. They thought they'd sealed it up well but our victim and witness had started to make it their home despite the barriers. People always find a way.'

'Have you interviewed the witness?'

'Briefly. Her name is Rita Court. Her formal interview will take place later at the station. She's currently in shock and is being treated by paramedics. She's well known in the area by the authorities and the community drug team. From what they say, she's a very nice woman who has fallen on hard times.'

They followed DI Kempsey up a short flight of steps into what would have once been a huge production space. The smaller rooms positioned along the left of the building must have been offices once, occupied by supervisors and admin staff. She spotted the broken wood at one of the windows. 'Is that how they were getting into the building?'

'Yes.' DI Kempsey pointed to a room right at the back. 'Rita told us that she and the victim were entering through that window. She stayed in a hostel last night and we have verified that. Her case worker confirmed that she got a bit argumentative and told them she was leaving at around five this morning. She wanted a fix and there's a no drugs rule at the hostel. As soon as she got here, she found the victim, ran outside, flagged someone in a car down and got them to call us.'

'What is the relationship between Rita and the victim?'

'They just agree not to enter each other's space and some-times talked in passing. She said he was moody and got angry if she went near him.'

Gina stopped outside the room and the lights on stands almost blinded her. 'Does the victim have a name?'

'Not yet. His fingers have softened and swelled up so finger-printing him has been a bit more challenging. We're working on it though. Hopefully when we get the chance to properly search the scene, we'll be able to get fingerprints from his personal items. There's always dental records to fall back on, but we haven't started that process yet. Are you ready to go in?'

Gina adjusted her face mask, to stop the elastic pulling at her hair. 'Yes.'

The crime scene manager called them in and beckoned them to stand on the plates by the entrance.

'Sheila, can you fill DI Harte and DS Driscoll in on what we have so far. They've come from Cleevesford Station and are working on a similar case. We have reason to believe they're linked.'

The tiny woman stood by where Gina imagined the wheelie bin had stood earlier. 'There is a tap at the far end and we've already bagged up the hose that had been fixed to it. There are no prints at all on the sink. It has also recently been cleaned.'

Gina glanced over. The sink was wide and deep. It reminded her of the sink that she used to clean her paint palette in at school, in the arts and crafts room.

Sheila continued speaking. 'The body has been removed from the scene, along with the bin but I'll talk you through what we found. See the metal beams above.'

Gina nodded.

'The victim's legs had been tied together at the ankles using washing-line cord. Marks on the beam disturbing the dirt and dust along with the start of a groove have showed us that he was hoisted up above the open bin and lowered into it, head first. The cord has been taken to the lab but I can send you photos later.'

'I can't see any scuff marks on the floor.' Gina pictured the strength it would take to hoist a human body up like that. Had the killer wedged their heels into the floor while pulling hard?

'We can also confirm that the floor has been cleaned with a

bleach solution so the killer has made an attempt to clear tracks. As for the victim, we have a male, looks to be in his fifties and he was very thin. He was lowered into this wheelie bin when it was full of water. I can confirm that he drowned. There are a few defence wounds but not many. He died here after being submerged in that bin. The cold water would have slowed down rigor mortis. He was still stiff when we got here which is why he had to be taken in the bin. Estimated time of death, between seven last night and five this morning.'

'That's a kill gap of almost a week between victim one and victim two. Thank you,' Gina replied. A crime scene assistant nudged past her. She couldn't help but stare at the windowless room, imagining what their victim must have gone through.

'There's a water supply here?'

'Yes, in this room and the toilet blocks.'

'Any electricity?'

DI Kempsey interjected. 'None at all.'

'So, all this would have happened in pitch-darkness?'

He nodded. 'Unless the killer had a light source.'

The killer must have known that there was a water supply. Given that it looked like Kain Pickering had died in the bathtub, drowning seems to have been the killer's choice of death for the victims. The building had to work for the perp. She was picturing a male given the amount of strength it would take but she wasn't excluding a team of two or use of equipment to help. She shivered slightly at the thought of their victim being literally treated like rubbish. Was the bin symbolic? Kain had been dumped in the car boot belonging to a deceased woman but was that just out of necessity? Victim two had been left at the scene; Kain had been moved. She wondered if he'd tried to cover up the first one because it was closer to him and gave up on the second because the industrial unit offered no clues as to his identity. 'Where was the teddy bear left?'

DI Kempsey turned away from the bin. 'It was on the draining board.'

'What's upstairs?'

'Another huge production floor. I believe it used to be a printworks but there's not much left now. There's a room just off the top of the stairs where Rita said the victim had been sleeping. There are a couple of bags containing clothes and an almost empty bottle of white rum next to a rolled-up sleeping bag. We're obviously going to be doing a full search of that floor soon.'

'Can we take a look?'

They stepped out of the room and Gina took a deep breath underneath her mask. The heady scent of bleach and death combined had started to cause a throb at her temples.

She followed DI Kempsey and Jacob up what was left of the bare concrete stairs, the banister long gone. On reaching the top, she saw the sleeping bag next to an almost empty bottle of rum. 'Has someone been through his things?'

'Yes, there's nothing in there to help identify him. We will, however, hopefully have fingerprints and DNA from the bottle and other items. This is a huge building with a lot of nooks and crannies. It will take an age to search.'

'There's a lot of old equipment and office furniture.' Gina gazed around the building. An old press sat at the centre of the room with other hunks of metal around it. 'There are some cabinets and old cupboards back there.' It looked like most of the doors had been pulled away from the frames and a pile of mouldy files lay in a trodden heap all over a rotten-looking carpet.

'Again, you can see that we're still in the process of going through all these things.'

'May I take a look?'

Kempsey nodded. 'Of course. I'll come with you. We can't disturb anything though.' Once again, he led the way.

Gina glanced into the cabinets but saw nothing. She bent over and checked underneath. All she could see was a gathering of crisp wrappers. The press was nothing more than the hunk of metal she'd suspected it was. With her gloved hands, she opened the large industrial filing cabinet and stared at the edges of several sheets of paper. 'Has anyone been through these?'

'No.' DI Kempsey stepped in front of Gina and pulled them out. He gently opened them and started half reading bits aloud. '"To my darling Nettie, I should never have spoken to you like that. That day, I knew that I had to get out of your life. You're far too good for me. I hope the boy is doing fine. All those things I said to him about his YouTube channel were cruel. It was the drink but I know that's not an excuse. You know I didn't mean them. I was in a bad place. It's like this darkness comes over me and I can't escape it. You've all been better off without me all these years. If you knew the real me, you'd know that me leaving like I did was the best thing. I know you kept going on at me to open up, to talk about my past but in truth, it was too painful. I only know how to run, and I'm sorry I ran from you, and tell Aunt Alice that I didn't mean to ruin her party. I think of the day I blew up at you and him and all I can say is that he reminds me of someone from my past. I look at him and he becomes that person. Seeing him just brings everything back and I couldn't expect you to run away with me and leave your life behind. Run away from what? That's probably the question on your lips if this letter ever reaches you."' Kempsey scrutinised the paper. 'The rest of this letter is water damaged. There is nothing more than smudges and torn-up paper.'

'What's written on the others?' Gina needed to know more about this man's life. She watched as Jacob typed out a message on his phone, mentioning Aunt Alice, Nettie and the boy. YouTube. Someone had to be able to make a connection. Their victim had left lots of clues as to his identity.

Kempsey frowned then continued to the next piece of

paper. '"Aunt Alice, I'm sorry. I was a jerk, a drunken jerk. It wasn't the first time. You'll probably be reading this if I'm dead but I want you to know that I'm sorry and I'm sorry that I was never big enough to come and say that to your face."' Kempsey started reading the last letter. '"Hey Sport, It's your uncle here. You are amazing. You're talented and one day you're going to have your name in lights. Those things I said to you about your music were mean, all spawned from the hangover from hell when you started playing that bass guitar at nine in the morning. I didn't mean to crush your dreams. I was cruel and I want you to know I'm sorry and I love you. I tried to search for your name on the net, see how you were doing, but I guess you're in a band and you have a cool stage name." Again, that's all there is. There's only half a sheet of paper here. Maybe the writer finished on that note or there's more.'

'We can't even prove our victim wrote these notes but if he did, what was he running from?'

Gina leaned over for a closer look into the cabinet while Jacob added bass player to his message. 'Jacob, can you forward that to the team now, see if we can match any of that information to missing persons.'

'I was about to do that.' Kempsey's brows furrowed. She knew she'd just stepped on his turf but she'd lost herself in the moment.

'Sorry, we'd be very grateful for a photo of the letters.'

He raised his brows. 'No problem. We all have to work on this together anyway. Let's just get this murderer caught. There are two victims now. What's to say there won't be more.'

'Thank you. I'll make sure our team keep you in the loop.' Gina exhaled slowly from behind her mask. She scrunched her brows on seeing something caught at the back of the cabinet. 'What's that?' She pointed.

Kempsey reached right in and tugged at what looked like a bit of torn paper and an old photo. 'Nothing on the paper but it looks like the same paper the letters were written on. There's a photo.' He uncrumpled the photo that looked like it had been printed on regular printer paper.

Gina glanced at the man who looked to be in his early fifties, his arm around a woman who looked similarly aged. Her long frizzy brown hair fell over her shoulders. 'Is this him?'

'You didn't see his body earlier with what the water did to it. We need to head out and ask Rita.' Kempsey called a forensics assistant over. 'Can you search around here, see if you can't find any more letters or photos.'

She nodded.

Without hesitation, they all raced out of the building, removed their protective wear and signed out before heading straight to the ambulance. Kempsey waved through the back window at the paramedic. 'Can we speak to Miss Court?'

The paramedic opened the back doors and the frail-looking woman with huge pupils stared at them before speaking. 'What?'

'Can you identify this man?'

'That's him.' She pointed with shaky fingers. 'The dead man.'

'How can you be sure?'

'How do you think I knew who I was talking about?'

'Please tell us, Rita.'

'A month ago, he stole those shoes from a charity shop. He didn't want Ugg-like boots but they were left by the door and they were his size. On wearing them, he said he wasn't takin' them off again because they were so comfy despite them probably once belonging to a teenage girl. He'd complained that it looked like someone had trodden in yellow paint and when I saw that body, I really only saw the shoes which is how I know it was 'im. I gave you a description too, of 'im, and you've seen the body. Earring, dark-greying hair.'

Gina knew they wouldn't have seen the body properly if it had been taken away in the bin. 'And you don't have a name?'

'Nah. Not really but I called him Z. He said call him Z. I thought that was because he was always half asleep.'

Gina's phone beeped. She read the message from Wyre.

We've interviewed Justine and Danny Crawford. Still no contact with Craig, and Justine now claims that Craig did know Kain Pickering. He had put a deposit down on a home security system before he went bankrupt. Mrs Crawford claims that Craig was livid at losing the money. Craig's phone is off. We've checked with his workplace and they say he's been off sick the past two weeks with flu. We've put out an arrest warrant for Craig Crawford and a team are heading over to search the house. If the hoodie found at the scene is the one in the photo, there won't be one at their house. There is a distinctive snag in the material of the hoodie that shows on the photo and the hoodie found at the scene. We'll find out soon.

A crime scene assistant began taking off her crime scene suit by the inner cordon. 'Sheila told me to catch you all before you left.'

'What is it?' Kempsey asked.

'I found another piece of paper. It's torn from a larger piece and it has names on it.'

'And the names?'

The woman began scrolling through her camera. 'I've left the paper where it is for now but take a look.'

Gina leaned over Kempsey's shoulder and clearly saw two names.

Kain Pickering and Chris Briggs.

NINETEEN

JUSTINE

Justine sat in the family room at the police station waiting for Danny to join her. She started pacing up and down, not that she could really pace far given that they were holding her in an oversized box room that stank of old kebab. A tension headache started to spread across her forehead. She needed to get out of this oppressive building and give her stupid son a good shake. As for her husband, when she found him, she was going to be arrested for murder because she was going to kill him. How dare he simply vanish and leave her with all this on her plate?

Her mind wandered back to the hoodie that the detective kept asking about in the interview. Why did they want to know about some blue hoodie that Craig owned? That hoodie was bought from a shop and those shops were in almost every town in the country. Lots of men owned that exact design and colour. Anyway, as soon as they'd ransacked her beautiful house, they'd find the damn garment and leave them alone.

She couldn't help but think about Danny and what he had asked her to do that morning. As instructed, she'd removed his laptop from the garden room and it was now in her mother's hobby room. Her phone beeped.

The police seem to be at your house. Is it your son again? Has he been joyriding in some other poor soul's car????

Great. Number five, the woman she'd been at war with over their bins was now relishing the fact that Justine's home was being ransacked. She punched in her response.

With respect, mind your own business for a change.

No way she was being nice, despite always arguing with Craig over how things with their neighbour had escalated. She knew that the retired busybody would now be having tea with number seven. Goosebumps formed on her arms as she imagined what they might say if they found out her husband or son had been involved in a murder. Would Lindy hate her? They hadn't been friends for long, but they'd all got along. Pia and Lindy would turn their backs on her. It wasn't even her fault and she hated herself already.

Her body started to ache from all the tense pacing. Only yesterday, she'd been living her almost best life – almost only because of Craig – and now she was at the police station and all she could think was, what have her son and husband done? She couldn't let the detectives hound Danny which is why she'd lied and forced Danny to lie too. She nervously bit her longest nail, tearing the gel layer off with her teeth. Danny was everything to her, despite spending all that time being annoyed with him for leaving his football boots lying around. This was bigger than that, so much bigger. If only she had nothing more to worry about than Craig having an affair with Simeon and Danny leaving his boots lying around.

Had she done the right thing? After all, her son told her he'd done something terrible and with her being a fixer, she had to correct his mistake.

Her stomach swirled with nerves. She spotted a plant and

wondered if it would be okay to vomit in the pot if she had no choice. She found its presence slightly reassuring. She gasped and allowed herself to succumb to the overwhelm that had been threatening to burst out during the interview. She was on her own. It was okay to feel like this when no one was looking. She inhaled and exhaled rapidly and deeply until she was dizzy, then she sat back on the couch, thinking long and hard about what she'd just said to DC Wyre and she was so glad she'd told Danny to say the same thing.

It's Craig. He hasn't been himself lately. He's always angry and shouts a lot. It all started when he paid a deposit in cash to Kain for our new home security system. He went to Maura's house and argued with Kain...

TWENTY

'I relayed that information to the team while we were back there,' Jacob said as he drove.

'How would the victim have Briggs's name? And Kain's too?'

'That's what we need to work out.' Jacob continued along Cleevesford High Street. 'Kain was in policing years ago, wasn't he?'

'He did six months and left. I checked.'

'And DCI Briggs is off the case.'

Gina nodded, knowing she couldn't mention that Briggs had called her. 'I wonder if the DCI and Kain worked together back then.' She paused. 'And what about the other victim? It looks like he'd written both of their names down.'

'Male, fifties. The age fits.' Jacob shrugged.

Fraser had told them to stay on schedule and visit Sheena May. All Gina wanted was to head back to the station and see what he had to say about Briggs. Her fingers itched to message her ex-lover and tell him about the names on the note. She pulled her personal phone out, not being able to resist the urge any longer. She had to risk messaging the phone he usually used, just as a concerned friend.

Hey, are you okay? Do you need anything? Maybe I could pop by, see how you are?

Jacob pulled up on the high street, right outside Sheena's house. It had been slotted in between a solicitor's office and a funeral home. Gina's phone beeped. It was a message from Briggs.

We can't message.

She understood and placed her phone away again. The best thing she could do was to get on with her job. Her phone beeped again. It was a message from Brodie.

Do you still like Mexican food? I remember that one time, we went to that restaurant and you had the enchiladas with extra spice because I dared you. Your eyes were streaming and you demanded an emergency glass of milk.

She smiled at the memory. The thought of going out and having a good time while Briggs was about to be dragged into something hideous felt wrong. Even though she felt like they were over, she wasn't sure she could go on a date right yet. Brodie hadn't called it a date but she wasn't stupid. She could see what he was trying to do and it was working. The thought of him and how they'd enjoyed each other's company back then sent a pleasant shiver through her and she hated that she was thinking about Brodie when Briggs was in such big trouble.

'She's in, guv. I saw her walk past the window.'

'Great. Let's see if she can shed any light onto what's going on.'

Jacob led the way this time while Gina took a deep breath and caught up. He knocked and a woman with short cropped blue hair opened the door. 'Hello.' She frowned and placed a hand on her stomach.

Gina guessed she was about six months pregnant. Her black dress with white lace trim at the neck showed her tiny bump off. 'Are you Sheena May?'

'Yes.'

'I'm DI Harte and this is DS Driscoll. May we come in?'

Sheena opened the door, letting them into a cosy cottage-style lounge painted in emerald green. 'It's about Kain, isn't it? Lindy called me.'

'It is.'

'Take a seat.'

Gina sat next to Jacob on the tiny couch that faced the fire-place. After initial introductions, Gina started questioning her. 'Can you tell me a little about what your relationship with Kain was like?'

'Turbulent. He came up with one mad moneymaking scheme after another. His moods – ups and downs – were exhausting. If I wasn't on board with these silly schemes, I'd be public enemy number one. He could be mean when he didn't get his own way, which I didn't like. He wanted me to be named as a director when he set his company up but, at the back of my mind, I didn't trust him with money. He ran up credit cards and I always bailed him out. When I refused, he said that I hated him, that I wanted him to fail and that any good wife would support her husband. Anyway, I had enough of his bullshit so I told him we were over.'

'When was this?'

'A couple of years ago now. Twenty-five-year-old me put up with all that but not thirty-seven-year-old me. I realised time was slipping through my fingers, and...' She took a deep breath. 'I met someone through work and we clicked. I did the right thing and ended it with Kain before starting anything. My feelings for this other person made me finally realise my marriage was over.'

Gina knew she needed to bring the interview up to the present day. 'Was there an incident between you and Kain about a month ago?'

Sheena leaned back in her chair and placed her hands on her bump. 'I posted a photo on Instagram, showing my bump and telling all my friends how happy we were to be having a baby. It was the first time I'd broken the news online because of Kain.'

'And what happened after that?'

'He turned up at my house drunk, banging on my door, shouting about how I'd denied him a kid then got knocked up as soon as I'd left him. I didn't want kids with Kain because he acted like a kid, but I didn't say that. Anyway, I was getting upset by all Kain's shouting on the high street so we just shut the door. Eventually Kain staggered away.' Sheena bit the inside of her cheek before continuing. 'I heard about Maura's death shortly after. Lindy called me but I didn't go to the funeral because Kain would have been there. I liked Maura, a lot. He was so lucky when it came to family.'

'Can you tell me where you were between one and ten p.m. on the fourteenth of November?'

She nervously smiled and pulled out her phone. 'That's an easy one. I was buying a car seat for the baby, then me and Mum had an evening meal there and I went back to hers for a while.' She leaned over and showed Gina the receipt. The shop was in Birmingham. 'This is me in the shop, with my mum.' Sheena showed Gina a Facebook photo of them in a baby shop, smiling. She clocked the upload time and it was fifteen minutes after the time on the receipt, one thirty that afternoon. 'The restaurant sent me an e-receipt. Here it is. We ate at five thirty.'

'Thank you.'

'I don't know if this is relevant but Kain used to meet up with someone once a year at a bar in Kidderminster, just for drinks. Same time, same place, every year. This man was an old friend, apparently. I thought it odd that Kain never introduced us and he always seemed tense whenever they were due to meet. I never met this friend at all and he'd go off at me if I asked any questions about him.'

'Do you know his name?'

'No, I don't know what it's short for but Kain called him Zed.'

'When did they meet?'

'I can't remember. Around this time. November, early December.' She shrugged.

Gina glanced at Jacob. Kain and victim two met up regularly. They had their link. 'I know this might sound odd, but did Kain have a small blue teddy bear?'

She frowned. 'No, definitely not.'

Gina's phone buzzed and O'Connor's name flashed up. She pressed on the message.

Search is underway and there is no sign of Craig Crawford's blue hoodie at his house. We have however found something else. We've put a warrant out for Craig's arrest.

TWENTY-ONE
JUSTINE

After Justine and Danny left the police station, she couldn't help but stop her son as soon as they'd turned a corner. 'You said what I told you to say, didn't you?'

He nodded.

'What have you done, Danny? Tell me about the message.'

Her son rubbed a bit of fluffy stubble on his chin. His eyes were purplish underneath from lack of sleep and the hangover he was obviously carrying with him. 'I told you already and I don't want to talk about it anymore.'

She grabbed his arm. 'I don't care what you want. I hid your laptop. I've just lied to the police and they are gunning for your dad. You do know that, don't you?'

'I can't do this, not now.' He pulled nervously at the edge of his T-shirt. 'Mum, just drop it.'

'I will not drop it.' She clenched her fists. A man walked past them with a dog. She awkwardly smiled until he turned the corner. Now they were making a public spectacle of themselves. Her neighbour would love to be a fly on the brick wall that her son was leaning against. 'Not until you tell me about the message. What can't you live with over your head? What have you done?'

Her son's Adam's apple bobbed up and down and he ran his finger through his sweaty hair. A few specks of rain fell on his cheek. 'It's nothing. Just leave it, Mum.'

'Don't treat me like an idiot. Answering with *"It's nothing"* is not an option. Do you know how bad it is? How about your dad?' She shivered as the pathway became a slight wind tunnel. A used chip wrapper blew past her head.

'Poor Dad. Poor, poor Dad.' Her son pulled a phone she didn't recognise out of his pocket.

She began to shake. 'What do you mean by that?'

'He's sleeping with someone else, Mum. I'm sick of the way he comes and goes. Even I can see that he's not always needed at work. The constant stench of his aftershave should give you a clue but you're too dumb to see it.'

She heard the slap before what she did registered in her head. 'I... I...' She didn't know what to say. She'd never slapped her son – ever. He stared deep into her eyes and his began to water up. For a second, she saw her little, sweet boy with his goofy grin, the one he always pulled when he said, I love you, Mummy, and she had just slapped him. 'I'm sorry.' She reached up to stroke his cheek but he flinched and before she had a chance to say anymore, he ran as fast as he could. 'Danny, wait.'

Despite being in her trainers, she couldn't catch her strong, athletic son. He'd darted off between the newsagents and the snack van. She could only hope that he wouldn't go missing, like his father. Her phone rang. She snatched it from her pocket, hoping that Craig had finally surfaced but it was Lindy.

'Hi.'

'Hi, Lindy. I'm sorry I didn't call and I'm so sorry about what happened to Kain.' Justine didn't know how much to say to her friend but she couldn't help the guilty tears that were starting to fall. Her son was acting suspiciously; her husband was definitely sleeping with someone else and even her son knew. She'd lied to the police and they were searching her home. She couldn't go home until they'd finished and she couldn't face her mum.

Lindy filled her silence. 'That's okay. It's hard to know what to say and there's nothing any of us can do. I know he wasn't the best of brother's but we can only hope the police do their job and find the person who hurt him.' She paused. 'Are you crying?'

Her sobs came that hard, she couldn't even answer Lindy because very soon, whenever the truth of it all came out, Lindy was going to hate her.

'What's wrong, Justine? You can tell me anything.'

She wanted to cry about how she suspected her son of having something to do with Kain's murder. Danny was certainly acting suspiciously enough. She wanted to unburden herself with how she'd lied to the police, putting Craig in the picture to take the heat off her son, but she couldn't say anything about all that, not to Lindy. 'Kids, they break your heart.'

'I'm sorry, you're going through a tough time too.'

'I'm not about to make this about me, Lindy, not with what's happened. How are you?'

'Do you fancy coming over for a tea or coffee? It would be nice to see you.' She paused. 'Are you okay?'

'Err, yes.' Everything was not okay. Her son was hiding things from her. Her husband was cheating. Both of them, like two peas in a pod. She began to shake, realising that her husband and son could be in this together. Her phone beeped with a message.

Where is hubby now, lovely Justine? Wow, my bed is so warm and look at you, so sad with your world falling apart.

She glanced up and down the path, struggling to swallow the lump in her throat. Her husband was a lying scumbag. She frowned and wiped her teary eyes with her sleeve. How did the messenger know she was sad?

TWENTY-TWO

Gina stepped out of the car on the road outside the Crawfords' house and headed towards O'Connor. A police officer stepped out of the hall carrying a box containing several evidence bags. Jacob followed a PC inside while Gina stood to one side by O'Connor. 'Can I take a look?' She called the PC over and peered into the box. 'What's in there?'

O'Connor reached in and held up a clear bag. 'This is the newspaper clipping from the nineties. We found it under the bed amongst Craig's personal items. It's a photo of Kain in a local paper in the congratulations section with a little message from his sister, Lindy. He's in his police uniform. As you can see, he looks to be in his twenties back then.'

She shook her head. 'Why on earth would Craig have this?'

'Indeed. And we couldn't find the hoodie from the photo. We spoke to someone from the lab where the evidence is being processed. A red hair was also found on the hoodie from Maura Pickering's house. It matches Craig's hair colour. We have his comb too so we'll know for definite if it's his hair soon enough.'

Gina knew that would take a while. 'We could do with more coming back on the forensics front but I guess they have a lot to process. At least there's a warrant out for Craig's arrest. Did you find anything else?'

'The search is still going on. There's still an upstairs study to go through and it's stuffed to the brim. I heard that Justine and her son left the station after being interviewed as there wasn't enough evidence to keep them there for now. Justine gave us her mother's address and said that she and her son would stay there until after we'd finished the search. Given that there was some conflict over money between Kain and Craig, it's not looking good for him at all.'

'Justine didn't mention that before. Any news on Craig's phone?'

'We are waiting for records but I do know we can't trace it. It's not in use any more.' O'Connor moved over to let PC Smith into the house.

'Thanks for the update. I'll go and take a look at the study while I'm here.' Gina stepped into the hall.

'And I'll ask that woman at the end of the drive to move on, yet again. Definitely a nosy neighbour.'

'It was probably the son. He's a right tearaway,' the woman shouted as if she could tell they were talking about her.

Gina left O'Connor to deal with the neighbour. Dog barks came from behind the kitchen door. PC Smith called back. 'It's okay, guv. The dog's a softie. We had to put her in the living room while we searched the kitchen and now she's back in the kitchen.'

She peered into the large lounge that had been zoned into a library area at the back with a comfy reading chair overlooking the garden. The lounge was pristine and all white. A huge silver Buddha sat cross-legged in a disused fireplace.

Jacob came up behind her, making her jump. 'Are you ready to take a look through the study?'

'Yes, I was just on my way.' She snapped on a pair of latex gloves, ready to leaf through anything she came across. On reaching the top of the stairs there were three rooms coming off the left side of the landing. PCs kept coming and going.

'Study's on the right, next to the main bedroom,' he said.

She glanced through the door of Craig and Justine's bedroom. Again, the décor was mostly white. Built-in wardrobes and a dressing table filled the one wall. A huge bed with what looked like an antique lime-washed bed frame stood proud in the middle and a long chaise longue had been placed at the end of the bed. The only sign that someone lived in the room was the inside-out pyjamas that had been left dangling off crumpled bedding. Her gaze continued to the Juliet balcony then it stopped on the only thing that broke up the aesthetic of the room. She pointed to the item sticking out from under the long curtain.

Jacob called out to one of the PCs.

'Can you please bag this up and log it into evidence immediately? It's a teddy bear, exactly like the one we found at Kain's and victim two's murders scenes, only it's pink. We need to get hold of Justine. That teddy bear isn't a good sign.' Gina's heart thumped. She didn't know if they were searching the house of a killer, a potential victim, or both of the above under the same roof.

TWENTY-THREE
UNKNOWN

As I dig deeper into her life, I know that I have to finish what I started. You get to a point in life where you don't care anymore and that's me. I. Don't. Care. Actually, I do care, too much, but I don't care what happens to me. This is all much bigger than me and the world will see that when everything comes out into the open. My burner phone is tucked deeply in my pockets and I've just turned it off.

There is one more person I need to deal with, or should I say, there was one more. I can't leave a job half done. There is just too much injustice in the world, and so many do-gooders who can't help but absolve bad people of the bad things they do. Having nothing to lose is liberating. Knowing where this is all going to end makes it all worth it. I have nothing to lose and all to gain.

My insides tingle because I'm so close to her. If only she knew. She sits alone on a kitchen chair and cries. I wish I could say it breaks my heart, but it doesn't. She holds that pink teddy bear in her arms, hugging it like her life depends on it. I had to give her something and the teddy seemed apt because why not?

It's my gift to her, a warning of what's to come. I'm close enough to smell her and her sweat makes me feel sick to the stomach. She makes me sick. They all make me sick.

She drops the teddy and heads to the fridge where she pulls out a can of kombucha. Its scent escapes as soon as she opens it – sort of vinegary. I can see her back door from here and I do feel safe because she never opens the cleaning cupboard. Her cleaner comes on a Monday, same time every week. I've made it my business to know everything.

She takes several swigs. She keeps scratching her wrist and then she takes her smartwatch off and leaves it on the draining board next to the empty drinks can.

In my excitement, I accidentally step back and tap the mop bucket with my foot. She glances in my direction so I stay back. I don't think she can see me through the tiniest hole in the wooden grain of the door but the last thing I need is her opening it while I'm in here. It means my plans for her will have to come forward.

Her footsteps get louder as she steps closer towards me. The scent of her jasmine perfume hits my nostrils.

Quickest way to drown her? Think!

Option one. Smash her head against the wall to instantly stop any screaming. Fill the kitchen sink up and finish her off.

Option two. There's a bag in front of me and it's stuffed with tea towels. I could ram one into her mouth, drag her into the garden and plunge her head straight into the water butt next to the back door. I'm wondering if she'll fit into it if I break a couple of bones. That's a better idea, more befitting of what she deserves.

These options weren't what I'd meticulously planned for her but I might not have a choice. I had a better plan that lies in wait which is why I'd rather do this later.

My heart is banging ten to the dozen as she stands outside the door, then her phone goes. Saved by the ringtone.

Great, I don't have to compromise. The plan still stands and my mantra never fails me.

All debts must be paid in full.

TWENTY-FOUR

Gina pressed her phone to her ear as she continued to update Brodie from outside Craig's study. 'We've found a teddy bear and it's the same make as the ones found at the other scenes. It's pink, though. It also looks like the Crawfords' dog has been chewing it.'

'Thanks for letting me know. I've been informed about the hoodie and the newspaper clipping. Keep looking.'

'There's something else. Jacob and I spoke to Kain's ex-wife, Sheena. She told us that Kain used to meet a man named Zed in a pub in Kidderminster, annually, around this time of the year, maybe a little later. She only knows the man as Zed and Kain didn't call him to arrange this; it was a long-standing agreement. Victim Two was known as Zed.'

'They could have met up recently, then,' Brodie replied. 'Great work. I'll update the team here and the system. Call again if the search turns anything else up. Our priority is to find Craig Crawford, but keep looking. Let's not close the investigation on him alone, not yet.'

Gina ended the call and entered the study. Piles of boxes, old tech magazines and books filled the room. She started with his desk while Jacob began rooting through the metal office wardrobe at the far end of the room. Splashes of rain hit the window. Gina peered out to see O'Connor walking the nosy neighbour back towards her house across the road. Several other neighbours had gathered around for a look.

She slid open the top drawer and it contained a stapler, several pens and a hole punch. The next drawer wasn't any more exciting. It seemed to be stuffed full of plugs and chargers. There was nothing in the bottom drawer either. She lifted up his in tray and spotted lots of paperwork from the company he worked for with details of jobs he had scheduled and places he was meant to go to. None of the paperwork mentioned Newcastle. Where had he been? Gina started leafing through the magazine pile, looking for any clue as to where Craig could be and not a single hidden sheet of paper dropped out.

'Guv, I've found something.' Jacob held up an empty burner phone box. 'Probably pay-as-you-go.'

'Is there a number attached to it?'

Jacob began leafing through the box and smiled. 'Yes.'

'Read it to me. I'll message it straight to the station. If we try to call he might hang up on us. We need to see if we can trace the number.' Adrenaline began to shoot through her body as Jacob read the numbers out. She hit send. Wyre messaged back.

I'll get onto that straight away. I'll call you as soon as we know.

'Is there anything else in that wardrobe?' she asked as she walked over to Jacob.

He placed the box on the desk and stepped aside. 'It's rammed full of all kinds of things.'

Several old porn magazines slipped off the top of a pile. She reached underneath them and pulled out a stack of photo albums. After flicking through a few pages, she could see that they were mostly filled with photos of a red-haired teen wearing a combination of *Ghostbusters* and Led Zeppelin T-shirts. He was with his parents and friends on holidays. She flicked to a photo of him with a girl. She had a tiny brown mole just above her lip. He had his arm around her and she was in the middle of dotting ice cream onto his nose, and they were laughing. 'We should bag these up.' Gina turned the page and saw another photo of the same girl doing a handstand on the edge of a rock with only the sea in the background.

Jacob let out a roar and shouted, 'Yes.' His one hand shot up victoriously into the air.

'What?'

'Look what had got caught behind the printer.'

Gina took the sheet of paper. 'It's a short-term rental agreement with Jordan and Harper.'

'And they're only down the road.'

'Let's head there now. We are this close to finding Craig.'

TWENTY-FIVE
JUSTINE

She sat on the couch in Lindy's lounge and sipped tea.

'I know Kain wasn't an easy person to be around but I miss him. I can't help it. You did so much for him, Justine, and I'll always be grateful that you tried to help him.' Lindy's eyes watered up.

'He was family and you loved him. We also have to remember he was sick. Alcoholism isn't an easy thing to battle. It's okay to feel upset.' Justine sipped her tea and listened. Guilt turned her stomach. She knew that very soon Craig would be found by the police. Soon everyone would be blaming her husband for Kain's murder and Lindy would likely never speak to her again. She swirled the tea around her mouth, scared to swallow it just in case it wouldn't go down. She held the teacup to her mouth and discreetly spat the tea back into it as Lindy wiped her eyes.

'But I hated him,' she yelled. 'I told him I hated him and that I wished he was dead because all he did was hurt the people around him. I said all that to him a couple of weeks ago and then someone murdered him.'

Justine hated to see Lindy torturing herself like this. She

walked over to the other couch and sat next to her, placing her arm over her shoulder. 'We all say things we don't mean when we're upset.' Justine couldn't control the breaking up of her voice and tears pricking at her eyes. She couldn't cry. She had to force that feeling away. After taking a couple of deep breaths, Lindy sank into Justine's chest and broke down while Justine stroked her hair.

Lindy pulled away and blew her nose.

'Here, let me take your cup. I'll make you another drink.'

Lindy grabbed Justine's arm. 'Can you stay with me. I don't want to be on my own. This house feels hollow and it scares me. I keep hearing things that aren't there, and freaking out. I swear I'm losing it. There's also so much to arrange and I don't know where to start. First Mum, now Kain. I haven't even got on top of Mum's stuff.' She began to weep. 'I don't know what to do. I need to sort out a funeral but I don't know when the police will release his body.'

'It's okay, I won't leave.'

Justine felt her insides turning to mush. Where had her son stayed and where had he run away to? *Can't live with this shit over my head any longer.* The words that she'd seen on Danny's screen swam through her head while she let Lindy cry on her. She swallowed at what she'd done to Craig, setting him up for a fall to protect Danny. Confusion was her best friend right now and she didn't know how to ditch it.

'Justine, you look sick. Are you okay?' Lindy dabbed at her red-rimmed eyes.

'Err, yes. I just remembered I have to do something. It completely slipped my mind. Pop your feet up. I'll make you another drink before I go and I'll take these dirty cups out.' She heard Lindy blowing her nose from the living room. As she carried the cups through the long hallway, she jumped at what sounded like the kitchen door quietly closing. 'Hello,' she said.

She stepped back into the kitchen and almost dropped the

cups at the sight of the pink teddy bear on the draining board, the same as the one she'd found in her house. She opened the back door and looked out at the garden. There was no one there, just like there had been no one at her house the previous night. A part of her wanted to scream and call Lindy in, ask her if anyone else could be here, ask her about the teddy bear but without knowing what Danny was hiding from her, she couldn't. Whatever her son was playing at was scaring the life out of her.

TWENTY-SIX

A bell rang as Gina pushed the door of the lettings agency open and Jacob followed her through. She was glad to catch them open after seeing on the door that they closed at five. Yes, they had Craig's computer but it could take the tech team ages to get into it and find that document, and that was only after it eventually reached the station. It was much easier to head here themselves and ask about the lease. She held her identification up. 'Can we speak to a manager, please?'

The receptionist peered through her aviator glasses. 'Yes, but we do close in two minutes. Is it anything I can help with?'

'It's about a short-term lease that has been arranged through your company.'

'Okay, I'll call Mr Jordan. Go through and wait in there.' She pointed her long-nailed index finger at the door to her left. They went through and sat in the faux-leather, bucket chairs.

Gina searched on the system so that she'd have all that she might need in connection to the warrant for Craig Crawford's arrest.

A man in a grey suit with a bun twisted at his nape stepped through. 'Follow me, we can talk in my office. So, you're police?'

'Yes, we need to speak to you with regard to a tenant.'

'Okay, we don't give personal information out.'

'We have a warrant for your tenant's arrest.'

'Ah, okay.' He nudged open a door at the end. 'Have a seat.'

Gina and Jacob sat at the one side of the desk and Mr Jordan walked around and slumped in his chair. 'Okay, name?'

'Craig Crawford.'

'What's all this in connection with?'

'We're in the middle of an investigation, so I can't disclose anything as yet.'

'Helpful – whatever.'

Gina estimated Mr Jordan to be in his late twenties.

'My dad, the other Mr Jordan, normally deals with this stuff but he's on holiday so you've got me.' He clicked his mouse and peered at the screen. 'He's at Nightingale House, number eight on Stirling Street. It's a short-term for three months. He's two months in and...' Mr Jordan peered at the screen. 'My dad has had to have words with him. He upset the downstairs neighbours about a month ago.'

Gina knew where that estate was. It was a new build. 'What did he do?'

Mr Jordan grinned and leaned back in his chair. 'Noisy sex.'

TWENTY-SEVEN

Gina frowned as they headed towards Nightingale House, passing several mid-rise apartment blocks. She checked her personal phone quickly. She hadn't missed any messages or calls and that was making her even more anxious. She hated being kept in the dark.

The November darkness had fallen, casting a grey-black hue on the estate.

Jacob ended the call to Brodie after updating him. 'They're sending two backup cars, guv. We can't go in until they arrive in case Craig tries to escape. He owns a grey Citroen estate which we should look out for.' Jacob reeled off the registration number.

'Great.' She pulled over a little way back so that Craig wouldn't see them approaching, not that he knew what she drove or who they were. 'I suppose, given what the letting agent said, we have to be prepared for him to have company. We also have to consider that they might be working together?'

Two police cars pulled up and four officers got out and stood away from the glow of the street lamp above. One walked around to the boot and pulled out a battering ram. PC Ahmed nodded at Gina as she stepped out to greet them. A police van followed, perfect for detaining Craig in until they got to the station.

'Are you ready to go in, guv?' PC Ahmed asked.

She nodded. 'I can't see his car anywhere.' As they stood outside the block, she looked up and wondered which flat number eight was.

'My mate lives in one of the identical blocks over there. He's number eight and it's on the top floor,' PC Ahmed said.

She glanced up. A light was already on in one flat and another light flickered on in the other. Gina hated that the curtains were closed but it didn't matter. Someone was in both flats and it was time to bring Craig in. 'There's no way he'll be jumping but can two of you head around the back just in case there is another door he can escape from? If there isn't, come back here. We might need all the backup we can get.' Two PCs nodded and left. Gina pressed number one on the intercom.

'Hello,' a woman with a crackly voice said.

'Hello, police. Can you please open the door?'

'Hold your ID up to the camera.'

Gina did as she was asked and the buzzer told her that the door had been released. As she, Jacob, and two uniformed officers entered, the woman came to her door. 'Is it him, the one staying at number eight? I hope it is because something needs to be done. I hate these people who let their apartments out to someone new every five minutes. Always trouble.'

'Thanks for letting us in. Please go back inside. An officer will speak to you in a short while.' They had more pressing things to do right now and the best thing for the woman was to be safely behind her locked flat door.

'Okay.' The woman frowned before going back inside.

Gina beckoned the rest of the team to follow her up the stairs. As they ascended the steps, the lights automatically came on with a click, illuminating the whole stairwell. She inhaled the mixed scents of new carpet and gloss from the paintwork.

On reaching the top floor, she took a moment to get her breath back and adjusted her stab vest. They had no idea what kind of a situation they were entering into. 'Ready?'

The team nodded.

She knocked hard. No answer. She knocked again. There wasn't even a letter box to peer through. They were going in blind, which she wasn't relishing when potentially dealing with a desperate double murderer. 'Police – open up. If you do not open the door, we'll have no choice but to force entry.' Again, there was no answer. She couldn't even hear the creak of an internal door or the gentle creeping of a person coming from behind the wood. She glanced down and caught sight of the tiniest bit of light bleeding under the door. It didn't flicker like it would if someone was lurking around the other side. 'Let's get this door open.' She stepped aside so that the PC with the battering ram could take over.

The weight and power of the enforcer shook it a little. The PC pulled it back and rammed the door two more times before the locks finally gave way. Gina swallowed and unclenched her sweaty hands. It was never cold in a stab vest and she was particularly nervous at what they might find. Her underarms felt clammy. What if everything they thought was wrong and they were about to find a body? Who had Craig been shacked up with in this flat? She inhaled deeply in the hope that she wouldn't detect the scent of death and she couldn't.

The PC stepped aside. 'All ready to go in?'

She nodded, allowing him to lead the way through the magnolia painted hallway. There were four closed doors. She pressed the handle and opened door one, the bedside lamps glowed a warm yellow. A man's clothes were strewn across the floor. T-shirts, jeans, chino-type trousers and a couple of pairs of underpants. Hardly the tidiest of love nests. 'Clear.'

Jacob had already passed her and opened the door to their

left. 'Bathroom, clear.' She noted that the bathroom was in darkness.

She opened the next door to her right and there was another bedroom which was a lot tidier but the bed was ruffled. Again, the lamps were on. Gina wasn't sure whether this room had been the passion pad and the other room had been more of a dumping ground for Craig's dirty clothes. The large picture of flowers the size of heads that looked like they were tracking them was a touch unnerving.

Whirring started up from behind the final door which Gina knew had to be the main living quarters. She'd seen a lot of flats like the one they were in and they mostly had combined kitchen lounges. Her hands were beginning to tremble at the thought of Craig bursting out at them. She knew that Craig's main motivation would be self-preservation. They had him in a corner. He'd either come cleanly and admit what he'd done in the hope of receiving a lighter sentence or he'd try to fight them in order to escape, regardless of the cost. She took a deep breath as the PC placed his hand on the last door, awaiting her instruction to go. It sounded like someone was scooting across a carpet, then there was a bang. They were all in place, ready for whoever was behind the door. 'Go.'

The PC pushed the door open, stepped into the room and stumbled onto the floor with his arms out. Gina glanced down and let out a long breath. The noise had been coming from a robot vacuum. The round gadget had turned upside down, possibly damaged by the PC. 'I'm okay,' he said as he stood and shook his arms out, then they all stared. On the table was a smart speaker, a piece of washing-line cord, a bucket of water and a pink teddy bear; but that wasn't why they were all staring. There was a small collection of photos that had to have been taken at the warehouse where they'd found Zed. They were pinned up on one side of the wall. There was a photo of a wheelie bin and one of Zed looking right into the camera, smiling and holding up a pint. She turned her attention to the photos of Kain that had been stuck all over the other side of the wall. Kain in Maura's house, going about his life. Kain walking down the street, unaware that he was being photographed. Kain in bed, sleeping. She shivered as she pictured Kain lying in bed while someone stood so close, watching him sleep. Why? This wasn't screaming a revenge kill in the name of debts, not unless the person owed was a member of the Mafia. This screamed up close and personal. It involved stalking. They hadn't looked deeply enough into Craig and Kain's relationship and who was he having an affair with, or was it casual sex?

'Bloody hell,' Jacob said.

Gina looked away, not wanting the last blown-up photo to remain imprinted into her mind. She felt her hands starting to shake. The murderer had been in this flat and everything was pointing to Craig Crawford. She forced herself to look at the last photo. Their victim didn't deserve to be on display like that. She swallowed and swore in her mind that she was going to find Craig and bring him in. Kain lying dead in the bath, his limbs all floppy and his eyes glassy and bulging. She would never forget that image. She looked down as she thought of Briggs and she wondered more than ever, what the hell had he got involved with?

Gina gasped and all the lights went out.

TWENTY-EIGHT

Jacob spoke. 'It looks like all the lights were on a timer using the smart speaker.' He flashed his torch at the wall. The photos looked eerier under torchlight.

Gina stepped out of the room and back into the light of the hallway. The neighbour opposite came running up the stairs and he stared at her. His satchel almost hit her as he removed it from his shoulder. 'What the hell is going on? One of the neighbours said there was a loud banging sound coming from upstairs and I thought it was my flat.' He placed his hand over his chest. 'What's going on?'

Gina nodded and held her identification up. 'Do you know where the resident of this apartment is?'

'No, it's a short-term rental. I don't get to know anyone who stays here let alone where they go and when.'

'Can we speak to you for a minute?'

He creased his brow in thought. 'I guess. I don't know him, though.'

'Him?' That was a good start.

'Yes, man, red hair, forties, maybe older but I'm not sure. I thought he might just be here on business for a while. The people who stay here are normally contractors and such. Come in, I need to feed my cat.'

Gina turned to a PC. 'Will you call this in and get Bernard to send a forensics team here?' She thought of them already stretched with what they had to process but there was no getting around what needed to be done.

He nodded and led the way as Jacob followed them into the man's flat.

'Lounge lights on,' he commanded. The smart speaker lit up and all the lights came on. A tuxedo cat jumped from the top of a tower and stretched in the middle of the living area. The man quickly emptied a pouch into a bowl and placed it on the floor in front of the washing machine. 'Have a seat.' He threw his coat and bag onto the tiny two-seater kitchen table that was positioned against the wall.

Gina sat on the larger settee next to Jacob and the man slumped onto a giant beanbag.

'So, what's happened?'

After introductions Gina knew she had to get straight on with it before hurrying back to the station. 'Tell me a little bit about your neighbour.'

'Like I said, I didn't know him. He kept himself to himself. I know he's a temporary renter because they all are. It's managed by a letting agent in Cleevesford. I've crossed this particular guest on the stairs about three times. I said hello and I think he said hello back or maybe he just nodded. He always looks down... He shouldn't be here, should he? Is he on the run? Is that why he didn't want to look up?'

'We're looking for him in connection to a serious crime. If you see him or if he comes back, please don't approach him. Call us straight away.' Gina passed one of her cards to the man.

'My mum is meant to be coming over later. Should I tell her not to, just in case he comes back? Actually, scrap that. I'll go to hers. You've got me worried now.'

Gina wanted to say, *and you should be*, but she refrained. 'Have you ever heard any noises coming from his flat or seen anyone visiting him?'

'I think he's been here for a couple of months, not that I've been keeping track. I'm not here all the time so he could be having parties when I'm out, but I can only say what I've seen or heard. I've seen one visitor and it's a woman. I've heard her voice in the hallway through the door. About a week ago – can't remember which day – I heard raised voices. He was arguing with someone. I couldn't hear what they were saying but there was a bit of banging and door slamming. Then there's the other noises.' The man swallowed and raised his brows. 'They've become the talk of the block and I know some of the others have complained to the letting agent. It's the noisy sex, screaming and headboard banging. The woman below them has a little kid. It's a bit embarrassing for her to hear all the time. The noisy sex is normally followed by the arguing. I really haven't heard anything else.'

Gina waited for Jacob to catch up with the notes and continued. 'You've been really helpful. Now, are you sure you haven't seen anything else? It doesn't matter how big or small, and it might seem like nothing.'

'I briefly saw her, once, when I came back after choir practice. It was around ten in the evening on a Thursday night about three weeks or a month ago. We crossed on the stairs.'

'Can you describe her?'

'Very slim, wearing a long black coat belted around the waist. She had an elegant silhouette. I thought something was odd as she was wearing sunglasses. It was dark and it was October. It screams affair, don't you think?'

'Did you see the rest of her face?'

'Lipstick, dark pink or red – I'm not sure. A white scarf. I've remembered more than I thought I would. I must admit, I found something about her attractive, that's probably why I remembered those little things.'

'Height?'

'I don't know, we were on the stairs. It was hard to gauge.'

'Hair colour?'

'She was wearing a white beanie hat. All her hair was tucked into it. Oh, there was one thing that stood out. She had a tiny mole on her upper lip.'

TWENTY-NINE
JUSTINE

Justine called Danny again but still he wasn't answering. His absence was going to make him look guilty and she was sure the police would be back for more and when they did, she'd have to tell them that she had no idea where her son was. There was no use trying to call her husband again. Her marriage was over. Pia tried to call but she let it go to voicemail. She couldn't talk to anyone right now, let alone Pia. She needed to have everything out with Craig first.

Her phone rang again and she hoped it was Danny, but no. It was Pia – again. She lounged back in the single bed in her mum's spare room. All she wanted was to go back to a couple of days ago. She wanted her perfect life, her yoga, and... panic caused her to jolt up. She was meant to be editing a bridal shop video and she'd abandoned it. Her hands began to tremble. Had the police taken all her files and her computer? Why didn't she think to bring her laptop to her mum's to protect the footage? Her life was falling apart. She bit the rest of her polished thumbnail down, worried about Danny and hoping that he wasn't hurt. A yapping noise came from behind the door.

Justine was thankful that the police had handed Pixie over when she turned up at the house to grab an overnight bag. She opened the door. 'You want to go out, Pixie?'

'Love, you need to eat.' Her mum made her jump as she appeared at the top of the stairs. For the fifth time that night her mum had tried to thrust food her way which is why she'd retreated to the spare room. This time it was a cheese sandwich. She didn't eat carbs and cheese was too fatty. Her mum never listened though. The timing was suspicious, more like an ambush. It was as if her mum had been waiting in the hallway for her to leave her room. She wouldn't be surprised if her mum had encouraged Pixie to scratch at the door.

'I can't. I don't want to. I'm too worried about Danny.'

'Why won't you tell me what's going on? Is it something to do with his laptop, the one I found in my hobby room?'

Justine shook her head. 'No, he just didn't want to leave it at the house because you know Danny, can't live without his games.' She forced a laugh and raised her brows in the hope that the questioning would end. She hated all the lies.

Her mother sighed like she always did when Justine mentioned Danny and his games. 'He needs to grow up a bit, work out what he wants in life. His friends are all applying for uni or starting apprenticeships but I guess getting into trouble with the law makes things harder.'

As always, her mum put Danny down and Justine couldn't blame her. Danny had got into so much trouble which is why she couldn't tell her mum what was happening. She was staying there because of the 'boiler leak' at their house as far as her mum was concerned, and Craig was still 'working away'.

'I think I should take Pixie for a walk.' Her mum didn't have a garden, just a shared communal garden in which dog walking was forbidden.

'Okay, but it's dark. Take my torch. It gets a bit creepy out there.'

She grabbed her coat from the coat rack and popped Pixie's harness on. 'Thanks, Mum.' She gratefully took the torch. Being alone in the dark would definitely creep her out. If anyone came at her, at least she'd have a weapon.

On stepping outside into the cold night, the white mist that was her breath coiled as it reached for the sky. She soon left the safety of her mum's lit up porch for the back of the houses. How could everything have gone so wrong? Sick of Pia trying to call, she popped her phone on silent and buried it in her pocket. She couldn't face anything Pia had to say until she had the full story but obtaining that information seemed impossible. Where was Craig and where had Danny gone?

A small path led to what her mum called the secret garden. She could just about see several bird boxes hanging from branches. Benches had been randomly dotted around and the trees around her swayed in the gentle breeze. She pulled the zip of her puffer coat up as far as it would go. Pixie yelped. 'Okay.' Justine bent over and unclipped the little dog who ran off behind the trees, snuffling and peeing. She felt in her pocket just to make sure the dog mess bag was still there, and it was. She could no longer hear the dog. 'Pixie,' she called. Pixie never went far. The dog's little legs rebelled against too much exercise which is why she preferred to sleep on a couch all day. 'Pixie.'

Justine turned the torch on and held it steady. She flinched at the sight of the scarecrows peering through the trees, cursing the day that some of the tenants from her mum's community made them in the name of fun. There was nothing fun about the faces with their button eyes staring at her, all soulless and sinister, each having their moment in the spotlight as she waved the torch around. Nerves jangling, she called the dog again. 'Pixie, come back to Mummy. Pixie,' she said in a sing-song voice. Her heart was thrumming. She tried to breathe like she did in yoga class but it wasn't working.

Heavy footsteps brushed the fallen leaves behind her and

she held her breath. Her phone vibrated in her pocket. Did she have time to grab it before whoever was approaching from behind reached her? She let out the breath she'd been holding and began to greedily gasp for air before running towards the scarecrows as fast as she could. She dropped the torch on the floor as she fumbled for her phone. The footsteps were catching up. On peering between a tree and a scarecrow, she saw exactly who was following her and for the first time in her life, she was terrified of him. The manic look on his face told her that he was going to hurt her unless she hurt him first. Bending down, she scooped the torch up, held it above her head and brought it down on his nose.

He backed away, holding his hands up. 'Put the torch down. I just want to talk to you.'

'Stay back,' she yelled as she snatched her phone with the other hand. Pia was calling yet again. This time she was going to answer. 'Pia.'

Her friend began talking at a million miles per hour.

'Say all that again, I didn't catch a word.'

'There's blood... it's everywhere. Please come. I'm so scared. I don't know what to do. I think there's someone here...' Her friend screamed and ended the call.

She stared at her pathetic husband, blood all over his face and hands, then she stepped forward and hit him again hard across the face, turned and started running.

'Wait.' He caught up with her and swung her around by the arm.

She went to scream but he threw her to the ground and placed his large hand across her mouth. 'Just shut up,' he said, saliva escaping through the gaps in his teeth and flecking her cheek.

She couldn't breathe. Her chest. The pain. He was crushing her. Gasping, she tried to wriggle free but he held her harder, using all his weight to keep her pinned down. Her heart. The man on top of her was not the man she knew. She was looking into the eyes of a monster and he was about to kill her. She tried to fight but he was crushing her, then the wooziness took over. The last thing she felt was Pixie's tongue across her cheek.

THIRTY

Gina left the kitchen with a hot cup of tea and headed to the incident room. O'Connor and Wyre were putting their coats on and O'Connor swiped his car keys off the main table. 'Sorry,' she said. 'I haven't been around all day and Jacob and I missed the afternoon briefing. How did the post-mortem go?'

'I emailed you the details, guv, but I know you've been busy. It put me off my Bakewell tart. I ended up giving it to Garth,' O'Connor replied. 'It basically confirmed what Bernard had deduced at the scene. Kain died by drowning. He did put up a defence which you'll see when you read the report.'

'That ties in with the murder scene at Maura Pickering's house.'

'Did he definitely die there?'

'We found photos at the apartment that Craig Crawford was renting. There is a photo of Kain lying dead in Maura's bath.'

Wyre glanced at O'Connor as she wrapped her scarf around her neck. 'We were just going to check in with Garth before heading home, just in case Kain or Craig's tech has produced anymore leads.'

'Thanks. If you find anything out, will you please let me know before you leave. I'll be in my office.' She headed out of the incident room with her drink, yawning and glad to be free of the stab vest. It played on her mind that Craig Crawford had not been in the apartment but she'd taken photos before leaving forensics to work the scene. A quick search of Craig's personal items in the apartment hadn't added anything else that was relevant to the case and there had been no visible clues as to who his affair partner was. Nevertheless, she needed to log on to the system and start updating it.

'Nothing to report from tech as yet. Garth said his team are ploughing on,' Wyre said, calling through Gina's office door before leaving.

Jacob peered through. 'I'm in the main office, guv. I'll do my updates and head off home. I've just checked in with the team at the Nightingale House scene. Officers are conducting door-to-doors and, obviously, all units are on alert looking out for Craig and his car. PC Smith has arranged for around-the-clock sentry duty outside Justine and Craig Crawford's house now that we've finished up there for tonight. Justine came for her dog apparently, but she left again and is staying with her mother. It goes without saying, if an emergency crops up call me and I'll come back here straight away.'

There was so much happening in the pipeline. Gina picked up her phone and was about to call DI Kempsey to see if he had any information on the murder of the man they only knew as Zed, then Brodie knocked and smiled as he stood at her door. 'Can I come in?' He held up a takeaway bag.

'Of course. I was just about to see where we were with the Kidderminster scene.'

He pulled out two paper bags and placed them down on her desk. 'You must be hungry. Help yourself.'

She slid a tuna sub on multigrain bread out. It had been a

long time since she'd eaten. 'Thank you.' Her stomach growled with anticipation as she took a bite.

He took the other sub and sat opposite her. 'I already have an update from the team at Kidderminster. I was hoping I'd get to catch up with you before you left.'

'I rarely leave early,' she said with a smile as she took another bite of sandwich. 'Actually, I rarely ever leave here except to follow up on leads.' She let out a small laugh.

'I've kept DI Kempsey updated with everything you've been feeding back to me. We've managed to identify the victim.'

Gina sat up straight in her swivel chair. 'Who is he?'

'Zavier Sellers, also known as Zed, fifty-nine years old. He was ex police years ago. He went missing two years ago while struggling with alcoholism.'

'That's the link between him and Kain Pickering?'

'Yes.'

'Is there more?' She swallowed a bit more sandwich and placed the rest down on the wrapper.

'Only what you already know. Both of them knew DCI Briggs. We know that because Zed had written down two names, Kain's and DCI Briggs's. What we now know is that the DCI had called Kain's phone a day before he was murdered.'

No, how could this be happening? Briggs would never kill Kain and Zed; she was sure of it but that seemed to be where the investigation was leading. A lump of bread stuck in her throat. She grabbed a napkin and coughed hard, while going red in the face. However hard she tried, she could not dislodge the bread.

'Gina.' Brodie ran around her and began hitting her on the back. Then he grabbed her from behind and thrust his fist into the base of her ribs, shifting the bread.

The bolus of stodge freed itself and she spat it into the paper bag. She took a deep breath. 'I am so sorry about that.'

She felt her cheeks burning up at the embarrassment, then her mind went straight back to Briggs.

'Gina, it's okay. Are you alright?' He let out a long breath.

Her hands were shaking. She'd nearly choked to death. Swallowing a huge mouthful while receiving bad news wasn't recommended. 'I, err; it was just such a shock.'

He nodded. 'Hopefully I'll be able to share more with you soon. Please don't mention what I've just told you to the rest of the team but it's not looking good for the DCI.' Brodie looked down.

Gina knew then it was serious. What had Briggs got himself into? Her mind instantly flashed back to the time he threatened to plant evidence on her ex-brother-in-law, Stephen. Admittedly it was to save her skin but the deception had come to him with ease. She was no saint but this was all becoming too much to take in. Briggs had been her rock, the order amongst the chaos that had been her life.

'You're shaking.'

She snapped out of her thoughts, scared that if Brodie looked at her too long he'd be able to read them. His gaze met hers and for a moment she felt like that young woman again, looking into the eyes of the rookie who made her smile, who was so much fun. She trusted Brodie then and she trusted him now, but she'd never trust anyone with the secret of her and Briggs's past relationship and that of her ex-husband's death. Brodie waited for her to say something... anything, and she was struggling to fill the silent void. After opening and closing her mouth a couple of times, she spoke. 'Sorry, almost choking does that to a person.' She inhaled and exhaled slowly. 'Can you tell me anything else?'

Brodie swallowed. 'I'd love to but I can't. We go back a long way but my hands are tied here. It would be more than my job is worth if I was to go into the details of that side of the investigation. All you need to do is keep following evidence.'

'But what about Craig Crawford? It can't be anything to do with DCI Briggs?'

'We can't afford to follow only one lead at the moment.'

'And what about all the photos at the rental flat?'

'Again, I can't say anything.'

Gina knew what was going on now. Did they suspect that Briggs had set Craig up? Briggs would know exactly how to frame a person. She wanted to shake her head but refrained. 'I shouldn't have asked. I understand.'

'It's late and I am parched and tired. The press haven't stopped calling and asking questions all day. They were flooding the car park up until about eight this evening.' He glanced at his chunky wristwatch. 'I tell you what, would you like to grab a drink? Maybe we can clock off and catch up on all the missed years.'

A heaviness spread across her chest What she needed right now was to crack the case and prove that Briggs wasn't the person they thought he was. So, what if he knew the victims. What did that prove? She looked up at Brodie again. There was so much more and he wasn't going to let her in. He couldn't. 'I, err... I'd really like to take you up on that drink but I'm so tired. Maybe when things calm down.'

'No worries. I'd love to know how life has treated you over the past few years and I've got a few tales of my own.'

'Guv.' Jacob stood panting in her doorway.

'What is it?'

'Lindy Pickering is missing. It looks like someone broke into her house, took her and there's blood everywhere. We have to go.'

'Damn, I'm on my way.'

Jacob left her and Brodie alone again. 'Where is the DCI at the moment?'

'He's currently waiting to be questioned again at Birmingham as we speak and it's not looking good. I shouldn't have told you this so I'm relying on your discretion. The Birmingham team aren't ruling out him working with someone else. He's in big trouble.'

THIRTY-ONE

Saturday, 22 November

After updating Jacob with what Brodie had told her, they'd swiftly left the station and drove to the scene. Gina jogged alongside Jacob towards Lindy's house. She'd checked her personal phone again but if Briggs was being questioned, there was no way he'd be able to call her from whichever phone he'd been using. She wondered if he'd got rid of it.

A PC had dragged tape around two lamp posts to cordon off the area and another two PCs were knocking on doors opposite. Every house had a long drive and a hedged off perimeter that would easily block camera doorbells. She glanced up and couldn't see any CCTV either.

'You can head around the side path, guv,' the PC guarding the cordon said. 'Keith in forensics has already put the stepping plates down and the person who called it in is being treated for shock at the minute. She almost fainted so the paramedics are treating her as we speak. Keith also said that Bernard and the rest of the team were still at the flat in Nightingale House which is why he's here.'

Gina glanced back to check out the witness but she couldn't see who was sitting in the back of the ambulance behind all the bushes. All she could see was the light from the vehicle glowing. She'd tried to look as they walked past but a paramedic had been blocking the view. 'Great. I'll check out the scene and speak to the witness after. Has the house been searched for people?' She assumed it had if Keith was in there but she had to check.

'Yes, and the annexe. There is no one in either.'

The PC passed her a bag containing protective clothing. She pulled the crime scene suit over her clothes and popped everything else on so not to contaminate the scene.

'Keith said to keep to the plates alongside the edge of the path. We've also taken elimination prints and swabs from the witness. She went inside the kitchen.'

'Great, thank you. Do you have a name?'

'Pia Yates. The witness said that before she came over Lindy mentioned that she was home and when she arrived, she called us straight away.'

'Thank you.' Gina followed Jacob alongside the large house and headed towards the path, while placing the elastic from the face mask behind her ears.

She thought of Craig and Justine, and then Lindy. Lindy and Pia had to be good friends if Pia was visiting so late at night. It was a little past midnight now. On reaching the garden, Gina first noticed the huge egg chair and patio sofa set that filled the space. Leaves from the surrounding trees had gathered in piles along the one side of the tall fence. A breeze whipped past her neck, sending a shiver down her spine.

On reaching the back door, Gina knew exactly how the intruder entered the premises. The window had been smashed, just like at Maura's house. She stepped in first, her boot clunking on the first stepping plate. She took in the scene. The key was still in the lock, on the inside. No doubt it would be taken to the lab. A spray of blood reached up the back wall, thinning out as it got higher.

'There was definitely a struggle here.' Jacob stepped inside. 'Broken plates, a knife on the floor and a smashed empty wine bottle. Upturned chair. No phones here. Blood spatter.'

She took a deep breath, imagining the struggle that must have taken place. It looked like Lindy fought. The scene was screaming kidnap. Her biggest fear now was that a double murderer had taken her. Their main suspect was Craig Crawford and they'd failed to locate him. She swallowed as she thought of Briggs again. This must prove them all wrong if they suspect him. She wondered what motive he'd have for hurting Lindy. She wasn't on Zavier's little list. 'There's a fair bit of blood, too. Lindy is hurt. There isn't enough blood to show that she bled out.' She swallowed. 'I fear Lindy doesn't have much time. We don't know how long our killer toyed with Kain until he was murdered and the same with Zavier. How long has she got? Why? This eliminates the theory that the first murder had something to do with Kain being in debt to Craig, and I have to ask why Craig Crawford would want to take Lindy?'

Her head hurt with the lack of clarity on the case, that and the fact that Briggs was involved. What else might Brodie not be telling her? She tried to think about it all rationally. *If Craig had nothing to hide, he wouldn't be on the run and the rental apartment wouldn't have been full of those horrible photos. Briggs would not have done that. The phone call he made to Kain, it had to have been about something else, but what?*

Craig and Briggs. Those two names ran through her head over and over again.

Jacob scrunched his brow and poked a gloved finger at a bowl he'd just upturned on the draining board. 'Guv, look.'

'Another teddy bear. Pink. What the hell do they mean?' She had no idea where this was going within the context of the case. 'These are the type of teddies people give to babies. Cheap little bears that are often attached to bunches of flowers or in gift hampers. Pink, blue, girl, boy. Kain wasn't a father but his ex, Sheena, is pregnant. We don't know much about Zavier's family situation yet. There was one of these teddies at Justine's. Her son is a young adult and she didn't mention being pregnant. Lindy – again – I don't know. I think I'm barking up the wrong tree here.' She stared at the scene and sighed. 'A baby boy and a baby girl.' She shook her head and shrugged. She couldn't help remember the strained moments of her relationship with Briggs. He had longed for a child so badly at one point that he'd taken up with someone he didn't love, leaving her heart broken at the time; all because he lived in hope of becoming a father. She forced those thoughts out of her mind. They were still too painful to think about. Yes, she still had deep feelings for Briggs but she knew that she really had to find a way of moving on when the case was over and Briggs was out of trouble.

'There is something. At the scenes where we found blue bears, the victims are dead. The killer is leaving us clues and I don't know if finding the pink teddy bear at Justine's means we need to keep in constant contact with her to make sure she's okay. It might be that the bears are Craig's and the dog got hold of one but we have to cover all angles. We don't know that yet.'

Jacob nodded.

Nothing was making any sense. 'Let's go back to basics. Kain – he was ex police. Zavier – again, he was ex police.' She kept her next thought in her head. *Briggs – police – not ex police.* She tried reframing Briggs's potential involvement and sent a quick message to Brodie. How could they not have all thought what she was thinking? It seemed obvious.

Could DCI Briggs be a potential victim?

Of course, Brodie hadn't confirmed or denied anything,

only that Briggs was in big trouble. Her own mind had jumped to the conclusion that he was a suspect for the actual murders. Maybe he was in trouble for withholding information, but why? At the very least, she hoped that the man she'd spent so many years loving wasn't a murderer.

She messaged Brodie again.

We need to look into the professional pasts of Kain, Zavier and DCI Briggs. Lindy seems to be an anomaly, but the past might hold the key to the present. I think we need to contact Wyre and O'Connor, see if they are able to come in early to look into this.

Keith stepped in, all hunched over in his crime scene suit. 'I'm going to have to make a start.'

'Sorry, we'll get out of here now. How's the back?' Gina asked, knowing that Keith always appreciated her concern.

'A bloody nightmare. I'm all dosed up on painkillers so I need to get going here before they wear off and I'm good for nothing. I've taken a step back on working the scenes but short-staffing and all that. Don't think I'll ever be able to retire.'

'Well, thank you. Your attendance is much appreciated. I don't know how we'd have coped without you this week, Keith. Let me know if you come across anything that might help us.'

'Will do. I'll call or message if I do.'

With that, Gina followed Jacob out and back alongside the path before discarding their crime scene suits into the box provided. A paramedic stepped out from the back of the ambulance.

'Is it okay to speak to the witness yet?' Gina asked.

'Just give us a moment and then I think she'll be fine.'

He stepped back into the ambulance, leaving Gina with her thoughts and Jacob annoyingly tapping his foot on the pavement. No amount of thinking was helping.

'Shall we interview her in the car, guv?'

Gina nodded. A handful of neighbours had come out of their homes to see why the blue-lighted vehicles had turned up. She flagged down the PC as she left one of the houses. She hurried over to Gina. 'Anything useful from the neighbours?' Gina asked.

She shook her head. 'Nothing. This is a really quiet neighbourhood and there is a lot of distance between each house. They were all in bed or watching TV. Three camera doorbells only caught hedges and nothing more. A couple walked their dog an hour ago but didn't see or hear a thing. Lindy Pickering seemed to be much-liked but no one knew her that well. She's only lived in this house for about three months.'

'Lovely. Keep knocking on doors and if you find anything that will help us, let me know.'

The PC hurried off towards another house as a paramedic opened the back door of the ambulance.

A lithe woman stepped out with the help of the paramedic. Her glossy hair fell over her face. Gina walked up to her. 'Ms Yates. I'm DI Harte. We're really sorry to hear what you've been through tonight and we need to speak to you.'

'Okay,' she murmured as she looked up, her hair falling over her shoulders, revealing her face.

That's when Gina noticed the small mole just above the woman's lip.

THIRTY-TWO

A larger crowd had begun to form. A woman in pyjamas was talking to two men who looked older. One seemed to be messaging and another had started taking photos. Gina watched as a PC spoke to them briefly before asking them to move on. 'Can we step into the car to speak?' Gina asked Pia.

'Err, yes.' Pia visibly shook and a streak of mascara running down one cheek looked like someone had drawn a faint line on her face. Her deep-pink lipstick was smeared on her chin.

Gina took a deep breath, knowing she needed Pia at the station but also knowing she had to tread carefully if she was to get her to open up. She looked Pia up and down. There was no sign of blood spatter on her coat or her white scarf.

Once they were all settled in the car, Gina and Jacob in the front and Pia in the back, Gina glanced back from the driver's seat as Jacob took notes from the passenger side. 'Can you confirm your full name?'

'Pia Yates.'

'What time did you get here?'

'Eleven forty-five.'

'And why were you visiting Miss Pickering so late?'

'I had a call from Lindy. She was really upset. She'd had a drink and you know what it's like when you've had a drink, everything seems good for a while and then it hits. She lost her mother not long ago and you know about Kain already, so I don't need to tell you about him.' Pia spoke fast with a nervous quiver to her voice. 'She was depressed. She asked me to come over. I was in doing a bit of work at home but she's a good friend so I quickly dressed and left my house straight away.'

'What do you do?'

Pia scrunched her perfect high-definition brows. 'My husband and I run a drinks company. We're working on new flavours and product lines. I'm not an early bird so I generally work a bit later into the evening.'

'What time was the call?'

Pia began to scroll through her phone. She showed Gina the call time and duration. 'You can take a look.'

'Two minutes, fifteen seconds starting at ten minutes past ten.' Gina spoke the words for Jacob. 'But you called the incident in at eleven fifty.'

Pia bit her plump bottom lip leaving a smear of lipstick on her front teeth, then she wiped a tear away. 'I had work to finish and I said I'd be with her as soon as I could.' She paused. 'If I left as soon as she called, I might have been able to help.'

'Or you may have been hurt.' Gina could see that Pia was visibly upset.

'Did she say anything else to you while on the phone?'

'No, just that she'd been looking at old photos on her phone, of her mother and Kain. I remember her going quiet and saying she heard a noise coming from the back garden. I waited while she checked it out but she said it was nothing. I ended the call and carried on finishing my work. When I looked up again, nearly an hour had passed so I ran out the door. I stopped off at the garage thinking we might have a drink and I grabbed a bottle of wine. It's in my car.' She dug in her pocket and pulled a receipt out. 'I bought the wine at…' Gina leaned out of the car light so that Pia could look closely. 'Eleven thirty-seven.'

They had a time. The attack on Lindy had begun after ten past ten. Gina wondered if the noise Lindy had heard was her attacker. If Pia bought a bottle of wine, like she said she did, she could have a partial alibi for the evening. Gina knew it was time to get Pia to the station before discussing her relationship with Craig. 'We need to interview you formally in connection to the murder of Kain Pickering. We'll also need to take your clothes and some swabs to eliminate you from the scene.'

'What? How… I haven't… I wouldn't… Am I under arrest?' Pia raised her brows and stared wide-eyed.

'No, but we will need you to come into the station for a voluntary interview. It will be recorded and we do have something we need to ask you about.'

'Okay. It's late and I've had an awful shock. I need to go home and have a shower. I feel disgusting. Can I come in tomorrow?'

'It can't wait. I know you've been through a lot but as you can appreciate, it's important that we eliminate you from our enquiries. I am going to ask a PC to drive you to the station if that's okay.'

'Has Kain's murder got something to do with Lindy?'

'We would really appreciate your help. We can talk more at the station, during your interview.'

'Okay.'

Gina escorted her out and enlisted a PC with a car to take Pia to the station. They were about to find out what had gone on between her and Craig Crawford.

THIRTY-THREE

LINDY

As she started to come around, she could hear a drip, drip, dripping sound coming from somewhere above her. Hands tied behind her back; her face pressed against a cold hard wall... where was she? After prising her sticky eyes open, all she could see was pitch-darkness. Shivering, she went to call out but that was near impossible with the tape over her mouth.

Her blood pulsed through her body and her breaths quickened, making it so much harder to hear what was going on around her. There was another drip. Was it a drip? She shivered violently. It was so cold. She tried to kick out but her ankles were bound by something smooth but tight that was digging into her skin.

What happened? She had a memory blank. Her head hurt. Not just hurt, but pounded. Someone had hit her that hard, they'd rendered her unconscious. As her mind darted to thoughts of Kain, she knew that whoever took her had killed Kain. But... she didn't owe anyone any money. Was this all about money? All she had was questions. If it was about money, it could be easily solved, she'd sell her mother's house and pay whatever debt Kain had run up.

It was starting to come back. She'd been in the living room and she'd heard noises coming from the back garden but when she checked, there was nobody there. The call... she was on a call to Pia, begging her to come over. It had been the wine talking. She had been so embarrassingly drunk and sad. Who wouldn't be sad after losing their mother, then finding out their brother had been murdered, despite how horrible he'd been? That's it – she asked Pia to come over and then she'd heard the noise again. On reaching the back door, she spotted that a bit of the window had been broken but the door was still closed. Her heart had started hammering the moment she saw that the keys in the back door were still slightly swaying.

Earlier that day, someone had been in her house. Come to think of it, she had thought that her bag had been moved from one kitchen chair to the other.

Despite being in complete darkness, she felt the room spinning but this situation was sobering her up, fast. She kicked out at nothing, then she made a nasally noise behind the tape. She wasn't closed in. The room sounded and felt big, echoey even. She began to half-rock in an attempt to keep warmer, then she flinched as something crawled across her face. She wanted to scream and yell. The thought of an eight-legged-freak on her face was too much. All she could do was make that useless nasally sound, over and over again. She wanted to shout, *what do you want? Let me go. You can have money. Whatever you want. Just let me go.* She knew she'd give the psycho imprisoning her anything in exchange for her freedom.

A shuffling sound panicked her. He was there, close enough for her to hear him move through the sound of blood in her ears and her muffled screams. Was he enjoying watching her squirm? Maybe he was wearing night-vision goggles. She'd seen *The Silence of the Lambs* and thinking of that film in this moment was making everything worse. She had no way of hitting, kicking, screaming or even moving properly. She was a slave to his wants, needs and desires and she knew that murder was his endgame. She was going to end up like Kain.

She thought of Pia. Had she seen the state of the kitchen? She hoped she'd reported it. She hoped so. Blood – she had a flashback to her own blood being cast across the wall as her attacker hit her. She was about to investigate the door and look through the window to see if anyone was in the garden but the pink teddy bear on the table had distracted her. She had turned her back for a second. She scrunched her brows as she tried to remember. It had to be a man. She didn't see him; her back was turned. He had swiped her from behind and she'd just caught that glint of blue metal, like a pole, as she fell. Before she could catch sight of him, the lights went off and she saw a glint of green in the darkness. That's why she thought of night-vision goggles.

He must have been hiding in that cleaning cupboard while she was drinking alone in the living room. Her heartbeat thrummed. She thought she'd heard a creak coming from that cupboard earlier that day before Justine came over but she'd given herself a talking to for being ridiculous. Another image came back to her; she was swinging over a shoulder with a blindfold on and something was forced into her mouth while her attacker held it closed. Had she been thrown into the boot of a car? A pill. She'd been drugged but it wasn't anything too strong because she was awake now. It had all happened insanely fast. Maybe it was a light muscle relaxant.

The shuffling got closer. She did all she could to keep her nausea under control and it wasn't helping that all she could taste was stale red wine at the back of her tongue. Was he going to rape her before he killed her? Would her body remain forever trapped in this dark hell, never to be found?

The shuffling stopped came to a halt next to her and she felt something brush against her thigh.

THIRTY-FOUR

'We've got Pia Yates in interview room one. Mrs Yates's family solicitor is on her way,' Jacob said as he came into Gina's office.

Gina stood from her chair. 'Great. It's time to learn about her relationship with Craig Crawford. We need to find him. The lack of leads on that count is beyond frustrating.' She paused. 'Where the hell can he be?'

Jacob walked with her towards the interview room. 'I spoke to Wyre when we got back. Garth is currently looking into Craig's bank accounts on his laptop and he hasn't used any of his cards for two days. He knows we're after him.'

'Where could he be keeping Lindy? There wasn't too much blood at Lindy's house and no sign of a drowning which seems to be our killer's MO. Then again, he could be planning to drown her somewhere else.' Gina continued talking through the modus operandi. 'The two murder victims were drowned. Kain was killed at home, yet the killer decides to move the body. The thinking is that the killer may have planned to come back later to clean up but we got to the scene first. He made mistakes and moved on or got distracted with his plans to take Lindy. Some elements seem well planned; others seem disorganised. He killed Zavier in a disused industrial building, on location, so there was no reason to move him. This time, with Lindy, he's taken her offsite like he did with Kain. The perp needs a place to take her, a place where there will be no interruptions. How long had he been watching Lindy? Why was there a teddy bear at Justine's house? At the moment my thinking is that Craig might have left it there by accident but the whole case is a confused mess.'

Jacob shrugged his shoulders and checked his beeping phone. 'Hopefully Pia will be able to help with some of those questions now that her solicitor has arrived.'

'I hope so. Time is against us. We need to find Lindy before the killer makes her murder victim number three.'

Gina stood outside interview room one and opened the door. Pia sat rigid against the back of the chair, both feet planted on the ground. Her clothes had been booked into evidence leaving the standard issue sweater and track bottoms swamping her petite frame. She inhaled through her nose and blew the breath out slowly through her mouth, with her eyes closed. Then she opened them. 'I feel sick.'

Her suited solicitor whispered in Pia's ear.

'Do you need a moment?' Gina asked.

She shook her head. 'No, I'm not actually going to be sick. It's just, I can't stop thinking about the kitchen and the blood. I keep thinking of Lindy.' She gasped and rubbed her red-rimmed eyes. 'It was just... so horrible. I've never seen anything like it and Lindy is my friend.'

'We know you've had a shock but we need to find her, and we need your help. Time is against us so please tell us all you know.'

After introductions for the tape, Gina kicked off with the questioning. 'I know you have already described your evening and you've explained why you went over to Lindy Pickering's house last night, but can you do it again for the tape?'

Gina waited while Pia relayed everything she said in the car outside Lindy's while her solicitor sat back and watched. The woman's pen scraped across her pad as the heart pendant on her necklace kept knocking the table.

'We need to talk about Kain Pickering next. We are currently looking for Craig Crawford and we have reason to believe you know him well,' Gina said.

Pia swallowed and once again, her solicitor whispered in her ear. 'Know him well?' She raised her brows as if fishing for more information.

'Can you tell me a little about your relationship with Craig Crawford?' Gina hated that they were wasting time when Lindy's life was on the line, but the last thing she wanted was for Pia to start saying no comment.

'Relationship. We don't have a relationship. He's my friend's husband and what has this got to do with Kain?'

'Craig is a person of interest and we need to find him. That's all I can tell you at the moment.' Gina paused, knowing it was time to show their hand. 'We know you've been in a relationship with Craig Crawford. A witness saw you leaving his rented apartment in Nightingale House.'

She inhaled and slowly blew out yet another slow breath, then repeated the action twice more with her eyes closed. Her calm exterior gave way to her biting one of her French manicured nails, then she opened her eyes and looked directly at Gina. 'It's got nothing to do with Kain.'

'We have reason to believe it does.' Gina couldn't erase those photos from her mind; all stuck to the apartment wall.

The solicitor placed her pen down and whispered to Pia once again. 'Okay.' She puffed up her cheeks and sighed. 'I'm married and I love my husband.' She scrunched up her nose for a second and continued. 'Craig's wife, Justine, is my friend. We've been friends for years.' She pressed her lips together and her eyes started to water. 'I didn't mean anything to happen.' She shook her head and sniffed. 'Please don't tell Justine.'

'Mrs Yates. Our priority is Lindy's safety. She is also your friend and her life is in imminent danger. This is serious. Do you understand what I'm saying?'

Pia began to shake and tears started spilling from her eyes.

'Tell us how it started, from the beginning.'

She uncomfortably scratched her stomach area and pulled the sweater down towards her knees. 'It was February. I'd had a fallout with my husband so I popped round to speak to Justine, but she was out. Their son was also out and Craig asked me if I wanted to come in and wait for Justine.' She went to speak but closed her mouth.

'How long have you known Craig?'

She looked down. 'Since I was fifteen. We dated when we were about seventeen, but only for a term. We never mentioned that we knew each other to our spouses. We didn't think it mattered and we definitely didn't want to ruin our dinner party nights with petty jealousies. I thought we had no feelings left... It just happened. One thing led to another and we kissed. That was all. We didn't see each other for two months after that kiss.'

Gina couldn't help but think how easy it was to pick up from where you left off with a person from your past. 'Is that when the relationship started?'

'We started texting. We have these phones. He bought me one, just like, err, I don't know, a pay-as-you-go. We sent jokes and shared memories – that kind of thing. Then he asked me if I would meet up with him. We went for a walk, in Warwick – far enough away from Cleevesford.' She looked to the side and paused.

Gina didn't need the full detail of how they got together. 'Then it got more serious?'

She nodded. 'Yes, about June. My husband was always busy working and we're not...' She scratched her head. 'We haven't been close in our relationship for a year or two but I still love him. It was stupid, irresponsible and I regret it.' She paused. 'Craig would tell Justine that he was working away. He'd book an apartment and we'd make dinner and watch films, pretending we were a couple.'

'Is that what the apartment in Nightingale House was for?'

'It started off that way but Craig told me he wanted me to move in so I said we were over. My husband and I have been having counselling sessions for our relationship, he doesn't know about the affair, and things have slowly been getting better. I thought I owed it to my marriage to give it my all.'

'What happened when you ended it?'

Pia whispered in her solicitor's ear with her hand covering her mouth. Gina watched as she frowned, then the solicitor nodded. 'Okay.' She swallowed. 'It was about a month ago, on a Thursday. My husband works a little later on Thursdays as we send a lot of orders out on Fridays so he has a lot to sort. I went to Nightingale House to tell Craig it was over.' She wiped her wet eyes.

Gina nudged a box of tissues across the table.

'I don't want Simeon to find out.'

'Simeon is your husband?'

'Yes.'

'Does your husband know Justine, Craig, Danny and Lindy?'

'Kind of. Justine and Lindy are my friends but Craig and my husband have joined us at the pub before... Craig and Simeon don't hang out together outside of our friendship group and Craig and Justine have come over to ours for dinner in the past.'

'Tell me what happened when you told Craig your affair was over,' Gina said.

'His reaction floored me. He shouted, telling me that he had done all this – the apartment – for me. He tried to convince me that we needed to leave our spouses that night and live there together and I flipped. I told him I didn't want to live with him, that it was all a mistake and I didn't want to hurt Justine or lose my husband.' She let out a sob. 'Simeon would be so hurt if he ever found out, which is why he can't ever know. Please don't tell him.' She hiccupped a little and blew her nose.

'You said that Craig's reaction floored you.' She wondered if Pia was referring to the shouting.

'He grabbed me and threw me to the floor. He's never acted violently before. I saw the rage in his wide-eyed stare and, for a second, I thought he was going to hurt me. I went to pull my phone out from my pocket – the pay-as-you-go – and Craig snatched it from me and trod on it. I have never felt so scared in all my life. All I could think was, I'm here in this flat. No one but Craig knows where I am and we communicate on phones that aren't contract phones. He could just kill me and make me vanish.'

'I'm sorry to have to ask you this, but what happened.' Gina felt her body tensing. She understood Pia's fear all too well but she needed to know what type of man they were dealing with when it came to Craig.

'He leaned over and said I was crap in bed anyway. He called me a selfish whore...' She grabbed another tissue and sniffed. 'He grabbed my arm and flung me along the hallway towards the door. There were bruises on my shoulder. I grabbed my coat and bag before leaving and he slammed the door. I don't know how I managed to put my coat on given the state I was in but I did. I put my sunglasses on to hide my puffy eyes and ran out the building as fast as I could... I don't want anything done about what happened. I don't want my husband to know but I do know one thing.' She paused. 'Craig is capable of hurting people and he has a short fuse.'

Gina noticed that Pia was grappling with the idea that

Craig could have committed such horrible crimes. 'We need to find him, Pia.'

She creased her brows. 'He said something else that night. He said we could make it work but she had to go. My mind has tried to erase that. She had to go – he had to be referring to Justine. I don't understand what that has to do with Lindy, though. I guess he could have been fed up that Lindy had asked Justine to help her brother with his alcohol issues.'

Gina sat next to Jacob in almost silence, giving Pia a little time and space to keep talking. The solicitor's necklace still scraped and bounced off the table as she made notes.

Pia continued. 'I should have said something earlier, about what Craig did to me at the apartment, but I've been so caught up in protecting my marriage. I didn't think, and I feel like such a shitty friend right now. I still don't want Justine or my husband to know but you have to help Justine. Her husband isn't a nice person.' She stared at Gina, her brow creased. 'Craig is a dangerous, unpredictable man who can turn in a second and I'm so scared for her. He also wasn't keen on Lindy because she asked Justine to talk to Kain. I wouldn't be surprised if he hurt Lindy.'

THIRTY-FIVE

JUSTINE

'Where are we going?' Justine's voice quivered as much as her insides were churning. 'Craig. Stop!' She wrenched her arm from her husband's pincer-like clutches and dug her heels into the earth underneath them. He'd dragged her all the way from the back of her mum's bungalow, through a thicket and out the other side before making her march across two fields to reach the lake. Her calves were killing and her toes were sore from being rubbed by pumps that weren't meant to be worn for hiking. She shook his hands off her.

He stopped and stared at her. She didn't want to upset him and end up pinned on the ground again. 'Just keep going.' He glanced behind her. 'It's not safe to talk here. We need to get further away.'

'How far?'

He turned to face her, the whites of his eyes reflecting the moon above. 'Keep your voice down.' He grabbed her again and pulled her by the arm. Pixie whined as she followed them, her little legs working hard to keep up.

'I will if you let me go. You're hurting me.'

Craig stopped. He turned and he moved in close, facing her, then he placed his hand over her mouth again. 'I said shut up.'

She snatched his hand from her mouth. 'Why, so you can wrestle me to the floor again and knock me out.' Right now, she didn't recognise her husband one bit, and this version of him was scaring her more by the second. She wanted her son and she wanted to go home to her mum's cosy house.

'I did not knock you out. You fainted. I didn't want to make you scream when I approached you and you were fighting me. I had no choice but to wrestle you to the ground. I had no choice!'

Charging into his chest, she began to beat him with her fists. He grabbed and parted them, moving closer until their noses met. 'I hate you,' she said. Scared or not. She wasn't going to let him see how much.

'Whatever. I have more to worry about than you being in a bad mood with me.'

'Bad mood.' She shook her head and continued walking. 'Right, so where are we going? Are we going to charge through another field or jump in the lake? What's it to be because I'm fed up and I just want whatever this is to be over.' She wondered if he knew that she and Danny had led the police to believe that he might have killed Kain.

'There, over there.' He pointed to the picnic table and benches next to the lake. A fox scarpered and Pixie barked and pulled. Craig pulled her back and threaded her lead through the wooden slats of the table. He sat on the bench in the dark and blew out a breath.

She sat opposite him, her heart beating ten to the dozen. The yoga retreat that she used was on the other side of the lake, all closed and dark, just as she'd expect it to be in the middle of the night. She glanced to her left at the old boarded-up building that she always looked at when she did yoga. From a distance, the rotting building didn't appear to be so sinister but close up, her nerves were getting the better of her. She couldn't stop her feet from nervously tapping. The imposing building caught the corner of her eye, the sky lit up as a huge cloud dispersed and the moon's milky light caught a damaged wall. It looked like a serial killer's haunt and the mere sight of it made her more uneasy. Heart banging to the point she could barely catch her breath, she kept imagining this moment being her end, and the only words coming from Craig's mouth were lies.

If she tried to run from him now, she wouldn't make it far. She needed to get her breath back and dislodge the end of her sock to stop it from rubbing her little toe. 'Where the hell have you been, Craig? The police are looking for you and you scared the shit out of me back there. Mum will be worried.'

'She won't. I sent her a message from your phone telling her that you've bumped into a friend and will be back late.'

He had it all covered. Her mum would go to bed and not worry at all. Her poor mum didn't even know that there was anything to be worried about. She needed Craig to help her find their son. 'Have you seen Danny? We argued earlier and he got upset and ran.' The last thing she wanted to tell Craig was that she slapped him in a moment of temper. She bent over and nudged her pump off with her other foot and pulled the sock tighter in the hope that it would rub less.

'He arrived home in a state but he didn't go into the house. I was around the back listening from the other side of the garden fence, hoping to catch you or him. He got spooked by the police presence so he almost bumped into me trying to hide from them. Then he told me what you both did and for the bloody record, I approve, okay? There's no way I want Danny to get hauled in over this. Something's happened and he won't tell me what. Do you know anything?'

She opened and closed her mouth, the words staying firmly inside as she thought back to that horrible message on his screen. 'I saw something on his computer. He sent a message to someone. He's in trouble and I know it's not just because he was horrible to someone on the internet. That's what he said it was about. I think he might have been involved in Kain's death somehow.' She paused.

'Don't be daft. This is Danny we're talking about.'

'Where have you been and don't say Newcastle. You haven't been working away, have you?'

He looked into his lap. 'No.'

'Who are you sleeping with?' She suspected Simeon but she wanted to hear it from Craig's mouth.

'That doesn't matter. Nobody.'

Her suspicions had been confirmed about the affair. 'It matters to me. I want to know. I'm sick of the lies, Craig.'

'It's over. It was nothing and I understand if you want to leave me but it's not what I want. I've been stupid and I will make it up to you.'

'You should have thought about that before you screwed someone else. Is it someone I know?' She held back. She really wanted to say, *just say his name...*

The breeze caught the lake, sending ripples all the way across to the other side, and the trees rustled. 'We have bigger things to deal with. Tell me about the message. I need to know everything if Danny and I are going to get out of this situation. Forget everything else right now and think of Danny. He needs us to stay focused.'

Pixie licked Justine's hand and Justine stroked her scared dog's head. 'It said something about needing to talk and how Danny couldn't live with whatever had happened any longer. I can't remember the exact words. It's not a case of who was involved, it's what he did and Kain is dead. I was so worried when I saw that message but I couldn't let him get interviewed by the police without a plan. I also took his laptop to Mum's before they searched our house.'

'Did you see the other messages leading up to that one?'

'No, I didn't. The police had just been and I waited in the

car until they left. I was panicking and I couldn't get hold of you.' She paused. 'Did you make Danny do something? Do you know about all this? What's going on with you and our son, Craig?'

'I can't say.'

'You know something, don't you?'

'Look, it's nothing. Just keep that laptop away from the police.' He frowned and ran a hand through his mussed-up hair. 'I'm being framed for Kain's murder and the murder of another man, and it looks bad. I had some cash that I kept for emergencies. I am not using my car or contract phone. Until I work out who is behind all this, Danny and I will stay in hiding.' He stared at her. 'You need to watch your back.'

'Is that a threat?'

'No, whoever is trying to set me up might try to hurt you. Tell the police you're scared. Keep staying at your mum's. Don't talk to anyone or tell anyone you're staying there and don't tell anyone you've met up with me or I'll tell them you've been helping me to stay on the run. What is it, aiding and abetting? They'll charge you, so just stay quiet. I will get to the bottom of all this.'

'Why did the police have your hoodie?'

'I don't know. I told you; I'm being set up. You have to believe me.' He looked away.

He was definitely lying. It felt like she was being played and she didn't know who or what to believe. Craig had lied to her for ages and he was still lying to her by not telling her the whole truth. He'd always ignored or neglected her when he worked away. Did he ever really work away or did he use that time to hook up with other people? Her mum always said he was no good but she didn't listen. She said, *you can't turn a compulsive liar into a good husband, and having a kid with him won't fix things.* She decided not to believe her mum. She wished she'd listened now because she didn't trust a thing coming out of

Craig's mouth but he had their son holed up somewhere, so she had to do her best to keep him onside. 'Please just tell me where Danny is.'

'No.'

'Can I just see him or speak to him?'

'He doesn't want to talk to you.'

'Why?'

'Because you keep badgering him. I'm giving him a bit of space to breathe and you think he killed Kain, don't you? He can tell.'

'I don't know what to believe any more. Please.' She started choking up. All she wanted was to talk to her son, get the truth out of him and protect him. If someone was setting Craig up, would this person use her to get to him or was he nothing more than a fall guy? Or was he just a liar? 'You're right about one thing, when this is over, I do want a divorce. He can have you. Actually, I bet he doesn't even want you because look at you, Craig. You're pathetic.' She stared at him. 'You make me sick. I hate you.' She reached down and untied Pixie.

'But—' He clenched his fists and the moon's light caught the veins in his temples throbbing.

It was time to make her escape. He wasn't going to tell her where Danny was and he was angry. She stood and sprinted as fast as she could, dragging Pixie along. He was right behind her, his pincer fingers pressing into her shoulders. A thought flashed through her mind, one of her husband and Simeon together. Her husband giving his bracelet to him. Craig stumbled to the floor and let go. 'You're disgusting, you know that?'

He didn't need to respond. She knew she was right and Craig knew that his world was about to come tumbling down on him in more ways than one. Once this was over, she was going to grovel like hell to Pia and Lindy to make things good between them. Maybe she and Pia could support each other through the hell of their shared experience of being cheated on.

'You say a word about seeing me tonight...' He stood up straight, brushing his hands together to get rid of all the dirt he'd just fallen in.

'And what?'

'You will never see us again. I will do anything to protect Danny.'

'You mean to protect yourself?'

'Both. Don't underestimate the lengths I will go to, Justine. Was it you who decorated the apartment?'

'What are you talking about? What apartment?'

'Don't give me that, you must have followed me. Are you setting me up? Getting Danny to lie like that came a bit too easy, didn't it?'

'What? You think I murdered Kain? Get real.'

'Innocent little Justine.' He paused and smacked his lips together. 'I know what you did.'

'What?' She scrunched her brow.

'You think I'm stupid, don't you? I'm not and I don't care but there are others who will care about what you did and it will blow your pathetic life apart.' He laughed. 'I will find a way out of this but you, I will make sure you get nothing when all this is over. You will never see Danny again because, guess what, he already hates you for leading the police to me and making him lie, and he chose to come with me instead of staying with you. Why, because you're a piece of shit and he knows exactly what you've done. I told him everything and he chose me. That hurts now, doesn't it, Justine?'

'What do you mean, what I did?'

'You know. You bloody well know.'

How? Justine struggled to swallow the lump in her throat. She knew how. Her cheating husband was in a relationship with the very person who would tell him everything. How his tone had changed. The man before her was some kind of monster given how he'd messed up. Yes, she'd done something terribly wrong but not as bad as the things he'd done. Was he trying to justify his behaviour or even excuse it? No, his was way worse than hers. Just looking at him made her want to throw up. If it wasn't for Danny and the fact that he'd be in big trouble without Craig to take the blame, she'd hand her husband to the police on a platter but she couldn't lose her son to whatever stupid mistake he'd made. She wouldn't say a word. Protecting Danny was her number one priority above anything else.

Heart pounding, she needed to get as far away from him as possible. She turned and ran, dragging Pixie along, choking on the sobs that filled her throat while hoping that he wasn't behind her because now he knew her secret, she was a sitting duck. And what did he mean by set-up and decorating the apartment? She tore through the trees as far away from him as she could get. She lost him and hurried back to her mum's, past the creepy scarecrows. That's when she heard the cracking of a branch coming from behind the hedge. Coils of vapour snaked up above the hedgerow. She knew that Danny had started vaping. She inhaled and was sure she could smell toffee apple, or something sweet and fruity. 'Danny, you're scaring me.' Had their son seen everything? Had he followed them or hid out while Craig attacked her? He'd stood by and let it happen – her own son. The coils of vapour vanished. Her every instinct was yelling for her to hurry back to her mother's and lock the door, but she couldn't help stepping forward to part the shrubbery. The only clue that someone had been there was the lingering scent of vape juice. He'd gone. Pixie whined and wagged her tail. 'Toffee apple,' she muttered. She knew Danny had used vapes despite her telling him she disapproved. He obviously didn't want to talk to her yet.

She dragged Pixie and darted to her mother's without looking back. Lindy was missing. Kain was dead and Craig mentioned that there seemed to be another victim. Was she next? Her phone beeped.

It was an Instagram message from an anonymous user with no profile or posts. Her jaw began to tremble. How could her own son do this to her?

The truth is coming out. Everyone will know what you did and they will all hate you. You're a skank!

THIRTY-SIX

The warmth of his hands caressing her set her senses alight. She reached out and touched him back – just his bicep. Her body tingled as he drew her in, closer to him, then his lips brushed against hers. Then Pia stood over her and spoke. 'You should just go for it. Briggs has moved on. He was getting too complicated and moody anyway, and he's made it clear, he doesn't want you. You could just have some fun. You deserve some fun, don't you, Gina?' She turned back to him knowing she had to give in to the pressure her own desire was putting her under...

'Gina, I brought you coffee and some breakfast.'

'What?' She lifted her head off her desk. Embarrassing – she'd dribbled on her notes. She took a couple of breaths and looked away from a very fresh-looking Brodie Fraser, in the hope that he wouldn't be able to tell that she'd just been dreaming about him. It had all seemed so real. Guilt tugged at her chest as she thought about Briggs. The not hearing from him had been the worst. She had no idea what was going on his end, all she knew was that he'd done something terrible. Was Pia's voice in her dream merely her inner self, trying to get through to her that she and Briggs were over? 'Sorry, I fell asleep. I was going to go home to grab a few hours and a shower but I got looking into all this and, next thing, I'm face flat on my desk.'

'You should head home for a bit. Wyre and O'Connor have just arrived and Jacob is on his way.'

She inhaled the woody body spray that Brodie wore and it made her tingle a little. That dream had really messed with her head. 'No, I'm good. What's in there?' She pointed at the paper bag next to the coffee.

'An almond croissant. I left some on the main table but I wanted to make sure you got one.'

Damn. 'The thought was there but I'll just take the coffee.'

'Don't you like croissants?'

'I love them, but my cholesterol doesn't. Too much butter. You have it.'

He burst into laughter. 'My cholesterol would say no too. I'll leave it on the main table. If only we could go back to those days when we'd come in at seven in the morning and eat pizza from the night before.'

'I'm surprised we didn't all die of food poisoning.' She smiled as she raked her hands through her tangled brown hair.

'You looked like you were dreaming when I came in. I didn't want to wake you but I was worried you might get a bad neck. By the way, there's a couch in the office I'm using at the moment. If you need it, it's yours. Hope you were having nice dreams before I interrupted.'

She pressed her lips together. They were sealed – for now. 'Any news on DCI Briggs?'

'They let him go in the night. He's home. He was at the station during the time Lindy was taken, but that's all I can say.'

'It can't be that bad if they let him go?'

'I can't say too much, Gina, but he's not off the hook. I will say that.' He smiled.

She leaned back in her chair knowing she looked like a hideous, sleepy-eyed mess but the show had to go on. Briggs was free, for now. She checked her personal phone. No missed calls. She hated that he hadn't even bothered to message her again even though he was out.

They had a murderer to catch and a briefing to head to. Panic hit her. How could she sit around talking about croissants, the past, and dreams when Lindy was still missing? She swallowed, knowing that still, Briggs had done something terrible. Maybe he should be facing whatever that was. Then she thought about her own past. She was as bad as him. She'd do anything to protect herself and still, she'd do anything to protect Briggs.

'Guv.' Jacob stood in the doorway.

'What is it?'

He held a croissant in one hand. A loose almond dropped onto her shabby-looking carpet. 'I've been looking into Sheena May and checking out her social media. Well, Kapoor started and I picked up where she left off. We know Sheena is engaged to someone called Fabien. He's on social media as Fabien Stone. He works as a debt collector and his brother died by drowning in a pool at nine. Fabien was thirteen. He was never a suspect but he had been looking after his brother at the time. He's been brought in for fighting in the past. The first time resulted in a caution and the second was thrown out by the CPS through lack of evidence. Most of his Instagram is full of photos of him flexing in front of weights at the gym and there's a cryptic message under a gym post about two weeks ago.

A man can't call himself a man unless he can protect his wife and then his children. A real man will do anything it takes. Are you a real man?

THIRTY-SEVEN

UNKNOWN

I'm exhausted from all the running around but I'm back now. This has grown bigger than I ever expected it to but I won't stop. Instead, my plan has changed and it is falling into place nicely. I am worried; I won't lie to myself about that. Having Lindy locked up is a concern and one I'm going to need to address soon. As I pace back and forth, my steps echo through the vacuous building. I headed downstairs a short while back and she was shouting. She can shout all she likes, no one can hear her. I told her earlier, 'When you hurt someone I love, you hurt me,' and she will feel that hurt soon, all in good time. I will look after my own. Okay, she might not have been there at the time but she was as bad as them. I wince as I remember champagne glasses being clinked together.

'Let me out,' Lindy shouts.

I know I should have gagged her instead of taping her mouth but then again, it doesn't matter. All she'll end up with is a sore, dry throat. I did think I should give her a drink but why bother? Why waste water when I intend to kill her? It will help me if she's weak, so no food and no water for her.

My phone beeps and I read the text. I'm needed and if I

spend too much time here while the heat is on, I'll arouse suspicion. My stomach kills. I run to the bin and vomit again before swilling my mouth out and popping another couple of pills. No one can see me in this state. I brush my hair with my fingers and take a swig of water from my bottle.

I check my phone. Actually, there's something I have to do later, something relating to the original plan. There is one person who needs to go now and I can't underestimate him.

Her shouting gets louder. Rage wells up inside of me and I can't help but clench my fists. It's time to shut Lindy up and I won't be held responsible for what happens now. She knows what she did or if she doesn't, I'll soon remind her.

Payment must be made in full and I'm ready to collect the debt.

THIRTY-EIGHT

Gina stood at the head of the incident room next to the boards. O'Connor tucked into a croissant and Wyre crunched on a pear. Gina's mouth watered. Wyre pulled out another pear from her bag and handed it to her. 'Thanks,' Gina said with a slight smile, the most she could muster given the desperate circumstance they were in.

'You're welcome, guv. I had my suspicions that you wouldn't leave the station last night.'

Bernard rushed in carrying a notebook and he held a folder under his arm.

'Glad you managed to join us.' Gina bit into the pear while Bernard got comfortable in a seat.

'I don't have long, unfortunately.'

'Would you like to go first?' Gina asked. Brodie stood beside her, his aftershave tantalising her nostrils again. That dream had done something to her and she couldn't let the feeling go.

'Thank you. Yes, please.' Bernard removed his scarf and placed it over the back of his chair.

'Can you talk us through what you got from the scene at

Maura Pickering's house and anything relevant from Tina Wild's drive?'

'Of course. I can confirm what we suspected at the time. Kain Pickering was attacked in his bed. There was a slight trail of blood leading to the bathroom and a bloody mark on one of the tiles. The height of this blood and the way that it had spattered shows it was likely from his head making contact with the tiles. There was also a wound hidden by his hair that would back this up. We know that the blood in the bathroom is a match for the blood in the bedroom. The knock on the head may have made it easier for the perp to get Kain into the bath. A bar of soap had also slipped into the bath, the same soapy water that had filled the victim's lungs so we can confirm that's where he died. Also, the perp was forensically aware. Not one print, speck of bodily fluid or hair found anywhere. The best we have is the disposable vape from the other scene. We managed to find some DNA and partial prints but the previous owner of that vape is not on the database.'

Gina had hoped for more but their perp was a ghost and it was possible that the vape belonged to someone who was unrelated to the incident. 'Okay, let's move on to the hoodie that was left at Maura's house, the one that looked to have been used to break the back-door glass in order to gain entry.' Gina turned to the rest of the room. 'We found the hoodie, Justine Crawford's business card and a red hair. This led us to the Crawfords and we have confirmed that the hoodie belonged to Craig Crawford who is now on the run.' Gina checked her watch. 'Wyre?'

'Yes?'

'Can you check with DI Kempsey at Kidderminster, see if you can get any more information from him. I've checked the system for updates but he may know more or may not have updated yet. Share what we have and see what they have.'

'Will do.' Wyre smiled.

Brodie interjected. 'I did ask if he could attend our meeting but he had something big but unrelated come in during the night. They're short-staffed over there but hopefully some more detectives will be deployed from another constabulary soon. Also, their uniformed officers are still conducting door-to-doors and following up witness leads. They have spoken to Zavier's wife and the family are said to be processing the news. He did say that they have alibis and aren't persons-of-interest so we can rule them out.'

'Jacob and Kapoor have looked into Sheena May's partner, Fabien Stone. He has become another person of interest. That doesn't mean we can let up on finding Craig Crawford. We need them both to come in. Jacob?' Gina said.

'Yes.' He stopped scrolling.

Gina frowned, wondering what he'd been reading. She addressed the room. 'We need to head to Sheena's next and bring Fabien in. Jacob found an Instagram account that belonged to him. Fabien wrote, *"A man can't call himself a man unless he can protect his wife and then his children. A real man will do anything it takes. Are you a real man?"* We know he's a debt collector. His brother drowned in his care when they were children. He has been brought in twice for fighting but nothing has resulted in a conviction. Kain went over to Sheena's place. He caused a scene and upset her. This could have triggered Fabien to attack Kain. We need to look into him. See if he has any association with Craig or Zavier. He might have known Lindy as Lindy is Sheena's ex sister-in-law. No link to Craig so far.'

'Guv?' Jacob held up his phone. 'Craig and Fabien follow each other on Instagram. There is a post that goes back almost two years. They both completed the same triathlon and took a selfie together.'

'Bring him in.'

Bernard cleared his throat and checked his watch. 'Sorry, I have to get back but there is one more thing.'

'I am so sorry. I should have let you finish.' Gina had let the briefing go off on a tangent knowing that Bernard couldn't stay long.

'The killer has slipped up.'

'How?'

'The forensics team found a tiny trace of blood under the cat's claws. It isn't a match for Craig's. We have the DNA of someone else who was at the scene.'

'And we know the cat had been trapped in the bedroom. Is there a match on our database?' Gina felt her heartbeat ramping up.

'No, but the DNA from the cat's claws did match that on the disposable vape.'

'Well, that is a breakthrough and links the two scenes nicely.' Gina paused and turned to Jacob as he'd been looking into Fabien that morning. 'What do we know about Fabien?'

Jacob popped his pen on the table and cleared his throat. 'Fabien was never convicted. His DNA is probably not in the database. Back then it probably would have been taken and then destroyed. As for Craig, he's never been arrested.'

'Is Fabien Instagramming at the moment?' Gina asked.

'Yes.' Jacob scrolled. 'It looks likely that he's at his office, although he could be posting from another location. He's just this moment tagged Fab Stone Collection Services Ltd. Looking at the name of the business, he is the owner. I'm not sure if it's just him as he doesn't mention any other staff.'

'We have to go. Lindy has been gone since yesterday evening. I can't let myself believe that it's too late for her,' Gina said.

PC Smith ambled in.

Gina glanced across the room. 'We have to find Craig. Keep all units on alert.'

PC Smith nodded.

'And we need uniform to assist us. We're heading to Fab Stone to bring Fabien Stone in.'

'I'll get onto that now, guv,' PC Smith said as he turned around and left the room.

Brodie exhaled. 'I'll get on with the press release. We have a team of journalists waiting for yet another update. This case is getting hotter by the minute and the national press are here now. We have decided to put Craig's face out there.'

'But what if he has Lindy, and gets desperate and kills her?'

'We have looked into this and we believe she doesn't have much time either way. We need to find her and our last hope is that the public come forward to help.'

Gina swallowed. This was a risky strategy but he had made the decision. She only hoped they could get to Craig and Fabien first. 'Can you wait until we have Fabien? Please, just give us that.'

He looked at his watch. 'You have sixty minutes until we go public with Craig.'

Sixty minutes seemed like mere seconds. She grabbed her coat and nodded to Jacob to follow. She flung the last bit of pear into the bin. 'Kapoor?'

'Yes, guv.'

'I'm worried about Justine and her son, Danny. Get a family liaison officer over to be with them. She's at her mother's. The address is on file.' She mulled over the friendship group. Pia, Lindy and Justine. Justine was a concern with her being Craig's wife. Lindy had been taken and Pia had been having an affair with Craig. 'I also want someone to check on Pia. These three women are all connected to this case in some way and I don't want anything to happen to them.'

Gina glanced at her watch. Fifty-seven minutes. The clock was ticking. 'The race is on. PC Smith is arranging backup. Given Fabien's link to Craig, Sheena and Kain, we need to investigate him further and having a business premises might provide the perfect place to hide and hurt Lindy. We also can't risk that Fabien will warn Craig if they are in this together. On a normal day, we could have brought him in for questioning but a life is in imminent danger. Let's arrest Fabien and bring him in.'

THIRTY-NINE

Gina parked in front of a newsagent's shop alongside a busy road. She dashed out of her car with Jacob close behind, then she glanced at her watch again. Twenty-two minutes left before Craig's face went out to the press. The three-storey building next door with its slightly dilapidated warehouse attached to the right had a sign pointing to the car park around the back but Gina didn't want Fabien to see them coming. She glanced at the main space at the front and a Mercedes parked in the space marked up for the managing director. Fabien's number plate partially spelled his name. 'It looks like he's in.'

Gina watched PC Smith pull in behind her and then another two police cars followed. It was too late to stay hidden. One glance out of any front-facing window, and Fabien would know they were coming. She looked at the warehouse, knowing how easy it would be to hide two people in there. The main house also had a cellar. She could see boxes piled up through the tiny strip of a window below.

'Head around the back,' she called to PC Smith, 'and you two go with him.' She nodded towards uniformed officers.

'Make sure you cover the back of the main building and warehouse.'

She then nodded at Jacob, PC Benton and two more officers. 'Can you all cover the front and side of the buildings?' She pressed the buzzer and waited with Jacob on the front step. Two bay windows overlooked the frontage but the rooms seemed empty of life. Gina spotted a large boardroom table that seemed to be covered in archive boxes and crusty-looking mugs. The other bay window appeared to be an unsupervised reception with a dead spider plant on the windowsill. Eventually the intercom system crackled and a girl's voice came through it. 'Hello.'

'Hello, we're here to see Fabien Stone.'

'Who are you? He doesn't have any meetings booked.'

'Damn,' Gina whispered under her breath. She had no option but to disclose who she was. 'I'm DI Harte and I'm with DS Driscoll. We're from Cleevesford Police. We need to speak to Mr Stone.'

She paused and then spoke. 'Err, he's about to go out. Can I get him to call you later?'

'I'm sorry but this can't wait.'

'Who the fuck is on the intercom.' The loud voice of a man crackled through.

'Police,' Gina replied. 'Hello, hello. He's hung up on us.' She pressed the call button again before nearly being swept into the entrance room as Fabien pulled the front door open.

PC Benton ran over to assist. 'Fabien Stone. I'm arresting you on suspicion of the murder of Kain Pickering and the kidnap of Lindy Pickering. You do not have to say anything. But it may harm your defence if you do not mention when questioned something which you later rely on in court. Anything you do say may be given in evidence.'

Gina went to cuff him. He jabbed her in the jaw with his elbow and crashed past her, knocking her to the ground. PC

Benton and Jacob ran towards the road where Fabien was heading. A stream of cars stopped him crossing. Jacob tried to tackle the bulky man to the ground but Fabien was built like a truck. Between Jacob and PC Benton, they just about managed to cuff him. PC Benton's hat fell off into the road and she almost stumbled.

Gina opened and closed her mouth a couple of times and prodded her throbbing jaw. There were no broken bones or loose teeth but her chin ached like mad. She walked over, taking her time. 'Fabien Stone. I'm further arresting you on suspicion of assaulting a police officer.' She glanced up at PC Benton who had now retrieved her hat as a police van pulled up. 'Take him to the station.'

She and Jacob stood on the roadside as it took another two PCs to get Fabien into the van. He kicked and spat as he seethed and swore at the top of his voice. 'Let's get a spit hood on him,' another PC said as they forced it over his head while trying to avoid his kicking feet.

'We've got our work cut out with this one. He easily has the strength to manoeuvre Kain and hoist up Zavier,' Gina said to Jacob. He held his arm up and a flap of material hung down where Fabien had ripped his coat.

They watched as the van pulled away, taking Fabien Stone with it.

Gina addressed PC Smith and the officers that were still left. 'Right, we need to search this building. We're looking for Lindy, or any sign that she's been here.'

A girl who looked to be about sixteen came to the door. 'What's going on? I'm meant to be leaving to go to the dentist but there's no one else in the office and Mr Stone won't be happy if I leave the building empty.'

Gina headed towards her. 'Mr Stone is under arrest and we need to search the property.'

'Okay, I best cancel the dentist.' Her blonde ponytail

swished as she turned away to make a phone call. 'I think I should call my mum, too.'

'Do you work here?'

'Yes, I've only been here a couple of weeks. I'm an apprentice.'

'How old are you?'

'Seventeen.'

Gina let out a sigh. They also had a minor to interview – great. They'd have to wait for an appropriate adult to be with her before they could conduct an interview. She called one of the PCs over and she jogged towards Gina. Keeping the girl safe was also a priority. 'What's your name?' Gina asked her.

'Keri with an I on the end.' She bit the inside of her cheek.

'Keri, could you please stay outside here with PC Stainton until your mum arrives? We'll need you both to come to the station then. It's nothing to worry about, okay.' She hoped she'd reassured the girl.

Keri nodded.

Gina called Jacob to the front door. That's when she spotted the pale-blue men's puffer jacket on a hook. 'There's a streak of blood on the sleeve of that coat, and it's fresh.'

FORTY
LINDY

Four Hours Earlier

She had very little concept of time and her heart was still thumping from the rat that had squeaked around by her thigh. Had she been in the dark room with its drip, drip, drip, sounds for a couple of hours or a whole day? She wriggled back towards the wall, hoping that the rat had gone. However hard she tried, she couldn't remove the binds.

Tears slipped from her cheeks. She felt the wetness tracing down her face until the coldness hit her neck. She couldn't sit here and cry in the dark. She had to get away before he came back and killed her, but how? Thoughts swam through her head. Why was she here? Was it to do with Kain and the money he owed to everyone? Was there someone in her house before Justine came over? She didn't see anyone but she had felt a presence. It was weird, like the air pressure had shifted. Last night, she felt that presence again but she dismissed it, then she was taken. She scrunched her brows. A lot of it was still a blur. She remembered being hit, then her house had been in darkness.

The lights had been turned off, maybe from the fuse board in the kitchen cupboard.

Kain, it had to have everything to do with him.

A loud clunk came from the other side of the door and someone opened it. She couldn't see anyone in the darkness, just the glow of green around the eye area.

Without warning, two hands reached down and dragged her across the stone floor so fast she barely managed to process what was happening. Her head was woozy, like she was on a ship in the middle of a stormy sea. Hunger, thirst, fear – all ganging up on her, pulling her closer to death.

The beast dragged her along the floor that tore her clothes and flesh with every cold and painful bump. 'I'm sorry for whatever I've done. Please, I don't deserve this. I've never hurt anyone.'

He slammed her head into the wall and forced her into some sort of chair that suddenly came to life. She was on a stairlift, going up. Blood trickled down the middle of her forehead. 'Please let me go,' she yelled as the tears flowed.

The stairlift stopped with a jolt. Her eyes adjusted to the chink of light at the other end of the large, open room. He dragged her from the chair, back onto the floor where he continued to pull her along. The pungent scent of the room hit her nostrils, taking her breath away, making her want to heave. Arms and legs still tied, she once again tried to wriggle out of the binds but they cut through her flesh. There was no way out of this. She was at his mercy.

He manhandled her into some sort of restraint, wrapping something around her, linking what felt like thick straps through the binds and around her body. A mechanical noise echoed through the space and she slowly began to lift from the ground, higher and higher until her bound legs dangled. The light caught the top of his head but all she could see was a baseball cap. He looked up and the glint of his night-vision goggles stared back at her. All she could do was scream at the sight.

Her veins pulsed with blood as she gasped for air.

He lifted her higher and higher. The hoist mechanism jolted and began pivoting her as she dangled, then he climbed up something behind her, each of his steps clunking on metal as he ascended, until she could feel his breath on the back of her head.

'It's time to pay your debt. Kain has gone, Zavier has gone, now it's your turn.'

She recognised that second name and in an instant she knew why but not who. She opened her mouth to say how sorry she was, but she didn't get her chance. He undid the straps that were keeping her in place and she fell with a plop into a tank full of putrid liquid.

FORTY-ONE

As soon as the main building was cleared and the coat bagged for evidence, Gina followed a PC to where a large set of double doors led to the warehouse.

'We found the keys in the suspect's office upstairs,' the PC said as she pushed the doors open.

All Gina saw was a long, dark corridor with an oil-stained threadbare carpet that gave off a musty whiff as she stepped on it. 'This doesn't look like a debt collector's office.' She caught a glimpse of an old car calendar dated nineteen eighty-seven with a Ford Cosworth on the front and next to it was a huge photo of a shiny exhaust pipe. 'I wonder if this used to be a garage.'

Gina waved an arm to gather the team around. 'I don't know what we're going to find in here but I'm hoping it's Lindy. Check that everyone is in position. We are still looking for Craig.'

A PC spoke into her radio quietly and nodded. 'All ready to go, guv. Every entrance and exit is covered.'

Gina stepped deeper into the dark corridor, her soles slapping on concrete where the old carpet had completely worn away. She nudged three doors open and all were full of what she could only guess looked like Fabien's personal items. Each was piled up with furniture, some of it broken down into pieces. She followed the sign to the warehouse. 'Why would a debt collector need a warehouse?'

Jacob followed closely beside her. 'I don't know. Could he be a high court enforcement officer also?'

'Maybe, although I don't recall that being mentioned.' They reached the end of the corridor and the PC used another key to unlock the next set of double doors which opened out into another room. 'Police,' Gina called, expecting to hear some sort of commotion. She shone her torch ahead, cutting through the darkness – nothing. She flinched as she heard a scuttle to her right. The shaft of light pointed at a rat's tail.

Jacob shuddered. Gina knew he wasn't keen on rodents but they were going in regardless.

She reached for the light switch but it didn't work. Either the strip light needed replacing or there was no supply. There was another room ahead. She led the way and shivered, leaving Jacob a little further back. He flinched as a squeak pierced the silence. The deeper into the building they got, the chillier it was and the lack of light was eerie. She inhaled the smell of mould and damp. 'Lindy?'

No answer.

Gina nodded to the PCs, gesturing for them to take the room on the left as she stopped at a set of three steps that she knew must lead to the back of the building. After stepping down while avoiding getting caught in the old carpet gripper, she heard dripping coming from behind the door. 'I hear water. Stand ready.' She pushed the door open and pointed her torch ahead. 'Police,' she shouted but there was nothing but what looked to be a huge electroplating bath positioned against the wall. She ran over to it, grabbing an old wooden box to step up on and peered inside and let out a long breath. Jacob flashed his torch around the rest of the room but it was empty. There was about an inch of murky water that must have gathered from the drips coming from a leaky pipe above them. 'There's no one here.' Gina sighed, knowing they were still nowhere near finding Lindy and time was escaping them.

'Guv,' a PC shouted as he ran towards them. 'We've found something in the front room, near the roller shutters.'

Gina ran through the maze of a building keeping up with him and Jacob followed. The PC flashed his torch at the only item in the room, a cardboard box spilling over with an entanglement of items. She peered in and pulled out a smashed wedding photo of Sheena wearing a wedding dress. Underneath it was a jumble of musty clothes and battered CDs.

'There's something else, guv,' Jacob said as he reached in and pulled out some torn-up photos. He placed them face-up on the concrete floor and laid a few out.

'These are photos of Kain, and what's that?' Gina pointed right to the bottom of the box.

He shone his torch directly at it. 'It's a piece of blue metal. It looks like a piece of racking and it has what looks like dried up blood on it.'

FORTY-TWO

They finally had Fabien in an interview room sitting next to the solicitor who took an age to arrive. Gina leaned back in her chair and swigged a glass of water, knowing her jaw now looked a sight but recognising that finding Lindy was her priority. Her face pain could wait. She hoped the paracetamol and ibuprofen she'd taken would kick in fast. The recorder was rolling, the introductions had taken place and Jacob was sitting next to her, ready to begin.

Fabien ran his fingers along his short brown goatee and sighed as if bored. Light glinted off the large diamond stud in his left ear and his full head of dark hair looked stiffly brushed back like he'd used too much hair gel.

'Mr Stone, where were you between one p.m. on Friday the fourteenth of November and six a.m. on Sunday the sixteenth of November?' Gina knew she had to get the questions in thick and fast. Time was ticking and now Craig's face had already been reported in the lunchtime news and pasted everywhere online.

'Saturday and Sunday is family time. That week, I had a

long weekend with her. I didn't work Friday. I was with Sheena, at home, building a cot.'

She thought about Zavier's murder. 'Where were you on the twentieth and the twenty-first of November?'

'At the office and home at five each evening.'

'Was anyone else in the building?'

'Keri, the apprentice, and two other debt collectors.'

'Will they be able to confirm that you were in?'

He shrugged. 'I base myself on the top floor, the other collectors are on the middle floor and Keri does admin from the back room on the bottom floor. The cellar is used to keep the archives but you probably already know that. You can ask them but I don't answer to anyone because I own the company. I went home to work at lunchtime on the twentieth so I could be with Sheena. I stayed in all day after about one. She's pregnant and struggling, especially since that arsehole came by shouting his mouth off.' He licked his teeth and folded his arms.

'Who are you referring to?'

'Kain. She dared to post on Instagram about her pregnancy and that entitled prick came by shouting his mouth off a while back. He was mad that she'd apparently led him on and that she promised they'd have a family together.'

'And did that make you angry?'

'You bet it did. You'd be angry too if someone came by screaming their mouth off at the person you love. He spat in her face. Who does that?'

Gina wanted to reply, you, but she didn't. She'd seen him spit at the PC during his arrest.

'I don't know what she ever saw in him.'

Gina was struggling to see what Sheena saw in Fabien too, but her taste in men was none of Gina's business. 'Is that why you killed him?'

Fabien leaned forward and stared at Gina for an uncomfortable few seconds. 'Looks like you've already decided I did it. Really? Here I am, cooperating and not going no comment and here you are trying to trip me up PC, err... Who are you again?'

'Detective Inspector Harte,' she corrected him, knowing full well he was trying to get a rise out of her. 'Tell me where you were last night?'

'With Sheena, at home.'

The problem was, Gina knew that Sheena would most likely back his story up. 'Did anyone else see you?'

'No, because we were at home together, sitting on the sofa, reading and watching the TV. She was watching some sitcom on Netflix and I was reading Dostoevsky's, *Crime and Punishment*.'

Great, he was reading a book written from the perspective of a man who'd committed a murder against a pawnbroker. She wondered if Fabien saw himself as the protagonist in this real-life crime despite him being a debt collector – a bit of role reversal – and was doing no more than playing a game with her. Why even mention the book? 'How do you know Lindy Pickering?'

'Not well. Lindy still talks to Sheena and they sometimes go for coffee. They were in each other's lives for years and they got on so that's nothing unusual. Kain hated that they met up. Lindy told Sheena that Kain referred to her as the traitorous bitch when he'd had a few. That's the kind of man he was. I think he'd have had a lot of enemies.'

'He also had a lot of debt. Did you ever chase him for any of it? We will find out. There are officers going through your records as we speak.' She knew it would take days to go through all the paperwork but he had to know he couldn't hide that information from her.

'Why would I care? The people we chase don't owe us personally. What stupid logic you apply.'

Gina sighed and had to agree, but she had to ask the question.

Gina wondered if Sheena's ongoing relationship with her ex's sister caused Fabien to be jealous enough to make him want to hurt Lindy. After all, Lindy would have been keeping Kain in her life. 'Where's Lindy?'

He shrugged and smirked. 'Have you tried knocking on her door and seeing if she's in. Lindy makes a mean cup of coffee.'

Gina clenched her knuckles under the desk. 'Whose blood is on your coat?'

'Which coat?'

'The blue puffer coat that was hung on the coat hooks at your business premises.'

'That came from a dead rat that I trapped. We have a rat problem. That's hardly a crime. The corpse is in the industrial bin out the back.'

Damn. Gina knew they'd have to get that confirmed and they would before he left custody. 'Why is there a huge electro-plating bath in your warehouse?'

'Really?'

'Please answer the question,' Gina said.

He scrunched his neat brows. 'I was going to start a new business. I'm faddy, what can I say? I didn't buy it; it was in the warehouse when I bought it six months ago. The ex-owners used to electroplate car parts. I saw it as a potential opportunity.'

'"A man can't call himself a man unless he can protect his wife and then his children. A real man will do anything it takes. Are you a real man?" These are your words, aren't they?'

He frowned and recoiled.

Gina pulled out a photo and showed him his Instagram post.

'So, I'm not ashamed of taking my duties as a man and a father-to-be seriously.'

'Did you go as far as murdering Kain to protect your wife and unborn child?'

He let out a laugh. 'You are so bad at this.'

'How do you know Craig Crawford?'

He raised his brows. 'Am I meant to recognise that name?'

Jacob passed Gina the photo of their social media selfie. 'Well, you are here together, after just completing a triathlon and you both look to be friendly.'

Fabien's Adam's apple bobbed as he swallowed. 'That was ages ago. I know him from the gym.'

'So why didn't you say you knew him?'

'I didn't know his surname was Crawford and there are three Craig's at my gym.'

'When did you last see Craig Crawford?'

He shrugged. 'Don't remember.'

Gina pulled out another photo, one showing the torn-up photos from his warehouse. 'Why did you have clothes belonging to Kain Pickering and photos of Kain stashed in a box in your warehouse?'

'You really suck, sweaty ass.'

Gina felt rage building up inside. 'Answer the question, Mr Stone.'

'They are the items that Kain left behind when Sheena threw him out. He never came to collect them and she wanted them out of the house so I took them out of her way. I wanted to bin them but Sheena, being the good person that she is, wasn't having any of it.'

'How about this?' Gina pulled out a photo of the blue metal racking rod.

Fabien furrowed his brows, the creases at the bridge of his nose deepening as he tilted his head slightly. 'That wasn't in the box. I put those things in the box myself. What is this? You're framing me.'

'So, it won't have your prints on it?' Gina knew their perp

was forensically aware so the likelihood of prints was low but had the perp slipped up this time?

'That's not mine. I didn't put it in the box. Why is it there? Why?' He kicked the desk leg, nudging it.

Gina stood, not wanting to be on the receiving end of Fabien's violence for the second time that day. 'You're a violent man, would you say so, Mr Stone?'

'No, no, no. You lot are framing me.'

Gina had a flashback to Briggs threatening to frame Stephen a few years back, but that was to protect her. Knowing that Briggs had done something wrong was filling her head with thoughts, and she didn't like them. Briggs was forensically aware and he'd been in some sort of trouble and Brodie couldn't go into detail. But they had let Briggs go, for now. He had an alibi for the kidnapping of Lindy. She tapped her feet nervously on the floor. Briggs still hadn't messaged and she shouldn't call him. Her mind bounced to the article they'd found under Craig and Justine's bed. Briggs could not break into two separate buildings to plant evidence and be involved in killing two people and organising the kidnapping of another. Or could he? 'Did you murder Kain Pickering?'

'No.'

'Where's Lindy Pickering?' It had to be him, not Briggs.

'I don't know.'

His solicitor stood. 'Stop, my client needs a break. He's been more than cooperative with you. Either charge him or let him go.'

'We still have twenty-two hours left and he will be charged for assaulting a police officer after hitting me in the jaw earlier. Do you need a break, Mr Stone?'

'No.'

'What happened when Kain came by to speak to Sheena? Did you tell him that a real man will do anything it takes? Are you a real man? Did you permanently remove Kain from Sheena May's life? Did Craig Crawford help you? Where is he?' She was going over it all again in the hope that he'd slip up soon.

There was a knock at the door. Jacob spoke for the tape. 'Interview paused at twelve thirty-eight.'

She stood and opened the door to Wyre, and stepped out, letting the interview room door slam before speaking quietly to Wyre. 'What is it?'

'We're interviewing Sheena at the moment and she slipped up and told us that when Kain came to hers verbally attacking her and Mr Stone, Mr Stone punched him in the chest then kicked him to the floor. She started crying, saying she didn't want to get him into trouble as in her words "he wouldn't hurt a fly."' Wyre raised her brows. 'Anyway, she said some of the neighbours came outside and it would only be a matter of time before someone told us what had happened. She said Mr Stone shouted that he was going to kill Kain and anyone else who dared to upset his wife-to-be and that he should also tell his piece of shit friend Zed to not pop by theirs looking for him again.' Gina raised her brows at the mention of Zed. 'Then she said he went on about how Kain's family needs to keep out of her life now they're not together anymore. Sheena got upset and they argued after Kain had gone because she said she regards Lindy as family. I'm heading back in there to resume the inter-view. I just thought you'd like to know all that.'

'Thank you. That's brilliant.'

Jacob started the tape again. 'Interview resumed at twelve forty-three.'

Gina sat back, pausing for a moment and looking directly at Fabien Stone. 'Tell me about when you assaulted Kain. You hit him and then you kicked him to the ground.' Gina relayed everything Wyre had just said.

'No comment.' Fabien calmly sat back and bit the insides of his mouth but Gina could tell he was worried. 'I'm ending this farce now. No fucking comment.' He paused and shouted at the top of his voice. 'No comment, no more comments, no comment!'

FORTY-THREE

Gina sipped on a warm cup of chamomile tea in the hope that it would calm all her nerves. She'd tensed up while interviewing Fabien Stone and she was glad that he was back in his cell. On passing by she'd heard him hitting and kicking the door, claiming it was all a set-up and that he knew nothing about a blue metal bar. Exhaling, Gina knew that Fabien was well and truly in the picture but was he in it enough to take Briggs completely out of it. She needed to talk to him whether he wanted to talk to her or not. She had to know if he was involved.

O'Connor stepped into the kitchen. 'Guv, I've just finished interviewing the girl, Keri. Her mother sat in on the interview and they've just left. Keri claims that the blood on Fabien's coat was from a rat. She came in and screamed when she saw the creature escaping the broken trap under the boardroom table. Mr Stone apparently hit it with a hardback book, killing it. Apart from that, she didn't tell us anything useful. Stone keeps himself to himself on the top floor of the building and the other debt collectors quite often work from home.'

Gina frowned. Keri had backed up Stone's claim about the blood on his coat and she now had no doubt that they'd come across the blood-splattered hardback. The case was getting more deflating by the minute. 'Thank you for the update. Is Sheena still being interviewed?'

'Wyre has just finished with her. I saw her heading to the incident room. As suspected Sheena is providing an alibi for Fabien Stone on the night of Kain's murder and the other incidents.'

They'd partially ruled out Fabien with the rat blood but tests would still be done to corroborate his and Keri's version of events, however Gina had no reason to mistrust what Keri had said. Fabien did know all their victims and the levels of violence he'd displayed couldn't be ignored. There was still so much to untangle, none of it helping them to find out where Lindy was. Her stomach jumped at the thought of what the previous victims had been through. Both drowned within a short period of time after their attack. They needed a proper break in the case and she had to find it before it was too late. She thought of Lindy, just a few years younger than her. She couldn't help but picture in her mind the terror she must be going through. She imagined being plunged into a tub full of water and not being able to breathe, then she gasped before carrying on down the corridor.

She headed to the incident room where Kapoor typed on a computer in the corner of the room. Wyre stepped in holding a pile of files that she placed next to Kapoor. 'I'm just popping to the shop to grab some lunch. Do you want anything?'

Gina's stomach churned with nerves and worry for their missing person but it was also screaming for her to eat more than a pear. She pulled a ten-pound note from her pocket and gave it to Wyre. 'A tuna or egg salad would be great. Thank you.'

Wyre grabbed her coat and left.

On glancing at the names of the friend group and their husbands, Gina made separate notes on another board. There had to be another link she was missing. Their cropping up all over the investigation was no coincidence. She called Kapoor. 'Anything from the appeal?'

'Nothing, guv. Someone called about a red-haired man in Tesco car park but it wasn't Craig, sadly. He's like a ghost. Do you think he could be hurt? It just seems strange that no one has seen him.'

'If I hadn't seen those photos in his rental apartment, I'd have considered that.' Again, she thought of Briggs. He'd know exactly how to get into an apartment to plant evidence. He could easily work out how to frame Fabien, too. A wave of nausea flashed through her body. No, there had to be something else she was missing. Actually, she had to speak to Briggs now and sitting around trying to make sense of everything without having that conversation was holding her back. She hurried outside and stood at the other end of the car park with her personal phone held to her ear while she hoped he'd answer. A chilly breeze whipped past her legs and up the back of her jumper. She shivered.

'Gina. What is it? You're not meant to call me on this phone. I told you.'

He was slurring his words and Gina had never even seen him drunk. She knew to tread gently and Briggs knew exactly how to play the game – drunk or not. 'You need to tell me what the hell is going on. This investigation is leading me to you and I don't think I can hold back the tide and if you keep me in the dark, I don't know if I want to. I know I screwed up our relationship but you were harsh on me. Whatever. This isn't about you and me; it's about the case. Have you got anything to do with Kain and Zavier's murders and do you know where Lindy is?'

'I can't believe you're asking me this?'

'Well, I am. There's something that's niggling away at me. A big part of me can't help wondering if both Craig Crawford and Fabien Stone are being set up. You're involved but I don't know how. Both Zavier and Kain used to be police officers years ago. Have you met or worked with them in the past? Did you know them?'

He remained silent.

'Chris, this isn't the time to refuse to speak. It's me, Gina. You've held my darkest deepest secrets but I need to know what's happening your end, the end that Brodie won't discuss with me.'

She listened as Briggs burped and scrunched up a can. His dog whined in the background. At least he had company.

'Are you drinking?'

'I had nothing to do with all you're accusing me of.'

A shiver tickled the back of her neck as she was transported back to when Terry used to scrunch his cans up when drunk, mostly before he turned the television up loud and beat her to the floor. She gasped as she remembered her face being pressed into their old coarse carpet. As for Briggs, she'd barely even seen him merry so she knew it must be bad. 'I will always care for you, Chris. You have to talk to me. You called me and said you needed me to do something. You can't blame me for thinking the worst.' Briggs wasn't Terry. She refused to believe he could ever be like Terry but he wasn't himself.

'Gina, I shouldn't have called you and said that. You shouldn't be calling me now. Why do you have to make all this so hard?'

She glanced back at the station and up at the window of the incident room but no one was watching her looking all flustered with her phone pressed to her ear in the car park. The cold damp air began to seep through her clothes and she began to shake. Why hadn't she put her coat on?

'Me? You're making this hard. I'm risking my arse here talking to you. Those men were murdered and I'm scared something will happen to you. Did you know the other victims? Shit, help me out here. I'm not even meant to be asking about the side of the case you're involved in.'

'Well don't. Everything will all come out soon.'

'What's that meant to mean? What did you need me to do?'

'When I called you, I wanted to say, I need you to believe me.' His voice broke up. 'I need to get some rest.' He hung up.

'Chris... Chris...'

But he had gone, leaving her shaking and holding the phone. Maybe later, she needed to pop over, see if she could get any sense out of him. If he'd been drinking, now wasn't the time.

'DI Harte, have you made any arrests yet?' A reporter wearing a rain mac ran across the car park. She ignored him and hurried back into the station, back into the incident room where she stared at the board until her head began to throb with anger, frustration and the fear that Lindy would soon turn up dead if they didn't get their act together.

'Guv.' She flinched as Wyre placed Gina's salad and wooden spork down next to the boards. 'I'm heading back to the main office to update the system.'

'Okay.' Gina opened the box and speared some browning lettuce. What the hell was she missing?

She started making notes on the board.

Pia and Simeon Yates. Pia reported Lindy as missing. Pia had been having an affair with their main suspect, Craig, and his wife, Justine, was her friend.

Justine and Craig Crawford had a son called Danny. Craig was on the run and Danny and Justine were staying with her mother. Craig knew Fabien and they both had issues with Kain. One personal and one debt related.

Lastly, Lindy Pickering was Kain's sister and now she had been taken.

Zavier – his connection was that he was in the police too, just like Kain... and Briggs.

What did the teddy bears mean?

'Kapoor.'

She swivelled around in her chair. 'Yes, guv.'

'Can you do a deep dive into this friendship group. I want everything you can find on them. Internet searches, social media, anything. We're missing something that's right under our noses.'

'Sure, I'll get onto that now.'

'I need to speak to Justine and Danny. I'm going to grab Jacob and head to her mother's. Craig is keeping well out of view and that's a hard thing to do when half of the town is looking out for him now that his face has been aired. There's a chance he's been in touch with them. Justine might even be helping him. Is there a family liaison there with them?'

'Yes, guv. I know that PC Masondo said he was heading there a short while ago so he must be there now.'

'Great.' Gina did her coat up and threw the salad box in the bin. Just as she was about to head to the main office to get Jacob, she almost walked into Brodie's chest. 'Sorry, sir.'

'Gina, I'm going to let you in on the other side of the investigation.' He ushered her over to a quiet corner away from the bustle of the station. 'Something has happened and you know the case well. Victim two, Zavier used to be police and he worked with Kain.'

'I guessed that much and reading between all the lines, I'm guessing that Briggs knew them too. Anything else come back from the Kidderminster team?'

'Nothing that will help us or that we don't already know but something big has happened and we need to get to the hospital.'

'What is it?'

'DCI Briggs has been attacked in his home.'

A wave of dizziness washed through her. She reached out and steadied herself on the wall, trying not to let Brodie see how affected she was. She'd spoken to him a short while ago. He hadn't been himself. She should have sensed that something was wrong. Did Briggs even know he was about to be attacked? Her heart started banging. Despite what he might have done, she wanted to drop everything and be by his side. She had no option but to air what she was thinking. If she was thinking it, she knew Brodie was too. 'He worked with them, didn't he? It's obvious.'

Brodie took a deep breath and nodded. 'I can't confirm, okay? What we need to do is question him about the attack.'

A nod told her everything she needed to know. Briggs worked with Zavier and Kain. He was as much a part of all this as the people on their board, only now she knew he was a victim and not a perpetrator. It had all happened so fast. His dog had been whining while she was on the phone to him. Had the perp been there waiting for him to finish his call? She trembled at the thought and she hated herself for the way their conversation had gone and all he wanted was for her to believe him. She knew he needed her to believe that he didn't have anything to do with the murders of Zavier and Kain. 'How hurt is he?'

'It's bad, Gina. If it wasn't for the neighbour wondering what was wrong with the dog, he wouldn't be here. Uniform are on their way over to seal the scene.'

She swallowed the lump in her throat. They'd soon find out that she had called Briggs. It was best to tell Brodie now. 'I called him, on my personal phone, just before it must have happened. I wondered how he was, that's all.'

He opened his car door and they both got in. Brodie didn't speak. He stared out of his windscreen watching it as it demisted. 'I wish you hadn't.'

'Are you going to report me?'

'No, because I need you on the case, but it will come out.

Time is of the essence to find whoever is behind all this. I'll keep my mouth shut but if you ever say I said you told me, I will deny it.' His eyes met hers and he smiled warmly. He was still the Brodie she knew from back then, at least she hoped he was. 'Did he say anything that might help the case?'

'No, I asked how he was and he was...'

'He was what?' Brodie frowned.

'He was slurring and sounded really drunk and it's not like him. He barely drinks.' She added quickly, 'From what I know. And his dog was whining. I think the perp was already in the house.' She bit her lip and scrunched her brows as something hit her. 'I thought he was drunk but what if someone had drugged him?'

FORTY-FOUR

LINDY

'Help...' Lindy called out through chattering teeth. All she wanted was to hear someone's voice, to know that Pia had called the police and they were coming to help her, but that was impossible. No one knew where she was. She'd called into the void over and over again but she'd heard nothing.

With her hands still bound and legs still tied together, Lindy stood in the tank of revolting slop, back against the cool metal curved sides while hoping with all she had that her body wouldn't give in, or that she wouldn't slip. Head tilted back, she kept breathing fast as the liquid bobbed over her ears with each movement. How long she could stay in this position was another question she couldn't answer. Her breaths came quicker and faster. She yelled as another cramp contorted her calf muscle.

The liquid wavered under her chin as she fidgeted to fight the cramp tearing through her. She choked and heaved as a gulp got trapped in her lungs. Her stiff neck failed to move, and even if she wanted to move it, it felt locked in place. Warmth came from underneath her feet but it was barely reaching the top of the tank. Was he going to boil her alive? Was she the proverbial lobster in the pot? One minute the warmth of a nice bath soothing her, the next boiling to death. She gasped for air and wondered if she was sealed inside this huge metal coffin. It felt like it. Would the air run out? She needed to calm down but how could she when she knew that no one had a clue where she was. The darkness was the worst. Was her kidnapper trying to deprive her senses and if so, why?

His words rang through her head. *I always knew I'd get my day.*

She begged him to tell her what she'd done but all he could say was, *you know exactly what this is about, you just can't remember but this is going to make you remember.* She still couldn't remember.

Who was he? All she could see was his outline. His voice was hushed and low, like a loud whisper and she wondered if he spoke out loud, would she recognise it?

She called out again and choked on another mouthful. Her chest hurt, everything hurt. She racked her brains trying to think why she was there but nothing was coming to her. Kain had been murdered. It had to be because of Kain. She thought back, through their lives. She had spent so much of her time trying to help him, she'd barely had a life of her own. She thought of her poor mother, trying to fix him to the end. Her life had constantly been on hold because of Kain's many dramas.

She thought of her new life since the move. She'd wanted to be closer to her mum after Kain moved back in with her. Meeting Justine and Pia through their shared love of yoga, seemed like a dream. With her career on hold, she'd relished having more time to herself while she thought about her future – and now she was here, in a stinking tank of some description, waiting to die.

The gentle swaying of water around her ears reminded her of the lapping of the lake on a windy day. She'd do anything to be at yoga right now while gazing at that lake. The session before last, she'd sat in downward dog, staring out at that huge building on the other side of the lake and she'd wondered if it was being used for anything now. She'd fantasised that she'd renovated it, that it was her home and she got to enjoy the view every day. In reality, it was covered in graffiti and metal window shutters – it was an eyesore. She tried to imagine that she was in a yoga class, holding a pose. This was the same thing. She just had to hold the pose for a long time, and not lose consciousness, or fall asleep, or slip. If she slipped, her tied feet might never regain their balance. She couldn't move an inch despite the cramps. The drug had started to wear off, she was grateful for that.

Her breathing sped up. She had to find a way out. She thought of her once chubby-cheeked little brother whose big dream was to be a police officer. Kain did eventually realise his dream and join the police. She smiled and almost cried as some of her most precious held memories began to flood her mind. Then she thought of all the things she'd never get to do. She'd never found the one, never had the child she'd always dreamed of. She thought of Justine and her lovely son, how he'd helped her mum around the house, doing all the jobs her mum had struggled with for pocket money. If she'd had a son, she'd have wanted one like Danny. He'd stand in her mum's garden vaping. She could still smell the toffee scent. She'd never have that. It was too late.

Hold the pose. Keep it steady, she imagined their yoga instructor saying. She thought she heard a bang in the distance before the liquid swished over her ears again, taking away the only sense she had, her hearing. As it stopped lapping around her head, she realised her one ear was blocked. She could barely hear anything.

'Hello,' she shouted, in the hope that rescue was coming.

One loud bang came from afar but it sounded distorted through her one good ear, adding to her disorientation.

Heart racing, she waited with bated breath for whoever was out there to reveal themselves. She couldn't control the trembling. It would be her kidnapper. No one was coming. She closed her watery eyes and visualised being in yoga class and all she could see was that lake and that building. Then there was another bang. She called again. 'Help.' No one ran to her aid which meant one thing, he was back and he was going to kill her, just like he killed Kain.

FORTY-FIVE

Gina's stomach churned as she waited near the accident and emergency side room that Briggs was being treated in. She peered through the crack in the door. A nurse stood beside him, checking all the beeping machines. She gasped when the nurse moved aside, revealing the extent of Briggs's injuries. 'Are you family?' she asked. Gina couldn't take her gaze off his bruised, battered face.

Brodie stepped in and held his identification up. 'Police. Can we speak with him? He's a colleague.'

The nurse turned to her patient and he half prised an eye open. 'Mr Briggs, are you up to speaking?'

Briggs mumbled something that Gina thought might be a yes.

'Not too long, okay.'

'Okay.' Gina ran over to his bedside. 'Chris...'

'Is that you, Gina?' He could barely focus through his swollen eyes. He yelled in pain as he tried to move.

'Yes, I'm with DCI Fraser who has stepped in to work on the case.' She hoped he'd now know not to say anything too personal about their relationship.

Brodie stepped in and Gina moved aside. She was lucky to be there and one wrong word or move could get her thrown off the case. She had no option but to let Brodie lead. 'DCI Briggs, sorry to meet you under such horrible circumstances. Can you tell us anything about the incident and what happened to you?'

'He came up from...' Briggs paused, his words still a little slurred. 'I think he drugged my drink. There's a glass... I spilled most of it thankfully... there's a towel on the settee that I mopped it up with... it might be Rohypnol, maybe something like that...'

Brodie interrupted. 'The crime scene team are there at the moment.'

'I felt really weird so I opened a can of pop to replace the drink I'd spilled. I thought... maybe I was dehydrated... woozy...'

Gina knew the team at his house would probably find traces of her. She was glad she'd been on the case day and night; she couldn't possibly be considered a suspect. They'd made love in his bedroom. She'd used his shower and they'd lain together on his couch last winter while watching Christmas films. A lump formed in her throat. She swallowed it down. The love they used to have was in the past. She was there to investigate who had hurt him and she had to do her job. After pulling out a notepad, she sat on the plastic chair backed against the wall, poised to take notes.

'He came from behind and covered my head with a pillow-case. I fought... even though my head was spinning... he bashed me in the face with something. It might have been, err... I can't think... it felt like a smooth, hard, metal stick or pole. It felt solid, not hollow. I was hit over and over again...' He half opened an eye and flinched. 'Bloody hell, I feel like crap.' He closed his eyes again.

Metal stick – Gina noted that down while thinking of the piece of blue metal that had been found in Fabien Stone's warehouse. Gina fought the urge to go over to comfort him. Had

Brodie not been in the room, she'd have sat closer but Briggs didn't want that anyway. He'd protect her in her job but that was it. She'd always love him and she should have known something was wrong when they spoke on the phone. He was nothing like Terry. Being drugged had confused him and she'd jumped to the conclusion that he'd been drunk.

'Did you hear or see anything unusual in the run up to the attack?'

'I, err, my dog kept barking. I stumbled to the door to let her out, then I sat back down and knew there was something wrong. I came over woozy and nauseous and my phone, I couldn't find it and I knew I needed to call an ambulance, that's when I was hit...'

'Do you remember anything else in the run up?' Brodie asked.

Briggs flinched and placed a hand across the side of his face. 'Ouch... the run up. I don't know. I have had so much on my mind with the investigation and being questioned, I wasn't thinking. Uniform have been checking up on me and they'd just left...' He dabbed his sticky eyes and flinched. 'I must look like a monster.'

Far from it, for the first time in all the years she'd known him, he looked vulnerable.

'The neighbour must have scared him away. She heard the dog... she's my dog sitter so she knew something was wrong... She has a key and as she came in, he ran out the back...'

'Did you see him at all?'

'No.'

'How do you know it was a man?'

Briggs sighed and paused. 'His voice. He said all debts must be paid in full.'

Gina gasped for breath and held her hand over her mouth. She didn't want Brodie to turn around and see her coping badly with this news but they had Fabien in custody. It couldn't be him. He could be working with Craig Crawford but he wasn't the attacker.

Brodie's phone beeped. 'Bear with me a moment.' He stepped out of the room, leaving the door open while he made his call.

'Sorry, could you please make the call over there?' a nurse asked as she tried to wheel a gurney past him with the help of a porter.

They were alone. Gina stood and hurried over to Briggs. 'I was so worried. I'm sorry, I should have known something was wrong when I called.'

'It's okay. I wasn't myself. I don't know what came over me. It's all going to be okay. I didn't tell him you called but they're going to look at my phone so you have time to work it out.'

'I've already told Brodie. Don't worry about that now. I'm here now so it looks like they've cleared you.'

'You thought I could be involved in killing those men, Gina... did you really think that?'

'I don't know. It's a confusing case. I'm sorry. If you need anything when you come out, let me know, or I can pick you up. You can stay at mine if you need. In the spare room.'

'Gina, stop. My brother is coming down from up north to stay with me. I have it covered.' He forced his eyes open again.

'I only meant to help... nothing more.'

'I know.' He forced a smile that cracked a scab in the corner of his mouth. 'Ouch.' He exhaled slowly. 'I worked with Zavier and Kain in my twenties. You have to look up a name. Barry something. When he said that I had to pay the debt, it clicked because... Sorry, my mind is a total blank. It was about thirty years ago when I was stationed at Kidderminster, the teddy bears. I was a custody sergeant and I checked in a personal item. A bear, a small bear... Ahh.' He screamed and a nurse ran in.

'How do you know about the bear?' Gina leaned over him but Briggs screamed out in pain again.

'I'm sorry. I'm going to have to ask you to leave.' The nurse ushered her out while starting to prep a syringe.

Briggs screamed again. That's when Gina noticed that the dressing had come off his arm exposing a huge open wound. 'When can we speak to him again?'

'I can't answer that yet. We're trying to manage the pain at the moment. Call back later or in the morning.'

'I believe you, Chris,' she said quietly as the nurse ushered her out. She almost bumped into Brodie outside the door. He popped his phone back in his pocket. Gina blinked a few times to get rid of the tears forming in her eyes. Seeing Briggs like that had been a shock. 'Sorry, it got bad in there. Did you see his arm?'

'No.'

'It was covered up when we went in but it's all open. He must have got hit really hard. He just started yelling in pain and I... the nurse told me I had to leave.' She raised her brows and blinked a couple of times before looking up at Brodie. 'Was the message to do with the case?'

Brodie nodded. 'They found a small blue bear. DCI Briggs's neighbour was standing outside asking if he was okay and PC Smith saw it in the dog's mouth. We have a couple of officers on their way here. We can't leave the DCI alone while the case is ongoing.'

'Do you think they'll come back?'

'Yes, whoever attacked him wanted him dead. A hosepipe had been attached to the hot kitchen tap. I'm theorising that the killer was going to wait until whatever drug he'd given to DCI Briggs had taken effect before feeding the hose into his mouth and drowning him.'

Gina leaned against a cold wall as she fought the panic brewing up within her. Medical staff carried on about their duties all around her and all Gina could do was imagine the scene they could have been attending had Briggs not spilled his drink. 'We need to get to Justine's mother's, speak to her and her son again and see how the family liaison officer is getting on.' She realised she'd said all that at speed and wondered if Brodie had even properly heard her. 'The three friends, Justine, Lindy and Pia are the thread in all this, I know it.' She took another deep breath and tried to push the image of the hosepipe out of her head.

'Do you need a break, Gina? You and the DCI have known each other for a long time. It's a lot to take in when one of your own has been attacked like that.'

'The whole department has known him for a long time and no, I don't need a break. We need to catch the killer before Lindy's body turns up, so no thank you to the break.'

'But you and DCI Briggs worked closely, maybe closer than the rest.'

'What do you mean?' It was as if Brodie could read her thoughts. 'I just care, that's all. We're all like family at Cleevesford. You never stop caring—' There, she'd said it.

'I agree and I understand,' he replied, as if he knew. 'I never stopped thinking or caring about you, Gina.'

FORTY-SIX

JUSTINE

She'd bitten her nails down to the skin and now she was starting on the skin around her fingers. That word, skank, kept going through her mind. She kept replaying last night, over and over, like a glitch in a film. How could Craig know what she did and how could he tell their son? Danny was obviously upset enough to send a message like that. She needed to find him and fast. Whatever Craig had done to upset their family in the past with either one of his temper outbursts or the cheating he'd never admit to, she'd tried her best to keep Danny out of it. She'd never once slagged Craig off in front of Danny, but Craig was happily slagging her off to her son. Skank – she hated that word. It sent a queasy feeling through her. Maybe everyone was going to hate her when her secret came out. The neighbours already hated her son. Everyone was going to hate her husband and now her. Her whole family was a complete mess. She wanted a hug from her son, despite him scaring her half to death in the night. He was confused and he needed her too, not that he could realise that. He may have done something unthinkable and that message was mean, but she was his mother and she would help him to the end; she just had to see him to tell him that.

PC Masondo peered into her mother's living room yet again. 'Do you know when your son will be home?' It would have been easy to forget that the police officer was probably hanging around to spy on them, given that he was dressed in casual jeans and a light-knit jumper, no shirt or tie.

She shook her head, not wanting to give anything away and living in hope that he couldn't sense the plethora of emotions running through her mind. She forced a smile, but that didn't feel right, so she dropped it. How is a person meant to look in circumstances like this? She was no actor. 'Err, he's with his friends and he's eighteen. It's a bit hard to keep them close at that age.' She couldn't let on that Danny's phone was no longer connected and he was hiding out somewhere with her wanted husband, Craig. The enormity of it all made her bite the skin around her finger even more.

'I've just been speaking with your mum in the kitchen.' He sat opposite her, in her mum's chair. Pixie nudged her head under Justine's arm before using her lap as a pillow. The family liaison officer continued. 'DCI Fraser and DI Harte are due here soon. How are you feeling?'

No way – she didn't want any close scrutiny but she couldn't leave the house. She'd have to sit out their questions and prying. If she left the house, it would look odd and her mum wouldn't appreciate being left to deal with the police alone. It was bad enough giving her the overview of what was happening. Her loving, supportive mum couldn't believe for one minute that anything would come of all the fuss. Justine had convinced her that it was all a misunderstanding. 'I'm okay. I just want this to be over and I want to go home.'

The officer smiled sympathetically and stood, leaving her to her thoughts. Her phone beeped with a message. She snatched it up, hoping that it was Danny, but it wasn't.

What's happening? I heard the police searched your house. Is it your kid? What's he done now? Stolen a car, robbed a house? Some people don't deserve to be parents. It's the way you bring them up!!!

It was the woman who lived opposite. They were going to have to move when all this was over. The neighbours never forgave Danny for going off the rails in his teens. She wanted to sit there and cry but where would that get her? As soon as Craig's escapades came out, they were going to hate her even more and she still didn't know what Danny had done. The not knowing was the worst, or was it? A big part of her hoped that despite all Craig's flaws, he could find a way of fixing everything which is why she wouldn't say a word. However much she hated and feared him right now, he was their son's biggest chance of getting out of this and if there was anything to take the blame for, Craig would gladly do it to save their son. She went to message Pia but changed her mind. Besides, she couldn't face Pia yet and she wondered if she'd ever be able to face Pia again, especially if Craig was sleeping with Simeon. They'd definitely have to move. She could take Danny, go right up north or far down south, away from everyone. Her secret was fighting to burrow out from the inside, but she had to keep it in and do whatever it took to keep Craig's mouth shut. She pressed her lips together and frowned as she thought of what would happen when the extent of her lies came out. She'd deceived the police and at the end of the day, for all Craig's faults, she was no better than him. This situation felt like her punishment.

The detectives were coming again. Did they know she'd seen Craig? Maybe they knew about the laptop. She needed to make sure she'd deleted everything. Could there be a message left in his recycle bin or in a hidden file? She hated not knowing and Danny wasn't around to ask.

She nudged Pixie onto the floor and opened the cupboard

under the stairs. The officer was being distracted by her mum in the kitchen again. She snatched the laptop and dashed into her mum's craft room. She swiped her arm across the table, sending a half cut out dress onto the floor. The laptop came on straight away but the screen was plagued by the damn egg timer as it took its time to start up. The skin around her finger started to bleed as she bit it again. There was no doubting that the laptop was Danny's. It had his name written on the lid in permanent marker and there were band stickers all over it.

Her heartbeat skipped as the computer eventually came on. She tried to click onto the app that Danny was messaging through but she needed his password to be able to see everything again. She was sure she'd deleted everything while it was auto logged in but after, she'd logged out fully. Several options came to mind. She tried typing in Pixie, his birthday, her name, Craig's name, their birthdays – nothing worked. There were no files called passwords, not that she could see. On any other day, she'd think that was sensible, but not today. It looked like she'd never be able to access that account to see if she'd missed anything. Maybe she could throw the laptop out of the window and hope for the best. She ran over to the small window. It was locked. She searched for the key but it was nowhere to be seen. There's no way she could leave the room with it. The FLO would see her and wonder what she was up to, then it would be game over.

She peered into the hallway. The police officer was still in the kitchen and the kettle was on. She couldn't risk passing the door and him seeing her. Pixie ran back and forth playing with her rope pull. She closed the door and in turn shut the chaos out. There had to be more on her son's laptop and she needed to eradicate it. Had she known the detectives were coming to her mother's, she'd have taken a hammer to it and burnt it. In fact, that's what she should have done as soon as she saw that message. *Ouch* – blood began to drip onto the keypad as she clicked on the last folder Danny had been accessing. Again, the egg timer symbol appeared. She needed a tissue, something to catch the blood. Anything would do. She mooched through her mum's top drawer for a scrap of material. If she used her mum's expensive fabrics, she'd never hear the end of it. Pixie barked and played outside the door, getting louder and more excitable. Justine needed to hurry. She reached into the drawer and found exactly what she was looking for, a scrap of old material. Relief flooded her as she dabbed it on her bleeding finger.

PC Masondo opened the door with a cup of tea in his hand and Justine stepped back, mouth wide open as she almost toppled over her mother's chair. His smile dropped as he stared at the screen. After regaining her balance, she caught sight of her son's face full of rage as he kicked the hell out of the person who was taking the video. The man holding the phone begged him to stop but her son didn't stop but he carried on. 'Danny, you're going to kill me.' The phone panned to Lindy's mum, Maura, who was crying as she watched her son being kicked to a pulp.

'You deserve to die. Scum. I don't know why my mum has been trying to help a low life like you,' Danny replied. In the video, Danny then wiped the sweat from his brow and stared wide-eyed into the victim's phone, then there was a struggle but her son could not get the phone from the man. Danny turned and ran away.

Justine knew that voice, the one saying that Danny was going to kill him. It was Kain's. Her son had threatened to kill Kain. It was all captured on camera and Kain had obviously sent it to Craig, then Kain had been murdered. It was as if the world had tipped sideward. She felt like the room was swaying as she tried to process what she'd just seen.

'Justine. Can you confirm the name of the person your son is attacking?' the DI asked.

'It's...' She hiccupped a sob. 'It's Kain.' Justine couldn't breathe. She hyperventilated and clutched her chest before bursting into a sob. There was no covering for him and she wasn't sure she'd even want to. In her mind, she'd convinced herself that Danny had got into some sort of tussle with Kain and that he'd hurt him by accident and dumped him in the car boot. What she saw on that video was a frenzied, unprovoked attack. Did Lindy find out about the video? Could her son have done something to Lindy to keep her quiet? She gripped the edge of her mum's desk, pulling a dress pattern to the floor as she fell. She went to speak, but couldn't. In that moment, her son and husband disgusted her.

'Justine, breathe, okay.'

No, she couldn't breathe, not now a DCI and a DI had just come through the door. She was about to lose everything. She roared and cried for the loss of who she thought her son was. Her life as she knew it was over.

FORTY-SEVEN

Gina bagged up the laptop, ready for evidence, but she knew exactly what she'd seen from the hallway. She listened as Brodie relayed what had happened to Wyre over the phone. Danny was in the frame for Kain's murder. She didn't know how he tied into the murder of Zavier but Craig had to be involved too. Parts of the evidence weren't making any sense. There were two murders, Lindy's kidnapping and Briggs's attack. The thing that linked the friendship group was the video but so much was still unknown. The teddy bears were a link to the past and future, and who was Barry? She had to look into a case involving someone called Barry, thirty years ago at Kidderminster. Somehow, Lindy was the connection between the past and present.

She took the bagged laptop out of the sewing room and saw PC Masondo. 'We need all units on alert for Danny. We need to bring him in for the assault in the video and on suspicion of committing Kain Pickering's murder.'

'I don't know where he is at the moment. I asked Mrs Crawford, but she just said he was out.'

'Thank you. Can you get his number from her?'

He nodded and walked off towards the dining room where

Justine's mum was trying her best to find out what was going on. Gina headed to the kitchen and waited by the door as Brodie finished his call. She kept replaying the video over and over again in her head and the sound as Danny's boot met his victim.

Brodie popped his phone in his pocket. 'I think we need to speak to Justine back at the station. It looks like she was perverting the course of justice by hiding that laptop so I'm going to make the arrest.'

She nodded. 'I agree. We need to question her further and find out if she's hiding her son as well as her husband. This laptop belongs to her son and it wasn't in her home when we searched it.'

'Guv.' PC Masondo knocked and entered. 'I have her son's phone number. His nan gave it to me. I've tried to call but the line is dead.'

'Right, let's get Justine to the station now. You arrest her, I'll call it in,' Brodie said as he grabbed his phone again.

Gina followed PC Masondo along the hallway, back towards the kitchen and Justine's mother sat on her own at the head of the table holding the dog in her arms. 'Where's Justine?'

The woman shrugged. 'She said she didn't feel so good. She went to the loo.'

The dog escaped from Justine's mother's arms and ran through the hallway and into the living room. Gina and the PC followed. The voile that had covered the French doors at the far end was open. Gina ran straight to it and opened the unlocked door. The dog ran out and barked frantically at the back gate. 'Sir,' Gina called in the hope that she'd shouted loud enough for Brodie to hear.

He came running into the living room. 'What's happened?'

Gina pointed to the slide lock on the gate and it was unlocked. 'Justine has run.'

'She can't have got far,' he replied.

PC Masondo headed out to the garden and Gina followed.

She ran with him outside the back gate and along the lane. There was just a long row of back gardens with a road at either end. 'I'll head this way, guv.'

PC Masondo ran in one direction and Gina ran in the other, trying to take in all the cut throughs between the shrubs and there were loads. Eventually, she reached the end of the path which led to a small road that led out of the estate, neatly hidden behind a row of garages. That's when she spotted a bit of bloodied material tucked up against the kerb, the same bit of material that Justine had been pressing against her bloodied finger.

FORTY-EIGHT

JUSTINE

Justine's heart rate was barely normal as she tore through the backroads and pulled into a dirt track only normally used by horse riders. She was safe for now but the police were going to arrest her. It felt like her tablet was screaming at her from the passenger seat to check it again but she didn't have internet access. There had to be somewhere close by with Wi-Fi that she could tap into.

Leaving her car hidden away from her mum's drive had been a paranoid move but now she knew it was the smartest move she could have ever made given what had happened. Plus the previous evening, she'd bought a burner phone and put all her important numbers into it. A shiver passed through her as she thought of that video and the horrible message her son had sent her. As soon as she got hold of Danny, she was going to march him to the police station herself. She now knew her son and husband had been involved in Kain's murder. It wasn't just the video, it was the hoodie that the police had questioned them about and all the things that were found under their bed during a search of the house.

There was a sickness in her family and she had no idea of its origins. Her son's violent streak had been a shock to see. All she knew is that she didn't want any part of it. Her friends meant a lot to her and the right thing to do would be to find Craig and Danny and get them to go to the police but she couldn't do that if she was in a police cell. She had no idea where Craig was which meant she had to find him.

The stupid burner phone had no internet access. All she could do was text and make phone calls. She couldn't call Craig or Danny. The phone was shaping up to be pretty useless. She threw it into the glove compartment. Thoughts of Lindy's disappearance ran through her mind and she was even more confused. Had Lindy seen the video and threatened to go to the police? How far would her son go to save himself and how far would her husband go to save his son? She slammed her hands onto the steering wheel and roared.

Forty minutes had passed and she'd pulled up in the middle of a rural road maze. There was a garden centre close by where she'd met up with Pia and Lindy a couple of times for afternoon tea. Flowerpots Nursery, that's what it was called. The Wi-Fi code had simply been Flowerpots123, so easy to remember. She turned the car around in a clearing and began the bumpy ride back down the path. All she had to do was avoid the police.

She took a left and followed the windy road ahead. The woodland park came into view. She remembered taking Danny there all the time when he was little. There was nothing but trees, wildlife information signs and logs to sit on. Sirens blared in the distance. Her heart began thumping again. As soon as she reached the car park, she pulled in and drove right to the end, her bonnet edging under the trailing branches of a weeping willow. She waited for the sirens to pass. They were after her, she knew it. She was now a fugitive for the first time in her life. She opened the window and listened for any more sirens, but there were none. It was time to go. After pulling out, she took several more lanes until she reached Flowerpots Nursery. She pulled in and parked right behind a huge Range Rover.

After putting her sunglasses and woolly hat on, she jogged towards the side of the building, taking refuge on one of the many empty picnic tables. She glanced through the window to the restaurant and thankfully they had the bushiest Christmas tree ever concealing her presence. No one could see her. She breathed in and out until she'd calmed her breathing down.

With fingers that were getting cold fast, she turned her tablet on, praying that Flowerpots hadn't changed their code, and presto, she was in. She set her search to incognito, activated her VPN and hoped for the best as she logged in to Facebook and Instagram. A virtual private network was just what she needed, so she thought. She wasn't quite sure what it did really. Craig told her that it stopped people spying on you when you used the internet but he was always paranoid about people seeing what he'd been up to. She huffed. What he really meant was that she could never find out what he'd been up to.

Everything was taking an age to open and load. She stood and walked around the back of the building, eventually getting a better signal. She opened Instagram and checked Craig's profile first – nothing. Danny's – nothing. Pia – nothing. It wasn't like Pia not to make her daily post. Justine searched through everything Pia had posted over the past week. Her daily yoga poses and kombucha promotions stopped two days ago. Given that her poor friend had ran into a crime scene the previous night, it was understandable. Justine felt sickened that she'd have to tell her about Craig and Simeon soon. No way should her friend not hear the truth from her. Again, she couldn't help but wonder if their friendship would get through all this. As for Lindy, she'd never want to see Justine again. She glanced at Pia's last post which was yet another promotion of her drinks range.

Sometimes a girl just needs herself and herself only. We have to be at one with nature so we can heal. We have to hear the trees blowing in the breeze, listen to raindrops trickling and nourish our bodies. Reach out, give nature a chance to cure you and while you're at it, feed your gut.

Pia was sitting on a bed of orange and brown leaves in the lotus position. Whoever was taking the photo held a can of kombucha to the side of the frame. Craig's bracelet dangled from the photographer's wrist. It even had the little imperfection on one of the threads. She was in no doubt that it was Simeon's hand and Craig's bracelet.

Craig had caused all this. He'd failed to provide a secure life for Danny. All their arguments and his aggression had made Danny what he was now. It wasn't all her son's fault. She swallowed the lump in her throat. She hated herself because however bad her son had behaved, she couldn't hate him, but she could hate Craig. She only hoped that when the police eventually caught up with Danny, they realised deep down that he was the product of a terrible father. The right thing to do would be to go back to her mum's house and come clean about everything. Justine hoped that once she handed herself in and told the police that she knew nothing about the video, they would bail her and when the truth of her secret came out, Pia would forgive her.

Her body itched to leave but her feet were saying no. Palpitations came thick and fast. Handing herself in came with arrest, questioning and the removal of her freedom, albeit temporarily. She knew how that felt. As a teenager, she'd been locked up for two hours after being caught shoplifting, all because of the drink. Again, she thought of Kain and how her son was kicking the hell out of him. She didn't want to be locked into a sparse, cold room not knowing how long she'd be there. She thought of her future. Would she be sent to prison for hiding Danny's laptop? She saw all those faces staring at her in horror at what she'd apparently covered up. Would they all believe she didn't know about the video? She gasped and tried to get control of her breathing. Torn by what to do next, she took a deep breath, hoping that it would quell the tension headache reaching across her forehead.

She clicked on Lindy's Facebook account. Her profile had been tagged with posters asking people to look out for her. Word had already spread about her disappearance and she could see that Pia had made the first post.

The message icon popped up on her tablet.

As she was about to open it, a man in an apron holding a huge bin bag opened the door and stared at her. She screenshot a photo of the message and ran, knowing she could read it later. Right now, she had to find somewhere else to hide.

She jumped into her car and drove off as fast as she could until she reached the woodland again. She turned the tablet on and opened the photo. The sender had no name or profile photo but she knew who it was just by reading it.

I can't believe you're online. I've been trying to contact you for the past hour. I don't know what to do anymore and I'm sorry for how badly I treated you. You have to meet me tonight. Something big is going on and I know you need the truth. This is me being honest with you. I've been sleeping with Pia and I hate myself for doing that but we're past lying. Our family is falling apart. I have a lot to explain but nothing is what it seems so you have to hear me out. Please don't speak to anyone, just come. I have so much more to tell you but Danny and me are in danger. It's all to do with debts but I'll tell you everything in person later. The police are monitoring our phones and computers but I'm using the VPN and a fake account to send this message. I'm not staying at the address below; I will just be there later. I know you hate me

now but do this for Danny. Like I said, it's not what it seems.
Delete after reading. X

It was as if the breath was sucked out of her body. She'd suspected that Craig had been cheating with Simeon. He had been wearing Craig's bracelet. Her hands trembled as she thought of her husband and Pia. He had to be lying. They'd been friends for years and discussed every intimate part of their lives. Humiliation burned her cheeks. Pia, Pia, Pia – all she could think of was her pretty face laughing behind her back as she slept with Craig. She rubbed her watery, tired eyes. All she wanted in life was a family and a career. She thought she had it all and her husband had to ruin everything. As for her son... she had no words left. What wasn't what it seemed? How could a video lie? Her stomach dropped. Maybe the video was a fake. She'd heard about deepfakes. That's what Craig must have meant. Her head ached with confusion. She had no option but to do as instructed.

She read the address underneath the message and frowned. She knew she could drive to Fern Street and leave her car there and walk the rest of the way. If she parked any closer, she'd more than likely be into ANPR camera territory and the police would be on her in an instant. She read the last line of the message.

I'll be there at midnight.

Her stomach churned. She hated her husband with a passion but she had to know what was going on. The truth was worth the fear and the hiding out from the police. Denying the rage in her gut was too painful, she had to speak to Simeon, tell him exactly what had been going on. He deserved to know. She couldn't wait to see the look on Pia's face when she blurted it out. She didn't even care about her secret anymore. Everything needed to come out.

She opened the glove compartment and saw the small paring knife she'd taken from her mum's house tucked behind the stupid useless burner phone.

A million thoughts went through her mind but she knew she had to listen to her conscience. She was going to speak to Craig and Danny at midnight and persuade them to turn themselves in. If it was all a misunderstanding, it would sort itself out. This had to end. Another part of her shivered at the thought of confronting Craig with that. If she was wrong about the video being a deepfake... she trembled. She thought of the times Craig had got angry, the times he'd pushed her around and she didn't trust him. She still had scratches on her legs and marks on her arms from when he'd dragged her across that field. Also, that message had seemed all too honest and open. Craig was never that transparent. He was up to something and she didn't know what.

She had a weapon and she wouldn't hesitate to use it on Craig if she had to.

FORTY-NINE

Gina sighed as she drove down yet another street and followed another dead end when it came to finding Justine and Lindy. 'I'm thinking that Justine had a five, maybe ten-minute head start on us, that's up to three miles potentially given the type of roads available and the time it would have taken her to run to her car.'

Jacob nodded in agreement and ended his phone call. 'No one has seen her and her car hasn't been caught on any ANPR cameras. A couple of cars have been cruising the scenic routes but no one has come across her.'

'While they keep looking, we need to head to Pia Yates's house, see if Justine has tried to contact her. As far as we know, Justine doesn't know about the affair so she might try to confide in Pia. We need to find out what else was on that laptop so let's hope that Garth manages to get through all the files soon. Justine also hid his laptop, knowing we were going to end up searching her house. She's got a lot of explaining to do.'

'It's frustrating, isn't it, guv?'

She nodded as she accelerated along the road. 'Did you manage to update DCI Fraser?'

'Yes, I messaged him.' Jacob paused. 'They're also probably going to be letting Fabien Stone out in a short while. They're charging him with the assault against you and his solicitor is pushing for bail.'

'I guess it is what it is.' She sighed. Her face still ached and it was definitely going to swell considering she hadn't managed to ice it. 'He was in custody when Lindy was taken and Briggs attacked and however much I don't like him, everything he said stacks up. There was a solid link between him, Craig, Kain and Zavier, though. I'm struggling here. Do you have any thoughts?'

'I keep coming back to the friendship group and mostly Craig. Seeing that video has confused the situation more and has added his son to the mix.' He frowned. 'Danny Crawford hasn't been seen for a while?'

'Are you wondering if he's been taken too? I know he's assaulting Kain in that video but again, we need to think outside the box here if we're to make all the links. Although, it is logical that he's on the run and his father is in on it, or protecting him.'

Jacob shook his head. 'I just don't know. All I know is the next line of questioning is taking us to the only member of the friendship group who isn't missing, Pia. She had an affair with Craig and they parted under bad circumstances. She said he hurt her.'

Gina scrunched her brows. 'All debts must be paid in full. That's what Briggs's attacker said to him.' She paused as she mulled that over. 'I'm coming back to the teddy bears. The killer is using them to send us a message or mark their territory. It's one person or two people working together. If there's two, they're both on the same page. Can you call Kapoor, chase up if they've found out any more information on the backgrounds of the friendship group? This has to go back a long way. To when Briggs, Zavier and Kain all worked together. Pia has known Craig for years, since they were teens. Could this be a part of her past as she is clearly connected to Craig? We can't rule that out until we know for sure but we don't have anything else to suggest she's involved. She was with Craig and they were happily having an affair until recently. Maybe the guilt she feels for sleeping with Justine's husband might cause her to help Justine hide from us. I'm clutching at straws here.'

'It's something else to bear in mind,' Jacob replied.

'Equipment was used for Zavier's murder. Pia also had access to Craig's shag pad where she could have pinned all those photos to the wall, and she's friends with Justine, she'd have access to her house to plant the evidence under his bed, framing Craig. She could have easily got hold of his hoodie and Justine's card being in the pocket could have been a coincidence. A witness saw a man vomiting in a lay-by after Kain's murder, could it have been the hoodie and cap that made the witness think it was a man? We need a break in this case. Better still, we need to find all the missing persons of interest. Can you send Kapoor a quick message, ask her if there are any updates?'

Jacob nodded and began typing out a message as Gina drove in silence in the direction of Pia and Simeon Yates's house. Justine had to be somewhere and their house was a good place to start.

Jacob shifted in the passenger seat and faced her as he spoke. 'Kapoor has replied already. The two murder victims and DCI Briggs were all working at the Kidderminster station alongside each other thirty years ago. The newspaper clipping we found under Craig's bed was dated a year before. The same three worked there together for five months, July to November. We don't have any more information about their time there, again, that's an issue with records. Kapoor said that she found something that connects two of them.'

'What's that?'

'The mistreatment of a suspect in custody, Zavier and Kain were mentioned but nothing was done.'

'Do you have the name of the person who made the allegation?'

'Carol Tayne. She accused Zavier and Kain of spitting at her and pushing her but there was no proof. Briggs wasn't mentioned. Maybe we're on the right track.'

Gina found herself exhaling on hearing that Briggs wasn't mentioned. She thought about him in hospital and she hoped that his brother had arrived to be with him.

'I don't recognise the name Carol Tayne at all.'

'She died of a drug overdose three years later. She was originally arrested for possession of heroin.' Jacob blew out a breath.

'Great, I guess she can't help us then. Can you request backup, just in case we find Justine? We can't lose her again if she's here. We'll be a laughing stock if she's there and we lose her twice.'

After pulling up on the road, Gina knocked twice on Pia and Simeon's door. Pia answered and inhaled sharply while glancing over her shoulder as a man joined her. Her eyes widened. Gina knew exactly what Pia was thinking. She didn't want her affair to be brought up in front of her husband.

Simeon smiled. 'Hello.' He glanced at his wife.

'Err, this is DI Harte and DS Driscoll. I went to the station and spoke to them about Lindy.'

'Please come in. Have you found Lindy?' Much to Pia's dismay, Simeon chatted as he led them along the wide hallway into a huge open-plan family room. He gestured for them to sit on the couch that had the best view of their sprawling garden. Darkness was falling and bats flew around their mature trees. 'Take a seat.'

Gina sat on the couch with Jacob. Simeon pulled up a couple of chairs that had been placed against the back wall.

'Please don't leave us in suspense. My wife told me what happened.'

Pia stood behind Simeon and shook her head gently as if to say she hadn't. 'About going to Lindy's and the blood, and her not being there.'

Simeon broke the silence. 'Is she okay? We're really concerned. Pia has been so worried.'

Gina listened for a moment, trying to fathom if anyone else might be in the house but there wasn't a single creak. 'I'm afraid we still haven't found them but, Pia, could you talk to us again, down at the station.'

'Why?'

'It's nothing, just need to go over a few things.'

Pia didn't need too much convincing. Gina knew she'd want to talk there, rather than in front of her husband.

'Err, of course. I can drive and meet you there?'

Gina checked her phone messages. Backup had arrived. 'It's okay, we have a car outside.' She couldn't force Pia into that car but she didn't need the last woman in the friendship group going missing.

'Pia has been through a lot. Her friend is missing. We've arranged to meet some of the community to search for Lindy. Does this really have to happen now?' Simeon frowned.

Gina knew he was confused. 'It would really help us with our enquiries. First, there is something I need to ask you both.'

Pia raised her brows.

'Have you seen Justine Crawford today?'

'Justine? Is she okay?' Pia began to bite one of her manicured nails. 'I can call her. She can't be far. I messaged her to ask if she wanted to join the search but I haven't had a reply.'

'Her phone is off,' Gina replied.

Pia began to shake. 'Where could she be?'

'That's something we also need to talk to you about. You know her better than we do.' Gina let out a silent sigh under her breath. She couldn't see that Pia had any involvement but with

Lindy missing and Justine on the run, she hoped that Pia would just go with them.

'I'm coming to the station, too,' Simeon said. 'I'll drive the car and wait for you. Surely my wife won't be there for long.'

Pia exhaled slowly. 'Why don't you give me an hour then come? I'm sure this will take a while.' Pia raised her brows at Gina.

Gina nodded. 'There could be a bit of waiting around but you're welcome to sit in the family room when you get there.'

Again, Gina could see that Pia didn't want Simeon to be there. Hiding her affair had become Pia's priority. The clock was still ticking for Lindy. If Pia was hiding anything when it came to seeing Justine, she was going to get it out of her at the station.

'I'll do that. I'll be right behind you, love. Okay?'

Pia placed her head against her husband's chest and he hugged her like she was the love of his life. Gina felt for him. It was going to bring his world crashing down when he found out about the affair.

While Pia hurried through the house putting her shoes on and looking for her coat, Gina tried to picture Pia hoisting Zavier up and dragging Kain's dead body down a flight of stairs and loading him into a car, and she couldn't. This was all about finding Justine, then finding Craig and Danny.

As Gina and Jacob led her to the police car, she left Jacob standing outside with her. Gina leaned in and spoke to the PC. 'Can you call for another car to be here? I want the house watched in case Justine Crawford turns up.'

'Already on it. Another car will arrive shortly.'

Gina stood and saw Pia wiping her eyes as she showed her phone to Jacob. She hurried over. 'Is everything okay?'

'I got this message from an anonymous Instagram account from someone called BustYourAss. I didn't want to mention it in front of Simeon. I know it's Craig and he's angry. He hurt

Lindy because he said I'm next.' She passed her phone to Gina and Gina read it.

Bitch. You don't know what I sacrificed to try to make a life with you. Start looking over your shoulder because I'm coming for you next!

FIFTY

JUSTINE

After running through the housing estate and over a field, Justine pulled a twig from her hair. The easy route would risk too many eyes on her. Her only option had been to stick with the back roads, the single-track dirt paths and the woodland. Her mission was to get to Pia's without arousing any suspicion on the way. There were no police. It was dark and the estate was quiet. Anger and sadness competed for space in her thoughts. Craig had cheated and it wasn't the first time but Pia, her friend – how could Pia have done that to her? She swallowed the shame in her throat. She knew exactly how. Pia and Craig was different... or was it? She hated them and herself so much right now.

Simeon stood in the window pacing, the glow of the floor lamp creating a halo effect around his head. She ran up the drive, clinging onto her tablet in the hope that she could use their Wi-Fi. If there were any more messages, she wanted to read them.

She checked the time on her burner phone. It was getting later fast and she had an appointment to keep for midnight. Before knocking, she opened her tablet and, as expected, it instantly locked onto Pia's Wi-Fi just like it had done in the past.

> All debts must be paid in full, Justine. I know that now. I failed you and I'm sorry. There's a house by the lake where the kids like to party. You know the one, you do yoga on the opposite side. Get Danny's bag from upstairs in that house and bring it with you. Do this for Danny. See you at midnight.

She frowned as she knocked on the door and turned her tablet off.

'Justine,' Simeon said with a frown as he opened the door.

'Is Pia in? I need to speak to her... and you. I need to speak to you both.' Her hands shook uncontrollably. A confrontation seemed like a good idea while she was trudging from her car but now, she knew she was going to destroy Simeon and that didn't feel good at all.

His Adam's apple bobbed up and down. He stared at her in silence before turning and walking towards the coat cupboard under the stairs. She stepped in and closed the door, watching as Simeon mooched through the cupboard. 'I can't find my jacket.' He pulled all the coats out, throwing each of them in turn into a heap on the floor. 'My car keys are in my jacket.'

'Is Pia in? Her car is outside.'

'No.'

'Simeon, what's going on?'

He stopped and stared at her. 'You damn well know what's going on. The police are looking for you and they've taken Pia in for questioning. Where the hell have you been?'

'A lot has been happening and I've only just found out. I'm so sorry, Simeon.' She hated that such a gentle man was going through so much. He deserved more than Pia. He also deserved the truth.

Tears began to slip down her cheeks. All she wanted to do

was make things right. She placed her tablet on the stairs and touched his arm. 'Simeon, I'm trying my hardest to make things better. There is something I have to tell you—'

'Found them.' He dropped his shoulders and grabbed a jacket from the floor of the cupboard.

'Simeon, please. Just stop. I need to speak to you.'

'What is it, Justine? Which bit of my wife is at the police station and I need to be with her don't you get? This isn't a good time. Whatever you and your family are involved in, you need to speak to the police.' He walked through the living room and grabbed his scarf. 'You can do that now. A police car has just pulled up outside. Someone has been sent to watch our house in case you turn up.'

'You deserve the truth, Simeon. Just give me five minutes.' She couldn't let him alert the police. She had somewhere to be, a truth of her own to chase.

He tilted his head. 'Just tell me. I don't have time for this nonsense.'

Justine blurted it out. 'It's Pia, she's been having an affair with Craig. A great big affair that's gone on for ages. I can't believe it. I thought it was you who was having an affair with Craig.'

'What the hell would make you think that?'

She pointed to his wrist. 'You're wearing his bracelet.'

Simeon held his wrist up and took the bracelet in. 'So that's who it belonged to. I found it in my office and thought one of the suppliers had lost it. I asked around, no one claimed it so I kept it. He must have lost it when he set up the accounting system.'

'And it was stupid of me to think that, but I did because...' She shook her head not wanting to share what she was thinking.

He scrunched his brow and his jaw started to slowly drop. 'How do you know that Pia has been having an affair? That's absurd. Are you just trying to make trouble because there isn't enough of that in your life right now?'

'No. I would never do that to you. Someone told me.'

'Who?'

'Craig. I'm sorry. He also knows what I did and I wondered if Pia could have seen or did you tell her?' Justine put her shaking hands into her pockets. 'I kissed you, that was all and I said I was sorry but you didn't have to go and tell Craig. What was it, an anonymous message? My husband has always been a lying cheat with someone or another. I just wanted to make him pay and as soon as I did it, I knew it was wrong and I know you love Pia and you'd never cheat like Craig. Anyway, I thought you had the right to know about Pia.' Her mind had been thinking all sorts while she thought Craig had been having an affair with Simeon. Simeon had rejected her back then and her thoughts had jumped to the idea that he preferred Craig more. Justine could tell that she'd floored him with that revelation.

He took a few deep breaths and looked away. 'I guess I'll deal with all that later. Right now, I have to go and you're holding me up. Why are the police looking for you? They didn't say much? I need to know.'

'I'm on the run. The police think I'm involved but I'm not. I need the chance to sort this before they take me in. I'm begging you not to tell the police that I was here.'

He let out a long, slow breath. 'I just want all this to be over.' He looked into her eyes. 'If it's any consolation I was flattered when you tried to kiss me but I'm obviously not like my wife. I've always been faithful.' He paused. 'I don't believe for one second you're a dangerous fugitive, Justine. You can leave out the back. It takes you onto a football field. Cross it and you'll know where you are.'

'Thank you.'

His keys jangled in his trembling hands. 'Go.'

She darted out of the back door. She loved her son with all

her heart but it was time for him to face the consequences of his actions. Sometimes being a parent was about making tough decisions. She knew she'd been wrong to try to hide Danny's laptop and she was wrong to make Danny lie to try to implicate Craig. She didn't have time to question her own morality over the past couple of days, all she had time to do was put things right. At least she didn't have to think about what Pia thought of her any more. Their friendship was over.

As she ran through the woodland, she realised she'd left her tablet on the stairs. She pulled the burner phone out of her pocket and tried calling Danny one more time but like all the other times, all she got was the dead tone.

It was almost nine that evening and midnight would soon be on her if the next part of her plan didn't work out.

She had to get to the derelict house. After reaching the cover of trees, she stopped to feel for the paring knife in her pocket. She pulled it out and held it up against the moonlight. She had no idea what she was going to find at that house but she was prepared for anything.

FIFTY-ONE

Back at the station, Gina stood outside the interview room with Jacob. 'What did Garth say, about Danny's laptop?'

'There was a deleted message on an app that gamers tend to use from someone who calls themselves BustYourAss.'

'Charming.'

'That's what I thought. The message said, "Need to talk. Can't live with this shit over my head any longer. You have to meet me now." We're thinking that Danny was talking about the video. There are also other deleted messages in the run up to Kain's murder. Kain had been trying to blackmail Danny for money and threatened that if he didn't manage to get ten thousand pounds, Kain was going to show the video to the police. There are numerous credit card applications in Danny's name, which were all turned down.'

'So, Danny has a strong motive and Craig does too. He'd want to cover for his son. I also think that when we questioned Justine and Danny, they spun us a yarn about the money that Kain took from Craig as a deposit for a security system. Justine knows and she too was trying to cover for her son. That still doesn't explain Zavier's murder or DCI Briggs's attempted murder. Can we confirm who Danny was messaging?'

'It was Craig.'

Gina sighed. 'Craig is now hiding Danny somewhere. Do we know if Craig has used his bank cards recently?'

'I checked this with Garth, too. Not for two days.'

'He knows we're trying to trace him. Then he goes and sends that horrible message to Pia, ending it with, "I'm coming for you." We need to bring him in. Let's talk to her. See what she knows.'

Gina entered the interview room with Jacob and they both sat opposite her.

After Jacob introduced them for the tape, Pia scraped her chair along the floor to be closer to the table. 'That message, I couldn't stop reading it all day. Then I thought of Craig and how little I knew him. I have so stuffed up my life. I just want things to go back to the way they were before the affair and I know Simeon is going to find out. I can't keep this from him. You have to find Craig. I'm scared of him. I told you what he was like at the apartment.'

Gina interjected. 'That's what we're trying to do. Did Craig mention anywhere else that he might go? Favourite places? Places he went to be on his own? Friends?'

'No, I'm so sorry. I wish I knew more.' She paused. 'Thank you for not doing this in front of Simeon. I need to be the one to tell him.'

'How about Danny? Did Craig ever mention where Danny hung out?'

'He never spoke about Danny when we were together. Danny almost caught us one time because he came to meet his dad early. From this day onwards, I was never sure if he saw me or not, but he didn't say anything. Craig said Danny had accused him of seeing someone and they'd argued over it.'

Gina felt her frustration building up. Pia knew nothing of

any importance. She let out a quiet sigh. 'How well did you know Kain?'

'Not well. I met him at Lindy's house but that was it. I know what Lindy told me. Kain had always been trouble. Look, I don't know anything that will help. I had an affair with what looks like your prime suspect, that is all.'

'Have you heard from Justine Crawford today? We're really worried about her.'

Pia shook her head.

'Do you know where she might go?'

'Only to her mother's.'

Gina looked down. Justine had run from her mother's house.

'We're taking the threat in the message you received seriously. Do you have somewhere else you can go after this?'

She shrugged. 'I'll get Simeon to book a hotel when he gets here. There's no way I want to go home until Craig has been caught.' She bit her bottom lip and frowned. 'Simeon's not going to want to do anything for me when he finds out what I've done. I guess I'll be staying in a hotel alone.'

'We do have some more information. The message sent to you was from an account in Craig's name. I know you guessed it was from Craig but we can confirm it.'

'And I told you, he's dangerous.' She began to sob. 'He has this way of making you do things you don't want to do.'

'What do you mean?'

'When I went over to see Justine on the night the affair started, I didn't intend for that to happen but it did. I weirdly didn't know how to stop it, like I was under some sort of spell. I wanted to end it but... sometimes I didn't even want to be with him near the end but he'd threaten to tell Simeon if I didn't turn up and...'

'And what?'

Pia stood and started to do her coat up, trying to speak as

she choked back her tears. 'I want to go. I don't know anything else and I'm not under arrest. I'll let you know which hotel I end up booking a room at. Get Craig so I can go back home, please.' She shook her head and began doing the buttons up. 'I really do hate him now. He's ruined my life. He's going to pay for what he did. He hurt me in that flat. I want him charged with assault. He hurt me and all this is going to come out anyway. What have I got to lose? He owes me too. You need to catch him and punish him. All debts must be paid in full. When you hurt someone you have to pay and I want him to pay!' She scrunched up her fists and punched the door. Not an ounce of pain showed on Pia's face. 'I hate him so much, I wish that had been his face.'

All debts must be paid in full. Gina knew she couldn't ignore the mention of paying in full. 'What was that?'

'Sorry, I'm just so angry and upset by all this. I don't normally punch doors.'

'Pia, what did you mean when you say that all debts should be paid in full?'

Pia scrunched her brow. 'Why are you looking at me like that?'

'Like what, Pia?'

'Like you suspect me of something? I told you, I didn't mean to punch the door and I shouldn't have said what I said about wishing it was Craig's face. Look, I'm sorry I hit your door. There's no damage so we're all good. I best go. Simeon and I have a lot to talk about.'

A sick feeling welled in Gina's stomach. It didn't feel good to do what she had to do next but with Lindy's life on the line, she couldn't ignore what she'd just heard. 'Pia, I'm arresting you on suspicion of the murders of Kain Pickering and Zavier Sellers, along with the attempted murder of DCI Chris Briggs, and the kidnapping of Lindy Pickering. You do not have to say anything. But it may harm your defence if you do not mention when questioned something which you later rely on in court. Anything you do say may be given in evidence.' Briggs's attacker had said, *all debts must be paid in full,* just before trying to drown him with a hosepipe. She could not let Pia leave and vanish into the night.

Gina glanced at the clock. It was almost nine thirty that evening. She didn't know how much longer Lindy had. Then Gina thought, if Lindy was relying on Pia to stay alive right now, she'd just killed her by arresting Pia.

FIFTY-TWO

LINDY

Another loud bang came from afar. No one had come up close and spoken to her. Maybe the bang was down to the kidnapper loitering around, planning what to do next. All she could do was endure the revolting stringy things brushing past her legs, suspended in the liquid and swishing as she gently bobbed. In her mind, she imagined worms swimming. She screamed again. 'Let me out.'

Her stomach turned each time she inhaled the sulphurous air. The liquid in the tank had to be stagnant. She looked up, knowing that she'd tried but couldn't reach the top of the lid, or whatever might be containing her. Above, all she could see was a crescent of night-time hue, only marginally lighter than pitch-darkness. Was it a relief that her captor had left her with a little bit of fresh air? Maybe he had no intention of killing her or he would have sealed her in and waited for her to suffocate from the stench or lack of oxygen. She had tried to climb out of the cylinder, but she'd slipped back into the liquid. Her captor knew she had no way of escaping.

She yelped as another cramp distorted her calf muscles and she kept thinking, *stay upright. Don't drown in this revolting stew.* Was anyone missing her? Her neighbours all thought a lot of her and they'd been more than supportive when Kain had come by making a scene. She hoped that everyone was looking for her. But where were they looking? Where was she? She'd been standing for a long time and the warmth coming from below had now gone. Iciness spread through her body and the constant teeth chattering was making her jaw ache.

Think about better times. She tried to conjure up her safe and happy place in her mind. *It was always their first holiday as a family when she and Kain were kids, back when he was her adorable little brother. They'd jumped over the waves on the Costa Blanca and Kain had shrieked with delight each time. That thought never failed to maintain her inner calm. She tried to tap into the warmth of the sun, the smell of salt and the slapping noise her feet made on the wet, compact sand beneath them, then the tickle of seaweed as it brushed against her legs.*

She stumbled, losing her balance. As she ducked underneath the liquid, she inhaled a mouthful of slime. She gasped and started coughing the foul gunk from her lungs while trying her hardest to hold back her nausea. Her mouth had never tasted more disgusting. 'Why are you doing this to me?' she said in a quivery broken up voice, wondering if anyone was actually listening. 'Help,' she cried one more time. If anyone heard how feeble she sounded right now they'd have surely thought she was giving up. Was she giving up? Never, not as long as she had a breath left in her body. She wouldn't give up.

The sound of a metal door creaking sent her silent as she listened to the nearing footsteps. The scrape of a ladder made her hyperventilate and she worried her ordinarily healthy heart might pack up at any moment. She'd waited for ages in the hope that her captor would come back to free her but now that he was back, she hoped he'd go away again. But if he went away, she'd definitely die. Thoughts raced through her mind, making her panic even more.

Boots clunking up metal steps sent chills through her and that was followed by the scraping sound of the lid being moved. The crescent of grim light turned into a half-moon but it was still too dark to see anything. A figure leaned over and she could make out the goggles on his face and their devilish green lights again. She was almost blind but he could see like it was daylight.

'Water.' He unscrewed a bottle and held it above her.

Desperate to quench away the disgusting taste in her mouth, she opened wide so he could pour. Before she realised what was happening, he'd already dropped what felt like a pill to the back of her throat and the water followed – too fast for her to stop that and the pill from slipping down her throat. 'What was that?' she spluttered.

He removed the goggles and moved in closer, leaning over. That's when she saw the barely visible line of his squarish jaw, one she recognised.

'A sleeping tablet. How long will you be able to stand for now?'

'Please don't do this to me. I don't know what I've done to deserve this. Please let me go. I won't say anything to anyone. I just want to go home,' she said.

'All debts must be paid in full. You were on the wrong side all those years ago. All that rejoicing, champagne... It's all about justice, rebalancing the scales. Remember his name. Baz. Baz, Baz,' he shouted and she knew exactly who he was referring to.

How could she not know that name? She pictured the day that they'd all gone to the pub after the inquest had been heard at the court in Kidderminster. Kain had walked straight up to the bar and ordered several bottles of their finest champagne all while the teen was gazing through the window of the pub. 'You were the boy...'

He slammed the lid down, but this time, he closed it. The air was thickening with eggy fumes and however much Lindy wanted to force her eyes to stay open, she couldn't. They half closed and she stumbled.

Her breaths slowed and she began jumping over the waves again, her hand gripping Kain's so the sea couldn't sweep him away from her. A large wave came and weed began to wrap around her calves, dragging her away as she held on to Kain. She allowed the sea to take them both.

FIFTY-THREE

'I don't need a solicitor,' Pia shouted as Gina and Jacob sat opposite her. It had taken a short while to process her arrest but now they were ready to start questioning her. 'Let me go. This is absurd. How the hell are you arresting me for all that?'

'Mrs Yates, please sit. You will get your chance to speak in a moment when the recorder is rolling again.' Gina sat back down next to Jacob with one hand ready to hit the emergency panel now that she knew how hard Pia could punch when forced into a corner.

'But I don't get it. This is stupid. I swear, you're all just so bloody woke. A person isn't allowed to say anything anymore. Just because I said a few things when I was upset.' She folded her arms in front of her chest.

Jacob introduced them all for the tape. Gina glanced at the time. It was now almost ten thirty that evening and it had been a long day but she knew that Pia was the key to getting Lindy back. She was also the person who reported Lindy missing but even though she had proven that she'd stopped at the garage for wine, no one could really corroborate Pia's whereabouts.

'Pia, where is Lindy Pickering?'

'How would I know? It's your job to find her. You're the police, not me.'

'Did you want Kain Pickering to pay in full?'

'No, this is insane!' She slammed her hand on the table but this time she flinched as the pain of the second hit to the same hand flared up.

'Where is Lindy?' Gina paused. Pia didn't answer.

'What do the blue and pink teddy bears mean?'

'This is getting more absurd by the minute.'

'Please answer the question, Mrs Yates.'

'I don't know what the hell you're on about.'

'Is your husband still at home?'

Pia shrugged. 'He's probably on his way over here to be with me.'

'We'll need your house keys as we need to search your property.'

'You can't do that. No way you can go through my house on some stupid hunch or whatever you have me here on.'

'It's more than a hunch, Mrs Yates. We have reason to believe that you were involved in some serious crimes. Why did you use the words "paid in full?"'

Pia scrunched her brows and tilted her head before allowing her jaw to slacken.

That wasn't the reaction Gina had expected but she continued questioning. 'Mrs Yates, where are Craig and Danny Crawford?'

'I don't know and I don't care. It's them you should be arresting, not me. Craig is a nasty man.'

Pia wasn't helping herself. Gina sat back, feeling less threatened by the woman's presence and Jacob's shoulders dropped. She couldn't help but tap her foot on the ground. The last thing they needed was to be held up with Pia playing games when Lindy's life was at risk. 'Did you murder or were you involved in the murder of Zavier Sellers and Kain Pickering?'

'No.'

'Did you attack or were you involved in the attack of DCI Christopher Briggs?'

'No.'

'You didn't answer my earlier question about the use of the words "paid in full." Did you want Zavier, Kain and Christopher to pay in full?'

She tilted her head and stared at Gina, then at Jacob. 'I want a solicitor.'

Someone knocked at the door and Jacob spoke for the tape. 'Interview concluded at ten forty-eight.'

Gina stood and opened the door to Kapoor. 'I've found something, guv, and you need to hear it now. I've found the link to someone called Baz, Zavier, Kain and the DCI. An immediate and short briefing is about to start in the incident room.'

As Kapoor gave her a swift overview, Gina raised her brows as the person behind everything was revealed. 'Will you organise a team to search Pia's house. We can't rule her involvement out as yet. She's stopped speaking to us and I doubt a solicitor will arrive immediately. I'm going to Pia's house. I want you to dig up anything else while we're in the briefing, potential locations, places of work, leisure, etcetera. We're this close to finding Lindy, I know it. We can't have any more murders on our hands.'

Jacob opened the door to the interview room and Pia's sobs filled the corridor. 'Guv, she's just explained why she said, "paid in full."'

'I already know,' Gina replied. 'We know who killed Kain and Zavier and we know why.'

FIFTY-FOUR
JUSTINE

She held her hand to her thumping heart as she ran across the fields towards the derelict house, the knife neatly slipped into her back pocket. She glanced back at the trees rustling in the breeze.

After passing the picnic table, she reached the wiry perimeter fence around the building and wondered how she could get in. 'Danny,' she called, hoping to hear his voice. She knew she was meant to get his bag and meet at the prearranged location at midnight but if this could all be over now, she'd prefer that. Maybe, just maybe, Danny was hiding in that house.

While speaking to Simeon, she hadn't dared to let on where she was heading to at midnight. He'd have been alarmed and might have called the police. She'd already let him down enough and upsetting him like that wasn't an option. What was an option was Danny being cold and scared in the derelict house. As soon as they got to the police station, she was going to blame herself for the story that she made Danny tell them. It was only right that if she got her son to face up to his wrongs, she would too. Danny was already in enough trouble and on top of that, she'd encouraged him to lie to the police.

She called out again. Danny wasn't answering. She had to get inside the building somehow. A light flickered from an upstairs room and muffled sounds of people chattering came from inside. Danny had to be up there.

She ran around the building looking for a way in. The top of the fence was covered in barbed wire. A clattering sound coming from the treelined side of the house stopped her dead. With trembling legs, she took a few steps forward, trying to make as little noise as possible. In any other circumstances, she'd run away but her son needed her to be brave. She might not like Danny right now but as a mother, she'd never stop loving him or being there for him. She crept along the undergrowth. That's when she spotted a badger next to an upturned metal bucket, and just a short way from the bucket was a gap in the fence.

She pushed through the metal until it was stretched enough for her to step through, into the overgrown garden. She looked up again. The light still flickered. She shivered, wondering if Danny was huddled up around a naked flame, trying to keep warm. It was chilly at night. She pictured him terrified and freezing, but not alone. There were other voices. Maybe other teens were hanging out with him. Either way, she was going in.

On reaching the back door, she pressed the handle but it was locked. A thick woollen blanket had been draped over a window ledge where glass had once been. The wooden board that had been placed at the window to prevent intruders had been ripped out and lay in two jagged pieces on the grass. She sat on the blanket and shimmied around until she fell into a dark room.

After stepping into the darkness, she followed the sound of distant chatter, trying to listen for Danny's voice but she couldn't make out who the voices belonged to. She placed her hands out in front of her, feeling for the door and eventually she reached a doorknob. After slowly turning it, she stepped into the hallway. The stairs and walls were touched by a light glow from the upstairs light source. She could just about make out scorch marks on the stairs and walls. She remembered that the house had previously been fire damaged after squatters had taken hold. It had been mentioned on social media.

Her heart jumped. What if the people upstairs were squatters? She stopped on the middle of the stairs and took a few deep breaths. If they were, she meant them no harm. They were merely people with nowhere to live. Danny could even be squatting there with them. She pressed on, taking step after step until she heard the chattering clearly. It wasn't squatters or partygoers; it was the news coming from a radio. 'Danny,' she called out, her knees trembling.

As she stood outside the room where the light flickered from, she stepped forward and gasped. Danny's bag was lying on an old sleeping bag against the far wall. She ran over and looked through it. There were a few tops, an energy drink and one of the illegal disposable vapes she hated Danny using, but there was no Danny. She ran from room to room before realising she was alone in the house. Going back to the first room, she picked up the battery-powered flickering candle. The old wireless radio crackled as she got close. She turned it off and the silence felt deafening. 'Danny.' Next to the radio was another pink teddy bear, just like the one Pixie had been playing with and underneath the bear was an envelope with her name on. She opened it and started reading the note.

Justine. If you're not where I told you to be at midnight, you will never see Danny again. Go downstairs and you will see what happens when you don't do what I say. If you call the police or don't turn up, Danny dies. Or... maybe he's already dead... Do you think you can save him now, Mummy?

She half fell down the stairs with her son's bag in one hand as she ran into the room that must have once been a kitchen. She held the candle up and saw a boy with his hands tied behind his back on all fours with his head in a bucket full of water. She took the knife out, ready to release his hands. 'Danny.' She dropped the bag and pulled his head out, allowing the lump of a stuffed person in her son's clothes to tumble to the floor. Craig would never threaten Danny like that or play such a sick game. She held a hand to her banging heart, knowing she had no option but to be at the rendezvous for midnight if she was ever to see her son alive again.

FIFTY-FIVE

Sunday, 23 November

The team had already started on the search while Gina had attended the briefing. PC Smith stood outside Pia and Simeon's house, keeping the neighbours away. Jacob peered through the front door at all the police officers searching.

'How's it going?' Gina asked.

'You're needed upstairs, in the spare bedroom at the far end of the house.'

Jacob ran behind Gina, straight up the stairs. The crystal chandelier above them began to sway as a breeze whipped through the open doors. She hurried past the huge suite to her left, spotting more police officers going through the wall of wardrobes and searching under the bed. She passed another two rooms; one almost filled with cans of kombucha and another full of mobility aids, including a motorised scooter and a Zimmer frame. Then she reached the room at the end, that would sit above the garage. PC Benton had her back to them as she tended to a box full of bags ready to take in to the station.

'What have you found?' Gina spotted a toffee-flavoured

disposable vape in a box, the same as the one found close by to where Kain's body was discovered in the boot of Maura's car.

PC Benton turned. 'There is a loft hatch in here, guv. It looks like this suite was added on as an extension and the roof was extended too. After shining a torch up there, I found a box marked Baz.'

'What was in it?'

'You can see here.' She began pulling the clear evidence bags out. 'A blister pack of sleeping tablets.'

'What else?'

Jacob moved in a little closer to see what PC Benton had found.

'There's an empty night-vision goggle box. Several photos of two boys. There are files of notes on Fabien Stone and Craig Crawford. They were being stalked by the looks of it. There's also a small key ring with a blue teddy bear on the end. It looks really old and stained.'

'That's where the teddy bears came from. Also, there's an empty bag with a picture of those bears on the front. It looks like he ran out of blue ones and moved on to pink. There are only three of each colour.'

'I suspect he intended to use only three until everything grew out of hand.' Gina flinched as her phone rang in her pocket. She pulled it out and held it to her ear while Kapoor reeled off the Yates's business premises.

'Guv,' PC Smith shouted from downstairs. 'We've been looking at a tablet that was on the stairs and it appears to belong to Justine Crawford. There's a message with an address on it. We know where's she's going and she's already there.'

'Where?'

'The kombucha factory on Stokes Lane.'

'That's where Kapoor just said to go.' Her heart began to thrum as she and Jacob ran as fast as they could back to her car.

As she pulled out of the road, Jacob called Wyre to arrange

for a team to head there now. He ended the call and frowned. 'Why now? Simeon Yates knew that Zavier Sellers, Kain Pickering and Briggs had been brought up during the inquest for his brother's death. Why did he wait so long?'

Gina was as puzzled as Jacob when it came to that question. Only Simeon could answer that question and they needed to find him before he killed again.

FIFTY-SIX

JUSTINE

It was midnight and she was exactly where she was meant to be. The knife poked through her pocket, slightly jabbing her buttock. She pulled it out, ready to use it if she had to. Without warning, a figure darted in the darkness straight at her. She went to jab it with the knife but missed and stumbled to the ground. Her attacker kicked it out of the way and the blow to her head sent a white-hot pain burning through her. As she fought to stay conscious, all she could think of was how she'd failed Danny. The knife – it was gone. He struck her once more and she too was gone.

'Justine, Justine. It's time to wake up. I knew you'd come. I'm sorry I led you to believe you'd be meeting up with Craig.'

She gasped at the sight of him, her head throbbing with every breath. How could sweet, lovely Simeon have hurt her like this? She recalled him hitting her twice before dragging her out of the old unit. She'd been in his car but not for long.

The stench of something rotten turned her stomach. This wasn't the beery vinegary scent of kombucha, more like something had died. She inhaled again. It was like the back of a bin lorry.

This wasn't Pia and Simeon's unit. It was bigger and didn't look as sparkly and clean. She blinked a couple of times to clear the grittiness in her eyes. Light bleeding through the crack of a door lit up the side of Simeon's face. He looked down on her while gripping a blue pole covered in blood while she lay on the cold floor stiff from cold and pain. She could see where the pole had come from. Several racks full to the brim with cans of kombucha had been stacked up and those same blue poles held the racking together. A dismantled shelving unit had been neatly laid out with the blue poles next to the stack of heavy metal shelves. She spotted a tool bag and a crowbar. She needed to get the crowbar if she was to save herself and her son. 'You took Lindy and you left me that letter and you messaged me pretending to be Craig,' she cried.

'Their actions gave me no choice. It was easy with him out of the way and using a burner phone. I managed to convince Pia I was Craig too. I deceived my own cheating bitch wife, which is funny.' He paused and began to pace before hitting the racking, making her flinch. 'Do you think I wanted any of this? You had to bring Lindy into our lives. I blame you.'

The back of her head throbbed as she wondered what difference it made that Lindy was in his life, then she thought of Kain. It had to be him, something Kain did. She reached around and felt a sticky pool gathering. She knew it was best to try to diffuse the situation or she'd end up dead. 'Simeon. Please, whatever this is, it has to stop. You can't get away with it.'

'Getting away with it is no longer my intention. Do you know how the business all started and why Pia wanted to make kombucha?'

She shook her head, wondering how any of this was relevant but she had to keep him distracted. As soon as the room stopped swaying, she was going to dash for the crowbar and fight him.

He stood above her and poked the pole into her bare neck. 'No, she never mentioned it.' She swallowed the lump in her throat knowing that her and Danny's lives were in Simeon's hands.

'She believes crap she hears on the internet. Apparently, all my health issues were going to be fixed with bloody kombucha. She made it at home and forced me to drink it to the point it made me heave like mad. I won the battle against cancer many years ago but you know what, it's back, only this time in my stomach.' He stepped over her and whacked the racking with the pole. He swiped a pile of cans onto the floor and roared at the top of his voice. 'This shit cures nothing. You know what cured me the last time, surgery and chemo.' He held his stomach and yelled. 'This pain, it's always there. Pia kept telling me it was indigestion and IBS and all I had to do was drink more of that stuff and all will be fine. Leaky gut, she kept saying. I didn't need a doctor, she said; just a healthy wholesome life-style. I chugged away, can after can. Now it's too late for me.'

'I'm so sorry, Simeon. I didn't know.'

'Of course you didn't. No one knows yet, not even Pia. All this time I've sat back, lovely placid Simeon – never hurts or upsets anyone – then Pia brings home her new friend Lindy. I knew exactly who Lindy was. As a teen, I watched her cele-brating as Kain got off with killing my brother, Baz. Then all these years later, they end up in my life – again!'

Justine let out a breath. This went deeper than she'd ever have been able to guess. She had to wonder why he was so angry at her and Danny. From watching the video, Danny had hurt Kain but Craig, she knew why Simeon would hate Craig, he'd been having an affair with Pia. 'Simeon, please don't be angry at me and Danny. Craig cheated on me. I was cheated on, like you were and Danny, he hurt Kain. I saw a video on his laptop.'

'I've seen everything. Craig was so stupid leaving his iPad unlocked when he worked on our accounting system, and keeping all his passwords in a file marked passwords – rookie error. Your husband is stupid and your son is even thicker. I've been watching, waiting and learning. Everyone is so stupid.'

'Why me? Why am I here?'

'You just had to interfere, offer to help Kain. Where was the help when my brother was dying in a cell? Where was the help for me too, when I had to live with what happened? I missed him, I still miss him and it hurts knowing he died alone like that. I kept hearing it from Pia, how kind you were, how you were trying to help Kain get his life back and get help. You're just like all the other do-gooders, trying to help the people who do the most damage and I hate you for it. I needed help from the justice system and I got nothing. This diagnosis and Lindy turning up... I knew what I needed to do.'

'So, I'm here because I tried to help someone?'

'You helped the man who let my brother die. Rage bubbled inside me for ages but I kept a lid on it. You know, there's only so long a person can keep a lid on rage. It's like an explosion that goes off.' He stared wide-eyed. 'You have to unleash the beast. You have to be the one to get justice because the system stinks at it. You have to collect those debts in full, that's what I'm always telling Pia when she shirks her credit control duties.' He shrugged and continued. 'Kain was police at the time. Zavier, the other man who paid in full was police at the time. Another pig called Briggs, the custody sergeant, had booked him in. No one checked on Baz. No one cared. All three officers pleaded their innocence at the inquest and no one cared that my brother had died. He was labelled a troublemaker who ended up piling onto a fight outside a pub.' He swallowed. 'His best friend died because those other men were beating him up. My brother would have been trying to save his friend because that was what Baz was like. He was a good, kind person, nothing like they made him out to be just because he accidentally hit a cop in the nose.'

Justine struggled to control the trembling coming from deep inside. 'You killed Kain and you set Craig up because of what Kain did to your brother?' She didn't know Zavier or Briggs but from what he'd said, she knew they were the other police officers involved back then.

He let out a laugh. 'It seemed fitting and a part of me hoped it would work because I wanted Craig to pay, too. I knew about the affair he was having with Pia and I'd listened to Pia rattling on about you all. She prattled on about Kain, his ex-wife and every little intimate thing you and Lindy shared with her. I knew about the arguments that Lindy had with Kain over how he treated their mum. I knew that Kain had made a fool of himself with Fabien. When I found out about the fight where Fabien had attacked him, I knew he'd make a worthy person to also set up, besides, Craig and Fabien were acquaintances. You only have to look at Instagram to see that. Pia told me everything and I found out the rest myself by logging in to Craig's social media and keeping an eye out.'

Justine kept glancing at the crowbar as he went on, going into detail about how he'd constructed his elaborate plan, how he'd fit Craig up by using the key that Pia had to Craig's flat and how he'd easily got into Fabien's warehouse. 'Do you know why I'm telling you all this?'

She tried to hold her tears back.

'Because you are going to die tonight but you know that already. See that tank over there? That's what you get for helping someone as despicable as Kain and bringing Lindy into our lives.'

No, no, no, no, no. He wasn't going to put her in there. She tried to sit up but her head was swimming. Slowly, she nudged herself a little closer to the crowbar while Simeon continued unburdening himself.

'It was so easy to set Craig up. When I dropped that kombucha over that Pia told me to take to yours, I popped to the loo and put a few things to implicate Craig under your bed.' He laughed. 'As for the key I mentioned, I used it to enter his flat and I put photos of my kill scenes all over his wall. The teddies, pink and blue. Blue for the injustice against Baz and pink for the rest of you. I left one at yours the other night while you were in the garden but you didn't get the warning. You just gave it to your dog.'

She shivered as she thought of Simeon stalking her. 'It was you, loitering around by my mum's the other night with the vape. I thought it was Danny.' Her voice was wobbly now. All she wanted to do was cry.

'Don't be stupid. I have better things to do than to hang around throwing stones but I did take one of his vapes when I was in your house. He seems to have a stash of them but I guess Danny doesn't care that they're illegal. He has quite the record, hasn't he? I used to smoke and I miss it. It doesn't matter if I smoke or vape now. What's it going to do, kill me? Anyway, that wasn't me. If I came across you in the night, you would have been here sooner, believe me.'

She furrowed her brows. It had to have been her son. If only he'd come out and spoken to her, she might not be here now because she certainly wouldn't have risked herself like this for Craig. 'Where's Danny? Please tell me that he's okay? I am so sorry for what I did. You're right. I shouldn't have helped Kain and I should check who I make friends with. I am sorry for bringing Lindy into your life, really I am. Please let Danny go. He's made some stupid decisions but that's my fault and Craig's fault. We could have done better. You can do what you want with me.'

He laughed. 'You seem to be mistaken. I can do what I want with both of you. I don't have a life of my own anymore. I can't fight what's coming my way, all I can do is fight injustice. Make the evil of this world pay. That is my curtain call.'

'Have you killed Craig?'

Simeon let out a laugh. 'Craig has taken off and even I can't find him. He only cares about himself but at least you can see that now. You and your son are nothing to that man. I'm also sure that Pia wasn't his first foray outside of your marital bed. He seems to be a seasoned pro. Pia – well, let's say she was an absolute amateur, that's why I found out what she was up to. At least your son was trying to make things right when he turned up at our house. Stupid kid was angry, a little bit drunk and he wanted to have a go at Pia for ruining his family. I wasn't going to let him blow everything up so I stopped him. Your boy really does have a nasty mouth on him and a temper. It was lovely seeing him so powerless once I'd hit his skull with a metal bar. Do you want to see what it's like seeing your child looking so powerless?'

She shook her head.

'Tough. You get to see anyway.' He turned to face the door at the end of the room and clutched his upper stomach.

Now was her moment. She shot up and stumbled towards the crowbar. He reached out and yanked her back as he yelled in pain. They both landed in a heap, him on top of her, her face pressed to the floor. She reached for the tool then he yelled again. Her fingers brushed against metal then she gripped the crowbar tight. While wriggling underneath him to get free, he kept grabbing her clothes. Her coat ripped. She stood. He got up and ran at her as she swiped the crowbar at him. He ducked. She swiped another time but missed and then they were both on the floor again. He had her pinned down. For a sick man, he was still strong. He grabbed the crowbar and kicked her hard in the knee. She screamed as he dragged her across the polished concrete floor into the other room. 'Stand.' He pulled her by the hair until she was up on her feet, her knee throbbing. A hose had been linked to a tap in the corner of the room. The other end was in the industrial tank close by. 'Danny,' she shouted.

Justine heard a little murmur then her son was silent. The

sound of water trickling into the tank sent chills through her. 'Turn it off!'

Simeon smiled. 'It's so peaceful in there. The sleeping tablet has taken care of him and he won't feel a thing, not like Baz did when he was left to choke on his own vomit in a cell because Lindy's brother and the other two didn't do their jobs. You all get to feel Baz's pain now. In several minutes that tank will be full and your son will be at peace.'

He was crazy, blaming her son for what happened to his brother. He'd lost it and she didn't know what to do. She tried to hit Simeon then he punched her cheek, sending her with a thud to the floor. He popped the crowbar into his waistband and awkwardly started dragging her again. He almost tripped while groaning in pain. She grabbed his feet but he was as sturdy as a tree trunk. Simeon locked the door on Danny, held the key up and threw it behind the racking.

'Now it's your turn, Justine. Open your mouth. We'll get you in the hoist then you can be with your friend, Lindy. It has to be this way. The world needs less sympathy for the bad people.' He dropped to the ground. He lay her head on his knees and she looked up into the eyes of pure evil. He pressed one arm against her neck. She couldn't breathe. As she tried to gasp, he dropped the pill down her throat and clasped his other hand over her mouth until she swallowed. Danny had a meagre few minutes and she was never going to wake up again. She'd never be able to save her son or tell anyone everything she now knew. She and Danny were about to die in this hellhole and there was nothing she could do about it.

FIFTY-SEVEN

Gina stood back as PC Ahmed bashed the door open with the battering ram. O'Connor and Wyre stood back and Jacob kept close. Several uniformed police officers proceeded. As they stormed in Gina shouted, 'Police,' several times. PC Ahmed found the light switch. The vinegary aroma hit her straight away.

She gazed around the small unit, and saw several kombucha tanks.

'Check them all. He likes to drown his victims,' Jacob yelled as O'Connor and Wyre began to climb up the ladders attached to the framework.

'What's in there?' Gina ran towards the door that one of the PCs had come back through.

'An office and a toilet. They're clear.'

Gina hurried through and spotted a phone on the floor. She reached down and picked it up. 'It looks like a burner phone. There's only a couple of numbers in it.' She ran over to the desk and glanced at a letter in a tray. 'Simeon Yates is sick. He has stomach cancer.' She popped the NHS letter back down.

'Guv.' Wyre hurried in to her. 'We've checked all the tanks. It's just kombucha at various stages of fermentation. There's nothing else in there.'

'Where are they?' Gina did a three sixty degree-turn, taking everything in. She'd been sure that Simeon had to have brought his victims here. 'Justine's messenger told her to come here for midnight. We're too late.'

O'Connor hurried in. 'Guv, you have to see this.'

Gina darted into the kombucha room and stared at the barely noticeable streak of blood leading from the middle of the room to the door. The blood streak continued to where Simeon's car would have been parked. 'Where the hell has he taken her?' She called Kapoor. 'We've just gained entry. They've gone. Is there another premises attached to the business?'

'Not that I can see, guv.'

'Go and ask Pia. We need her to speak. There are lives at stake.'

As Kapoor left the call on hold, Gina took her phone back with her to the office where she began to search through all the paperwork with Wyre and O'Connor.

'Guv.' Kapoor was back on the call. 'She said they only have the one premises but Simeon had been looking into another. It's close to where their unit is but she doesn't know where. He was going to take her next week.'

'Thanks.' Gina ended the call and addressed the room. 'He has another premises. Keep digging through these files. There has to be a record of this other place.'

Wyre tried to turn the computer on but the password box came up. 'Damn.'

O'Connor began rooting through the desk drawers.

Gina opened the filing cabinets and nothing was marked up. She grabbed the thickest folder and a flurry of debt collector letters from Fabien's company spilled out. 'Their kombucha business is on its knees. Simeon Yates had a reason to set up both Fabien and Kain.'

'Guv.' O'Connor held a piece of paper up. 'The other unit is on Herald Road, about a quarter of a mile away from here.'

Gina ran to her car with Jacob. The others followed. Her heart banged at the idea of turning up to find more dead bodies.

FIFTY-EIGHT
JUSTINE

'In another life, I think we could have been a thing, Justine. I might have kissed you back and we could have got married. Pia was never right for me, but you care. You're all about family. I wanted a family but Pia didn't.' He set the hoist contraption that he'd obviously engineered to lift her up. It buzzed until it snapped into place. 'I knew we kept all this crap for a reason. It's come in handy thanks to Pia's poor dead mother.' He laughed as he turned the main light on.

'Please, stop this,' she said with a sob, knowing it was too late. A few bangs in the distance made her jump.

He tilted his head. 'We've gone over this already, Justine.' He paused. 'It's just death. We're all going to die. I'll die soon; you'll already be dead. By fighting death, we're just delaying the inevitable.' He scrunched his brow. 'A diagnosis like mine can make a person pretty philosophical.'

He went on about how he'd dragged Kain to the car, how he'd killed someone called Zavier. He mentioned another man she didn't know called Briggs. It got harder for Justine to understand what he was wittering on about as he became more erratic. 'You're insane.'

He shrugged. 'Maybe so but that's irrelevant. Thank you for the insult. Insane is leaving a man who can't even stand up, high on drugs and drink, lying on his back in a cell, but we don't talk about that. Insane is putting up with a serial cheat and insane is helping pond scum. Kain was beyond help but you were so nicey-nicey, just because you had a drink problem yourself all those years ago. I hate that no one was there to help me but I won't go on about that again. When I see you, I hate you. I hate that you couldn't do a better job of being a wife because if you had, your husband wouldn't be all over the place like a horny dog.' He began to turn her in the hoist.

She knew she'd be dangling over the tank very soon. Her eyelids felt heavy as the tablet started taking effect. Tears slipped down her cheeks.

He climbed up the ladder next to the tank and came face to face with her. 'I wasn't joking when I said you'd be joining Lindy. Look down?'

Justine opened her mouth to scream. Panicked breaths escaped through her lips. The stench of the slime that had mixed in with Lindy's floating hair made her baulk. She couldn't go in the tank. 'No, no, no, don't do this to me. I'm begging you, Simeon.' She grabbed him. 'One last hug for old time's sake.'

She sank into his chest, not wanting to let him go because as soon as she let go, she was going to die in the most horrible way ever. Her knuckle brushed the metal of the crowbar. She thought of Danny and the tank in the other room slowly filling up. Had it filled up yet? It was no use pleading with him. She was done with pleading. Simeon wanted both of them dead because he was losing his shit. She couldn't help the yawn she let out.

'Time to go, sleepyhead. I'll see you on the other side, probably in hell. You tried to help scum, you married scum and now it's time to die in scum and pay your debt in full.'

She reached across and snatched the crowbar at the same time he unbuckled her. She slashed his face before gasping as she hit the cold, slimy water. A huge splash followed as the liquid sloshed over the top. She listened for Simeon but she couldn't hear a thing. She wanted to scream as she came face to face with Lindy's dead-eyed stare. It was no good trying to climb out, her vision was already prickling. She let out the tiniest of snores and her eyelids closed. The fight was over.

FIFTY-NINE

The gust caught a tree's branches and they kept hitting the side of the building. Led by the battering ram, PC Ahmed burst through first. Gina and Jacob followed. Blue lights shining across the car park lit the entrance up. A pair of night-vision goggles lay on the floor against the wall.

'Simeon Yates, it's the police.' Gina ran through the reception area, then through another door into the main room. The light was already on. She saw a pool of blood around the crowbar sticking out of Simeon's eye. Stagnant water had sloshed over the top of the tank. 'We need a paramedic.' She kneeled on the floor and checked Simeon's pulse. 'He's dead.' She looked up and gestured to Jacob.

'The tank.'

He climbed up the ladder and recoiled. Gina watched as he reached in. 'Two women, one alive and one dead. Her finger moved. It's Justine Crawford.'

Wyre burst in.

Jacob pulled Justine up and let out a roar as he yanked her body towards the lid of the tank. 'It looks like most of the liquid is on the floor. She barely seems conscious but I felt a pulse.' He managed to manoeuvre her over his shoulder before climbing down and letting Wyre help him. 'Lindy's in the tank. She's dead.'

Gina pulled the strips of slime away from Justine's neck and face as they lay her on the ground. 'Her airways are clear.' Gina was sure Justine just tried to murmur something. 'Justine, where's Danny?'

'Danny,' she muttered as she let out a snore.

Wyre got down on the floor and shifted her into the recovery position.

'It looks like she's been drugged.'

'There are sleeping tablets on the racking over here,' O'Connor said.

Gina heard the sound of trickling water under all the commotion. It was coming from the door behind them. She stood and ran to it. It was locked. 'Shaf, you need to get this door open now.'

She stepped aside. After three crashes with the battering ram, the heavy door burst open. Gina ran to the tank and grabbed Danny by the shoulders, lifting his head out of the water. Jacob assisted and they lay him on the concrete floor. Gina stood aside as a paramedic nudged past.

Gina and Jacob left the paramedics to do their jobs. She placed a hand on her chest, over her banging heart while watching as the paramedics tried to revive him. She glanced at Justine, knowing she was going to have to break the news to her about her son's death and a lump formed in her throat. No one wants to tell someone that their child had died. Justine hadn't asked for any of this but then he coughed up a load of water.

SIXTY

Danny had made it through the ordeal. Another minute, he'd have drowned. Gina had left him in the care of a nurse with a police officer posted outside his room. First they'd treat Danny like a victim and when he was in better shape, they'd bring Danny to the station and interview him with regard to his assault on Kain, but now wasn't the right time. She sipped her hospital machine coffee.

'I'm shattered, guv.' Jacob stood there in his standard issue track bottoms and sweater after changing from his filthy clothes back at the station.

'Same. Can you head to Justine's room? I'm just going to update DCI Fraser.'

Jacob nodded.

Gina mulled over all that Justine had told to her. It was clear that Simeon was behind everything, all in the name of justice for his brother and then he got angry with Justine for helping Kain. Justine had cried when she said how she'd brought Lindy into their friendship group. She wasn't to know about Simeon's past and how Simeon had blamed her for bringing his past to his door. She went to call Brodie but tapped Briggs's number first.

He answered. 'Gina.'

'Hi, how are you doing?' She thought of the last time she saw him, all sore and battered.

'Getting there. I heard what happened. Congratulations.'

'So many people died or were hurt. It doesn't feel like a victory.' She thought of Kain, Zavier and Lindy – all dead.

'A very dangerous person is off the streets. We can't win them all.' He paused. 'I'm heading to my brother's for a short while, to help my recovery.' She heard him swallow. 'I'd appreciate it if you didn't call. I need some time to think about this week, my close brush with death, and I want some time alone. We need some time alone... apart... but thank you for being there and believing in me.'

A twinge of guilt made her wince. There was a time when she didn't believe he couldn't have been totally innocent and she would always wonder if he acted in a way that would make him ashamed to admit. She knew Briggs well enough to know he wouldn't purposely hurt anyone in custody, but did they all neglect Barry Yates? She couldn't help but feel for the poor lad after having his life taken away so young. 'Barry Yates died in your custody. The perp blamed you and the others.'

He paused. 'I know and I always wonder if I could have done more that day. I'll think about that case for the rest of my days.'

'Can I see you, before you go?'

'Like I said. I need some time alone.'

'Are you still angry with me over the last case?'

'I'll always be angry that you gave that memory stick up but no, I just need some time to myself.'

She took a deep breath. Was he telling her that what they had was definitely over? It felt like it and she wasn't going to beg him to see her. The kindest thing she could do was respect his wishes. He'd been through a lot and he didn't need her making his life complicated. 'Of course. Get well soon and I'll see you when you're ready to come back to work.'

'See you then.'

She swallowed. He didn't have feelings for her anymore, that much seemed obvious. Maybe they both needed to explore who they were, separately. 'Take care, Chris.'

'Take care, Gina.' He ended the call she was finding so hard to end.

After taking a minute to process everything, she quickly updated Brodie and hurried towards the ward where Justine was recovering. When she arrived, Justine was up and dressed in something the hospital had obviously cobbled together for her. The oversized pink jumper and black leggings looked like they belonged to another person. 'I want to get Danny and go home.'

Gina pulled up a chair as Justine sat on the edge of the bed. Jacob stood beside her. 'I'm sure you'll both be able to go home soon. Danny is still being treated. Is there anything else you remember now that you haven't already told us?' Gina had spoken to Kapoor who found out that there had been an inquest into Barry Yates's death. He'd died of asphyxiation in his cell after being left in a bad way, unsupervised. There had been rumours that Zavier and Kain had been mocking him. Someone in the next cell heard them. Briggs had booked Barry in on the night he died and Simeon had blamed all three of them, even more so when the verdict of accidental death was read out.

'He waffled on, just before he dropped me into the tank. He was so angry,' Justine said. 'He was sick and thought he had nothing to lose. Pia has been having an affair with my husband. Have you found him yet?'

Gina shook her head. She already knew about the affair.

'Simeon wanted to drown us all so we'd know how it felt for Baz, his brother.' She looked into her lap. 'I didn't know that video was on Danny's laptop...' She swallowed. 'What will happen to Danny?'

'He'll be interviewed at the station when he's well enough. We know he had nothing to do with Kain's murder so we'll just be speaking about the assault.'

Gina thought about how everything had unfolded a few hours ago. Pia had been released after helping them throughout the night and she'd known nothing about the box that Simeon had kept in the loft. He'd never even told Pia he had a brother and that he'd been estranged from his parents. Gina realised that the memories must have been too painful for him. Hiding them away and not speaking about Baz or his parents had been Simeon's way of coping, that was until Lindy came into his life.

Justine continued. 'Simeon kept muttering about how he found someone called Zavier. He'd gone back to the pub his brother used to go to. He saw Zavier and followed him to a warehouse.' She paused. 'I think I mentioned it before, but he knew all Craig's passwords. He'd known everything about Craig, about Pia, about us. He was able to log in to everything and pretend to be Craig whenever he chose. I don't think I'll ever believe a message again as long as I live.' She shivered.

Gina had informed Garth of this already, so he'd be able to look into all of that. From what she'd seen and the message Pia had received, she knew that Simeon had been creepily playing them all. 'Do you know where Craig is?' Gina asked. 'We know he also had nothing to do with Kain's murder.'

Justine frowned. 'I don't. I'm sure he ran to protect Danny and himself. He said he was being set up. He said he needed to get to the truth before you falsely arrested him and Danny. I honestly don't know where he's been staying.' She sniffed and wiped her watery eyes. 'I seriously don't want him back though.

We're over. His affair with Pia... I never want to see that woman again.'

Gina knew Craig couldn't stay hidden forever. 'Did Simeon mention anything else about Kain's murder?' Gina asked, trying to get all the information she could.

She frowned and took a moment. 'He, err, he kept going on about booking a parking space and having to wait a day for it to become free.' Tears trickled down her cheeks. 'He left the body in the car, parked up in the woods. He stole Craig's hoodie...' She held a hand to her chest. 'Simeon found the hoodie in Pia's car. Craig must have let her use it. He watched us all. He hated us all. After the inquest for his brother's death, he said he saw Lindy celebrating in the pub with Kain and he never forgot that moment. I can understand the pain he went through back then but I can't understand the pain he put me and the others through. But if what happened to Baz had happened to Danny, I think I'd also be full of rage. Can I see my son, yet?'

Gina nodded. 'I'll get a PC to take you to him.'

The nurse walked in. 'I need to ask you to leave for a short while?' She took Justine's chart from the pocket at the end of the bed.

Gina nodded. She and Jacob left the ward. She let out a long sigh. 'What a tangled mess this all is. I'm trying to think like him. His diagnosis along with Lindy coming into his life sent Simeon over the edge. He'd spent years living with the injustice of what happened to his brother and he finally exploded and now he's dead, so we don't get to question him.'

Jacob frowned. 'It's odd that he blamed Briggs. He just booked him in but I guess he was lashing out.'

Gina let out a long breath. 'Briggs is one of the most upstanding people I've ever met. I can't imagine him hurting anyone but Simeon obviously could. He blamed everyone whose names had come up in the inquest.' She looked away. Briggs had his secrets like she did. She knew he could lie, she knew he could play the game when he needed to. He'd kept her secrets, threatened people who were in danger of releasing them and she wondered, did Briggs keep Kain and Zavier's secrets too? Could Briggs have given a statement at the inquest, helping them get away with being negligent? It was a question she'd never be able to answer.

SIXTY-ONE

JUSTINE

Craig knocked on the door. The nurse placed Justine's medical notes back in the holder at the end of her bed and left. 'How did you know I was here?' She and their son had nearly died and Craig had run away.

He shrugged. 'Danny borrowed a phone and called me.'

Justine saw that the scratch on his neck had almost faded but his face still looked a little pink from where she'd hit him with her torch. 'Your number was disconnected.'

'I know, I had to get a burner.' He stepped a little closer.

'You still didn't tell me where you got that scratch?'

'Danny was in a state. He lashed out at me, then I calmed him down. That was all. You always were really paranoid, Justine. I had nothing to do with any murders and everyone knows that now. Are you okay?'

She shrugged. Paranoid was her middle name because her husband was a cheat with an impulsive nature. 'The police were just here. They'll want to speak to you.'

'I saw. I hid by the vending machine until they left.' He paused. 'I'm sorry about Pia and about running off like that. It was foolish but you know I had to protect Danny and myself.

Then, when I saw those photos up in the apartment, I knew the police would blame me for Kain's murder. I knew about the video too. Danny would have been as much of a suspect as I was. There is something else, I went over to Maura's and ended up arguing with Kain over what happened between him and Danny. Some of the neighbours saw me pinning him up against the wall. I thought one of them would tell the police and that they'd add two and two together and come up with five.'

Justine hated that her husband had pinned Kain against a wall and her son had kicked him. The violence had to stop. She needed to step up and stop Danny going down the path he was on and she would as soon as they were home. 'Why were you hurting Kain? You didn't even know him.' She just wanted to go home.

'There you go, thinking the worst of me and your son. You really are a piece of work.'

'Oh, shut up, Craig. I've had enough of your bullshit. You attacked him and Danny attacked him. Just tell me what happened.'

'There was an argument where Danny stuck up for Maura. You sent Danny over to Maura's to help her with some jobs.'

'Yes, she needed some help cleaning her shed out and Danny needed some money.'

'Well while he was there, he heard shouting and when he went into the hallway, he saw your paralytic friend pushing Maura around and swearing at her. He knocked her off her feet. Danny told me she was crying and begging Kain to leave and come back once he was sober but he kept shouting at her. Maura told Danny to get him out the house because she was scared. He did as she asked then Kain started trying to hit him, but missed. Danny threw him to the floor and kicked him a couple of times. Our son has an anger problem, I know that. But he did what he did for the right reasons and that bastard had to film him and try to blackmail him.'

Justine stared, mouth slightly ajar. How could Kain have done that to his mother and her son, after all the help she gave him?

'Anyway, I was angry after Danny told me what happened. I went over to tell Kain to delete that video and that he deserved what he got for treating Maura so badly but he refused and started to swing drunken punches outside the door, that's when I pinned him there. I just wanted him to stop. The man was an animal. I thought that was it but he followed me outside, shouting his mouth off and the neighbours were curtain twitching.'

'I guess we're all to blame. I brought Kain into Danny's life.'

'You can't fix everyone you know. Some people are beyond help.'

'I know that,' she scoffed, looking at her pathetic husband. 'You have to know when to give up and I know I want to give up on you, Craig. You were ready to ditch our family for Pia. That flat was for you both to live in, wasn't it? But she didn't want you. Am I right?'

He looked away.

'Where did our son stay on Friday night? He said he was at a friend's but I know he wasn't.'

Craig shrugged. 'He told me he stayed at that derelict house.'

She huffed. 'That's where I found his bag last night. Simeon could have killed our son. He'd been keeping tabs on us all and he found Danny there.' She fought back her sobs. 'You did nothing to protect our son. How could you let him stay there? You're all about yourself, aren't you, Craig? You always were and you always will be. My mum was right about you.'

He reached out.

'Don't you dare touch me. And that night when you dragged me from the scarecrow garden, I ran away from you because I was scared. You were there because that's where

Danny had been hiding out. Did you tell Danny to follow me, because I smelt his vape? I know it wasn't Simeon and it can't have been you. You turned my son against me and I will never forgive you for that.'

He shook his head. 'I told him not to go but he was so angry at you introducing him to Maura and Kain. He was trying to turn his life around after the car theft but that set him back.'

'Whatever. I want a divorce, Craig. We' – she pointed at herself and then him – 'are over.'

Her husband had failed her. They'd failed their son. She wasn't going to fail herself any more.

EPILOGUE

Two Weeks Later

Gina pushed the paperwork on her desk aside. Tonight, she was going home. She wanted to run a long, hot bath and snuggle up in front of the fire with her cat. The forensics report had come back. Simeon's DNA had been found under the cat's claws at the scene of Kain's murder. She'd heard from Brodie and he'd told her that Briggs would be back to work next week. She'd had no contact with him since that call. A message popped up from her daughter, Hannah.

Gracie wanted to know if you'll be watching her in her Christmas play. I have to book family tickets soon. I know it's early but I don't want you to miss out if you want to be there.

She smiled and replied. Without a doubt she was going to be there. Hannah replied with a photo of Gracie asleep next to their dog. Gina sent a heart emoji reply.

So much had happened recently and she couldn't help but think of everyone involved in the case. Pia had already packed up her house and gone to stay with her sister. She'd also put her house up for sale. Gina could understand why she needed to get away.

Justine had wasted no time in issuing divorce papers to Craig and she was helping her son face up to what he did wrong. She'd been worried that she might be in trouble for killing Simeon. A file of evidence had been prepared and submitted to the CPS. The scene had backed up what she had told them. It looked like she had killed him in self-defence so it wasn't looking likely that she'd be prosecuted. As for Craig, he simply ran to evade arrest so he was in the clear too. He'd come in and they were able to interview him. Gina was glad that Danny wasn't running from his part in all this. He'd admitted to assaulting Kain and that he'd done it to defend Maura. The video had done him no favours. He'd gone beyond reasonable force, kicking Kain while he was already down. Facing up to his crime was the only way to deal with it and she hoped he'd change for the better.

A cousin of Lindy's was waiting for Lindy's body to be released so he could plan her funeral but Gina knew these things could take a while. She didn't envy the heartache this caused for the families. Zavier Sellers's family had received the news and they too were waiting for his body to be released.

Someone tapped at her office door. Brodie peered around the corner. 'I'm heading back to Gloucester soon. It's not too far away. I was hoping...' He inhaled and looked away with a slight smile on his face.

She raised her brows.

'I was hoping that we'd be able to keep in touch if you'd be okay... if you'd like that. Or maybe you wouldn't like that. I mean, we were friends years ago and you're probably busy and all that...'

She stood and grabbed her bag and coat. 'I'd love to keep in touch. Actually, I only have a date with my bath and my cat tonight so do you fancy a drink first, or a bite to eat?'

'Yes, I'll grab my coat.' He ran out the door, leaving her stomach nervously fluttering.

She didn't want to be alone. She wanted to be happy and she wanted to find a reason to laugh again, and she couldn't help but relive the past in her head again. She giggled at the memory of them lying in a heap as young rookies on the pub toilet floor all those years ago. A woman who looked to be in her sixties had burst in a moment later. The woman had cleared her throat, then said, 'Have fun, kids,' before discreetly leaving. Gina had never laughed so much. Surely it was okay to laugh, to live, and to love. It had to be because if it wasn't, what was the point in living?

There would always be a huge place for Briggs in her heart but he didn't want her and she needed to accept that, and going out for a drink with an old friend was okay, wasn't it?

A LETTER FROM CARLA

Dear Reader,

I'm grateful that you chose to read, *Their Deadly Truth*. Thank you so much.

If you enjoyed *Their Deadly Truth* and would like to keep up-to-date with all my latest releases, just sign up at the following link. Your email address will never be shared and you can unsubscribe at any time. You'll also get a free story.

www.bookouture.com/carla-kovach

I hope you enjoyed reading it as much as I enjoyed writing it.

My husband and I have rented our drive out in the past to rugby fans mostly and I had this strange thought one day. What if someone rented our drive to dump a body? Simple idea: book the space for a while, use a stolen car and bank card, then there will be plenty of time before the police step in. That was the bud of an idea that turned into *Their Deadly Truth*. Thankfully the rugby fans who parked on our drive were no trouble at all.

I also loved exploring Gina's journey further in this book and I hope you did too.

I'm on BlueSky, Facebook, Instagram and, occasionally, TikTok as it's fun to hang out with other writers and readers. As a writer, this is where I hope you'll leave me a review or say a few words about my book.

Thank you,

Carla Kovach

www.carlakovach.com

facebook.com/CarlaKovachAuthor
instagram.com/carla_kovach
bsky.app/profile/carlakovach.bsky.social
tiktok.com/@CarlaKovachAuthor

ACKNOWLEDGEMENTS

I'd like to say a huge thank you to everyone who helped create *Their Deadly Truth*. Editors, cover designers, people working in every aspect of publishing from admin to management – you're all amazing. I know I say it every time but I'm so grateful and happy to be a part of team Bookouture.

My editor, Helen Jenner, is amazing and I couldn't have created this book without her. She's been with me from the start of my journey and I always look forward to receiving her input and her ongoing encouragement and support.

Thank you, Lisa Brewster for designing another smashing book cover.

I'd like to say a big thank you to policing expert, Stuart Gibbon, of Gib Consultancy. He answers my policing questions and without his knowledge, I'd definitely make a mess of the police procedures. Any inaccuracies are definitely my own.

Everyone on the Bookouture publicity team is fabulous. As always, they ensure that publication day runs seamlessly, is panic free and lots of fun.

Super thanks to the blogger and reviewer community. I'm always grateful to those who chose my book when there are so many brilliant books out there to read.

Thank you to the Fiction Café Book Club. If you're not in this Facebook group and you're a reader, check it out. This group is a friendly place for readers and authors.

As always, I love being a member of the Bookouture author

family. Huge thanks to them. My other author friends are lovely too. Authors are wonderful.

Big appreciation to my beta readers, Derek Coleman, Su Biela, Abigail Osborne, Jamie-Lee Brooke and Vanessa Morgan. Anna Wallace helps me at the proofread stage so great big thanks to her, too.

Lots of gratitude to Jamie-Lee Brooke, Julia Sutton and Abigail Osborne. I love our, 'Hot Dog Cringey Crew,' support group. This is still an in-joke, sorry.

Lastly, special thanks to my husband, Nigel Buckley, for the coffee, the admin, dealing with my website, photography at events, and all those other jobs I'm useless at, and mostly for being with me throughout the whole process.

PUBLISHING TEAM

Turning a manuscript into a book requires the efforts of many people. The publishing team at Bookouture would like to acknowledge everyone who contributed to this publication.

Audio
Alba Proko

Commercial
Lauren Morrissette
Hannah Richmond
Imogen Allport

Cover design
The Brewster Project

Data and analysis
Mark Alder
Mohamed Bussuri

Editorial
Helen Jenner
Ria Clare

Copyeditor
Jane Eastgate

Proofreader
Shirley Khan

Marketing
Alex Crow
Melanie Price
Occy Carr
Cíara Rosney
Martyna Młynarska

Operations and distribution
Marina Valles
Joe Morris

Production
Hannah Snetsinger
Mandy Kullar
Nadia Michael
Charlotte Hegley

Publicity
Kim Nash
Noelle Holten
Jess Readett
Sarah Hardy

Rights and contracts
Peta Nightingale
Richard King
Saidah Graham

Dear Reader,

We'd love your attention for one more page to tell you about the crisis in children's reading, and what we can all do.

Studies have shown that reading for fun is the **single biggest predictor of a child's future life chances** – more than family circumstance, parents' educational background or income. It improves academic results, mental health, wealth, communication skills, ambition and happiness.

The number of children reading for fun is in rapid decline. Young people have a lot of competition for their time, and a worryingly high number do not have a single book at home.

Hachette works extensively with schools, libraries and literacy charities, but here are some ways we can all raise more readers:

- Reading to children for just 10 minutes a day makes a difference
- Don't give up if children aren't regular readers – there will be books for them!

- Visit bookshops and libraries to get
  recommendations
- Encourage them to listen to audiobooks
- Support school libraries
- Give books as gifts

There's a lot more information about how to encourage children to read on our websites: **www.RaisingReaders.co.uk** and **www.JoinRaisingReaders.com**.

Thank you for reading.